## Praise for *The Unsinkable Greta James*

'Warm, funny, and bursting with heart.
A pitch-perfect story about the ways we recover love
in the strangest of places'
**Rebecca Serle**

'Beautiful, moving, hopeful. I loved this book
from beginning to end [. . .] A total triumph'
**Emily Stone**

'Filled with music, passion, and love of all kinds,
*The Unsinkable Greta James* is an unforgettable exploration
of family and the choices we make that shape our lives'
**Jill Santopolo**

'I burst into tears at the end of Jennifer E. Smith's
gorgeous, heartfelt *The Unsinkable Greta James* –
tears of surprised happiness'
**Amanda Eyre Ward**

'Thoughtful and tender and true [. . .] perfectly
captures the messiness of loving and being loved'
**Janelle Brown**

'It's about how family can misunderstand us,
grief can undo us and our dreams can save us'
**Christine Pride**

# *The* Unsinkable Greta James

*The*
# Unsinkable
# Greta
# James

*Jennifer E. Smith*

QUERCUS

First published in Great Britain in 2022
This paperback edition first published in Great Britain in 2023 by

QUERCUS

Quercus Editions Ltd
Carmelite House
50 Victoria Embankment
London EC4Y 0DZ

An Hachette UK company

A CIP catalogue record for this book is available
from the British Library

PB ISBN 978 1 52941 647 3
EBOOK ISBN 978 1 52941 645 9

This book is a work of fiction. Names, characters,
businesses, organizations, places and events are
either the product of the author's imagination
or used fictitiously. Any resemblance to
actual persons, living or dead, events or
locales is entirely coincidental.

10 9 8 7 6 5 4 3 2 1

Printed and bound in Great Britain by Clays Ltd, Elcograf S.p.A

Papers used by Quercus Editions Ltd. are from well-managed forests
and other responsible sources.

*For Susan Kamil, who believed in this book*
*long before I'd ever written a word*

We set out to be wrecked.

—J. M. BARRIE,

*The Boy Castaways of Black Lake Island*

# BEFORE

# Chapter One

Greta is standing at the window of a hotel in West Hollywood when her brother calls for the third time that day. Across the street, there's a billboard with a sleek white yacht surrounded by turquoise water, an ad for a new kind of beer, and something about it—that feeling of being adrift—makes it easier to say no when she finally picks up the phone.

"Come on," Asher says. "It's only a week."

"A week on a boat."

"It's a ship," he corrects.

"It's the last thing I need right now," Greta says, turning from the window, where the light outside is dreamy and pink. She's just come from a photo shoot for the cover of her second album, which has been pushed to July. If it were up to Greta, she would've moved it back even further, but apparently, that's no longer an option. Instead, she'd been summoned to Los Angeles to spend three days in a warehouse surrounded by flashing cameras and frowning studio execs in suits and sneakers, the pressure to get this right all over their faces.

It's been two months since she last performed live—not since the week after her mother died, when she fell apart onstage—but everything else has continued to march ahead, the business part of things still grinding forward mostly without her.

On the desk, next to the hotel stationery, there's a plate of chocolates with a note from the hotel manager that says, *We're so happy you're with us*. Automatically, Greta thinks of her mom, who no longer is, whose absence feels so breathtakingly final that even this is enough to make her heart drop.

"Why don't *you* go?" she says to Asher, trying to imagine spending all that time on a boat with her dad. The Alaskan cruise had been her mother's idea. It was all she talked about for nearly a year, right up until March, when an artery ruptured in her head and the whole world seemed to stop.

Now it's only a month away. And her dad is still planning to go.

"We can't let him do this alone," Asher says, ignoring her question. "It's too sad."

"He'll hardly be alone," Greta says as she wanders into the bathroom. "He'll have the Fosters and the Blooms. They'll take care of him."

She stares at her reflection in the mirror, her face still made up from the shoot. Red lips, white skin, green eyes lined with charcoal. Her dark hair, usually so wild, is now sleek and tamed. She sets the phone down on the sink and switches to speaker, then twists the tap and begins to scrub it all off.

"He'll be a fifth wheel," Asher insists, his voice bouncing around the bathroom. "It's depressing. One of us has to go with him."

"Right," Greta says. "You."

"I can't."

She straightens again. Her skin is now pinkish, but she looks more like herself, which is always a relief. She grabs a towel and pats at her face. "The thing is," she says, picking up the phone again and walking back out into the room, where she flops onto the bed, "he actually likes you."

"Greta," he says, impatient now. "You know I can't do it."

She knows this, of course. Asher has a wife and three girls under the age of five. He has a job with a boss and a regular work week, an HR department, and a set number of vacation days, which mostly get used up when the kids are sick. He hasn't been on a plane in years.

Greta's already been on three this week.

She sighs. "What are the dates again?"

"End of May, beginning of June."

"I've got to be in the city for Gov Ball on the fifth," she says, almost indecently relieved to have a legitimate excuse, no matter how much she's dreading it. But this does nothing to deter Asher.

"Lucky for you," he says, "it gets back on the fourth."

"You know this isn't just any show. It's important."

"More important than Dad?"

"That's not fair."

"It's not like I'm asking you to choose," he says. "You'll be back in New York in time to do your thing. And I've heard Alaska is beautiful this time of year. Still a little cold, maybe, but that was just Dad trying to save some money—"

"Asher?"

"Yeah?"

"I don't think I can do it."

"Sure you can. You love the water. Remember that time we took the canoe out on—"

"You know what I mean."

He goes silent for a moment, then says, "It wouldn't just be for him, you know."

And that's what finally gets her.

# SATURDAY

# Chapter Two

Greta stands beneath the wide shadow of an enormous ship, wondering how such a thing could possibly float. It's a hotel on rudders, a skyscraper tipped on its side, a monolith, a beast. And it's her unlikely home for the next eight days.

The name of the ship is painted across its broad white side. It's called the *Escape,* which is the only thing so far today that's made her want to laugh.

Hundreds of people are milling around her, fancy cameras dangling from their necks, all of them eager to climb aboard and begin their Alaskan adventure. To the left, the city of Vancouver disappears into the sky, which is now silver, heavy with the threat of rain. Greta was here once for a show, but as with so many of the places she travels to, her views were pretty much limited to the inside of a music venue.

"It's got eleven decks," her dad says, stepping up beside her with a map of the ship. He's wearing a too-thin windbreaker and a baseball cap he got for free when he opened a new bank account. It's been three months now since her mother died, and for the first time in his life, he looks every inch of his seventy years. "And eight different restaurants. Four of them buffets."

If her mom were here, she would've said: *Wow!* She would've said: *I can't wait to try them all.* She would've squeezed his arm and beamed up at the ship, all eleven decks of it.

But Helen isn't here. It's only Greta, who still can't believe that Asher managed to talk her into this.

"Cool," she says, an attempt at enthusiasm, but it obviously falls flat, because her dad simply gives her a resigned look and returns to his map.

This was supposed to be a celebration, a fortieth-anniversary trip; they'd been planning it for nearly a year and saving up for it even longer. Last Christmas—a full five months ago now—Helen gave Conrad a calendar with photos of glaciers, and he got her a new fleece to replace her old one, worn and thin from years of gardening in it. They bought a pair of binoculars to share, the kind that hang heavy around your neck, and every time there was an article about Alaska in the newspaper, Helen would clip it out, put it in an envelope, get a stamp, and then mail it—actually mail it—to Greta with a Post-it note that said "FYI," as if she were going too.

That new fleece—light blue and impossibly soft—is in Greta's bag, which is currently being carried aboard the ship. Her mother never ended up wearing it. She'd been saving it for the trip.

The ship's horn blows, and the line to board moves ahead. Behind her, the other four adults—even at thirty-six, Greta can't help thinking of them this way—are already making plans, debating between the casino and the musical for their first night out. They're longtime friends of her parents' and each couple has their own reasons for being here: the Fosters both recently retired and the Blooms are about to turn seventy. But everyone knows the real driving force was Helen, whose excitement about this trip was so infectious, she somehow talked them all into it.

A steward walks past, and Greta watches him pause and take a few steps back in her direction. He points at her guitar case, which she's had slung over her shoulder since they stepped out of the taxi.

"Would you like some help with that, ma'am?" he asks, and she tries not to flinch at the *ma'am*. She's wearing a short black dress with Vans and sunglasses. Her hair is tied up in a messy bun at the top of her head, and there's a leather jacket draped over the arm not carrying the guitar. She's not someone accustomed to being called *ma'am*.

"That's okay," she says. "I'll hang on to it."

Her dad grunts. "You couldn't pry that thing from her even if she fell overboard."

"I don't blame her," Davis Foster says as he comes up behind them, holding a map of Vancouver over his bald head as it starts to drizzle. "It'd be a real shame to lose it."

Greta has known the Fosters since she was twelve, when they moved in next door. They were the first Black family on the block, and Greta had immediately fallen in love with their youngest son, Jason, who was two grades ahead of her. Nothing ever happened until much later, when they both found themselves living in New York, and even then, it was never serious, mostly just when they were both between relationships. None of the parents ever had a clue, which was by design. If they had, they probably would've started planning the wedding a long time ago, which is the very last thing either Greta or Jason would ever want.

Davis nods at her guitar case. "I bet it'd be worth a fortune on eBay," he jokes, and his wife, Mary, gives him a whack across the chest. He doubles over in mock pain. "I was kidding."

Mary is tall and slender, with dark brown skin and a pixie cut that makes her eyes look huge. Right now, they're fixed on Greta. "We all know it's worth a lot more in your hands," she says, and there's something protective in her gaze. Right from the start, Mary and Helen had been instant friends. Davis used to joke that they should call the little garden path between their houses *the black hole*, since the moment one of them crossed over for a visit—a bottle of wine in hand, always—they were as good as lost. At least for a few hours.

Now Greta can almost feel Mary's determination to look out for her. It's comforting, like her mom is still here in spirit.

"You know what you should do?" Eleanor Bloom says in her faint Irish accent, looking all lit up at the thought. She's wearing a designer raincoat, and her long silvery hair is perfect, as always, even in spite of the dampness. "You should play a little show at sea. It would be brilliant to see you perform."

"I don't know . . ." Greta says, though of course she *does* know: there's no way she's playing on a cruise ship. Not ever, if she's being honest, but especially not now.

"I saw there's a variety show on the last night," Eleanor continues, undeterred. "Anyone can sign up. I'm sure they'd be absolutely gobsmacked to have a real professional turn up there."

"All the performers are professionals, honey," her husband, Todd, says in his usual mild-mannered way. Other than his wife, Todd's main passion is birds; he spends his weekends out in the marshes looking for egrets and other waterfowl. Once a year, his birding club takes a trip to some far-flung place that he views only through a pair of binoculars, but he's never been to Alaska before, and a field guide to the state's birds has been tucked under his arm all morning, already full of dog-eared pages. "They get pretty good people on these ships," he tells Eleanor. "Comedians, magicians, Broadway dancers."

"But not rock stars," Eleanor points out. "Not people like Greta James."

She says this last part like Greta isn't standing right beside her, smiling politely, like she's talking about someone else entirely: Greta James the guitarist, the indie singer-songwriter with a cult following, as opposed to Greta James, daughter of Conrad and Helen, who learned to play guitar in the open garage beside the shelves of tools, with only Asher's gerbils—banished from the house because of the smell—as an audience, and who now feels like a kid again as she waits to start this bizarre sort of family vacation, a poor replacement for the most important member of the group.

Across the way, she spots a man heading toward the end of another line. In a sea of older couples and young families, he sticks out. He has a trim beard and a square jaw and he's wearing glasses that are either incredibly nerdy or incredibly hip; it's hard to tell which. When she notices that he's carrying an old-fashioned typewriter—cradled under one arm like a football—she wants to roll her eyes. But then she sees him clock her guitar case, and there's nothing to do but exchange slightly sheepish smiles before he disappears into the crowd.

"Just think about it," Eleanor is saying, and Greta turns back to her.

"Thanks, but—"

"This is small potatoes for her these days," her dad says, arching an eyebrow. He doesn't say it like it's a compliment.

There's a brief silence, and then Eleanor—trying not to sound deflated—says, "I suppose you're right. It was only a thought."

"Not at all," Greta says, shaking her head. "I just . . . I don't get a lot of time off, so . . ."

What she doesn't say—what none of them say—is that all she's had is time off lately.

Mary fixes Greta with an admiring look. "I remember you practicing away in that garage all those nights—"

Davis lets out a booming laugh. "You were god-awful, kid. But you were certainly determined. Gotta give you that."

"That's just it," Eleanor says, turning back to Conrad. "How many people actually grow up to do the thing they dreamed of when they were young? You must be so proud."

Conrad's eyes drift over to meet Greta's, and they stare at each other for a long moment. Eventually, he nods.

"Yes," he says. "We're very proud."

Which is a double lie. He's not. And there's no *we* anymore.

## Chapter Three

The room is so tiny, she can sit on the edge of her bed and touch the wall. But Greta doesn't mind. She's spent the last fourteen years in New York City, where space is a luxury, so she's well versed in the art of living compactly. The bigger problem is the absence of any windows. By the time she booked the trip, all that was left were interior cabins. So while Conrad's room has big glass doors that open onto a veranda, Greta's looks more like something out of a minimum-security prison: small and beige and just barely functional.

*Seven nights,* she thinks. *Only seven nights.*

She sets her guitar on the bed beside a thick black binder. Inside, there's a day-by-day itinerary of the trip. They'll be at sea for the rest of tonight and tomorrow, cruising the Inside Passage (the inside of what, she has no idea); after that, they'll travel on to Juneau, Glacier Bay, Haines, Icy Strait Point, and then spend another full day at sea as they return to Vancouver.

There are separate laminated pages for each port of call, filled with recommended tours, lists of restaurants, suggested hikes, and points of interest. There's also a fairly ridiculous amount of information about the ship itself: floor plans and menus, instructions for making spa appointments, detailed descriptions of each club and bar, every lecture and game night. You could spend an entire week deciding how to fill your week.

Greta snaps the binder shut. It won't be long now until the ship sets sail, and she doesn't want to be burrowed inside it like a mole when it does. If she's actually going on this trip—which it would seem, at this point, that she is—she'd at least like to witness the beginning of it.

After all, that's what her mom would have done.

Outside, there are a few people bundled on Adirondack chairs beneath the low Vancouver sky, but most are dotted around the edges of the ship, peering either out at the city or at the hunched gray mountains that loom across the water from it. She finds a spot between an elderly couple and a group of middle-aged women in matching pink sweatshirts that say *Fifty Is the New F-Word*. They're laughing as they pass around a flask.

Greta leans on the rail and pulls in a deep breath. The harbor smells of brine and fish, and far below, dozens of tiny figures are waving up at them madly, as if they're about to set off on a dangerous voyage instead of an eight-day all-inclusive cruise with four buffets and a water slide.

A few birds circle above, and the breeze is heavy with salt. Greta closes her eyes for a minute, and when she opens them again, she can sense someone staring at her. She turns to see a girl—probably no more than twelve or thirteen—standing a few feet down the rail. She has light-brown skin and black hair, and she's staring at Greta with a very specific kind of intensity.

"Hi," Greta says, and the girl widens her eyes, caught somewhere between excitement and embarrassment. She's wearing pink Converse sneakers and skinny jeans with holes in the knees.

"Are you . . . Greta James?" she asks, her voice full of uncertainty.

Greta raises her eyebrows, amused. "I am."

"I knew it." The girl lets out a surprised laugh. "Wow. This is so cool. And so weird. I can't believe you're on this cruise."

"Honestly," Greta says, "neither can I."

"I'm obsessed with your album. And I saw your show in Berkeley last year," she says, the words tumbling out in a rush. "Dude, you can *shred*. I've never seen a girl play like that before."

This makes Greta smile. She hadn't been expecting much overlap in the Venn diagram of people who go on Alaskan cruises and people who go to her shows. She fills good-sized venues and her songs are played on the radio and she has fans all over the world; she's even been on the cover of a few music magazines. But she's rarely recognized on the street outside of New York or L.A. And hardly ever by anyone this young.

"Do you play?" she asks the girl, who nods enthusiastically. There's no sheepishness about it, no modesty: the answer is simply yes. She plays.

Greta remembers being that age, already full of confidence as she started to realize that a guitar was more than just a toy, more than even just an instrument. Already, she knew it was a portal, and that she was talented enough for it to take her somewhere.

Her dad was the one who'd bought that first guitar. Greta was only eight; it was supposed to be for Asher, who was twelve, but even then he had little interest in anything but football. It was acoustic and secondhand and much too big for her; it would be years before she'd grow into it. Some nights, when Conrad got home from work, he'd stand in the open mouth of the garage, the tip of his cigarette burning bright as he watched her try to work out the notes like a puzzle. When she landed on the right ones, he let the cigarette dangle from his lips while he clapped.

That was back when he loved that she played. When music was still a subject without controversy for them. Every night after dinner, he'd put on an old Billy Joel album while they did the dishes, the two of them singing over the sound of the faucet to "Piano Man" while Helen laughed and Asher rolled his eyes.

The girl picks at the peeling paint on the rail. "I've been trying to figure out 'Birdsong,' actually," she says, referring to a not-particularly-popular track off Greta's EP, a choice that makes her like this kid even more.

"That's a tricky one."

"I know," she says. "Way trickier than 'Told You So.'"

Greta smiles. "Told You So" was the first single off her debut album, which came out a couple years ago, and it's her most popular track by far, having achieved a level of success where people tend to know it even if they've never heard of Greta James.

"Not into the mainstream stuff, huh?" she says to the girl, who gives a solemn nod.

"I prefer the deep cuts."

Greta laughs. "Fair enough."

A horn blares once, then twice, and everyone on the deck startles and looks around. The engines have begun to stir, the water churning as the ship vibrates beneath their feet. Somewhere, invisible speakers crackle to life.

"Good afternoon, passengers," comes a slightly muffled voice. "This is Captain Edward Windsor. I want to welcome you all aboard and let you know that before leaving port, we'll be holding a safety briefing. Please collect your life jackets and proceed to your muster station."

The girl glances around at the receding crowds. "I guess I should go find my parents. But it was really cool to meet you. Maybe I'll see you again?"

Greta nods. "What's your name?"

"Preeti."

"Nice to meet you, Preeti," she says. "I'll look for you when I want to talk shop, okay?"

Preeti's face brightens at this; then she gives a wave and hurries off.

By the time Greta grabs the life jacket from her cabin and arrives at her assigned spot for the muster drill, her own little crew is already assembled. Her dad frowns at the way she has the vest slung over one shoulder. He was a naval officer during Vietnam, stationed on a patrol boat in the western Pacific, and he doesn't mess around with this sort of thing.

Around her, there's a sea of bright orange; everyone is wearing their life jackets, even Davis Foster, who is six foot seven with shoulders so broad it looks like a child's pool toy has gotten caught around his neck. Greta lifts hers over her head, fastening the clips and hoping there are no other unexpected fans nearby. The last thing she needs is a picture of this.

"While it's doubtful you'll ever encounter a real emergency, it's important to be prepared," says a man who introduces himself as their station captain.

Behind him, Greta can see the tops of the orange-capped life-boats fastened in a row along the edge of the ship like ornaments on a tree. The man's voice is even-tempered as he lays out all the worst-case scenarios, the many calamities that could—unlikely though they may be—befall them on this floating city. It's the same way the doctor had spoken after her mother's aneurysm, when Greta—stuck at the airport in Berlin, where she'd just played a festival for tens of thousands of people—had insisted on talking to him. Her mom was in a coma by then, and the disconnect between the awful things he was saying and the calm way he was saying them was so jarring it made her want to throw her phone clear across the gate.

"If you should see anyone fall over the side," the man says, his voice almost cheerful, "please throw them a life buoy, then shout 'Man overboard' and inform the nearest crew member."

A ripple of laughter spreads across the assembled passengers as they make whispered guesses about which of them will be the first to go over. Davis grabs Mary's shoulders so suddenly she lets out a yelp. Eleanor reaches for Todd's hand as if to anchor herself, but he's busy watching a small iridescent bird flit past what little sky is visible between decks.

"A purple martin," he whispers excitedly, fumbling with his binoculars. But they get tangled in his life jacket, and by the time he lifts them, the bird is gone.

Greta tugs at the straps of her own vest and looks around. Down the row, she spots the guy she'd seen earlier with the typewriter. As she watches, he lifts his phone to take a picture of this, the safety briefing, of all things. When he lowers it again, she can see him typing and wonders who he's sending the photos to. Then she wonders why she's wondering this.

"You're not listening," her dad says under his breath, giving her a nudge, and when the guy glances in their direction, Greta feels like she's about twelve years old. But he only smiles, and then they both turn their attention back to the station captain, who is still detailing all the ways they might possibly—but not probably—find themselves in peril over the next eight days.

# Chapter Four

Despite all the talk of buffets, her dad made reservations for the group at the most formal restaurant for their first night, a dimly lit sea of white tablecloths surrounding a dance floor. Out the window, the light is soft and hazy. The sun doesn't set until after nine here, and dusk takes its time, moving leisurely from orange to pink to gray.

"So, Greta," Eleanor Bloom says as their drinks arrive. She's wearing an elegant black pantsuit and has already had her hair done at the salon. It always seemed to Greta that Eleanor was a bit too glamorous for their little corner of Columbus, Ohio. She'd met Todd decades ago on a trip to New York City with her girl-friends from Dublin. He was there for an insurance conference, and she was sightseeing, and they got caught in a rainstorm in Times Square. Greta always wondered how a man like Todd—incredibly kind but extremely boring—had managed to inspire someone like Eleanor to move across an ocean for him. But apparently her first husband had been a nightmare, and in Todd, she found a steadiness that gave her the space to shine. Which she usually does. "How are things with that adorable boyfriend of yours?"

Greta takes a long sip of her wine, trying to decide how to answer. It's been nearly three months since they broke up, just after her mother's death, but even so, the *boyfriend* part throws her off-balance. As does the word *adorable*. There are a lot of ways to describe Luke—brilliant and edgy, sexy and infuriating—but *adorable* isn't really one of them.

"We're actually . . ." she begins, then stops and takes another quick sip of wine. "We sort of decided to . . ."

"They broke up," Conrad says with forced joviality. "Didn't you guys get the email?"

Greta feels the heat rise to her cheeks. She hadn't realized he was upset about that. The split had happened shortly after the funeral, and neither of them had been in a state to talk about much of anything then. But she'd wanted him to know, and to hear it from her, before Asher mentioned it. So she'd sent him a quick email.

He hadn't written her back, and neither of them had talked about it since.

"I'm sorry to hear that," Mary says as she reaches for a dinner roll, her bracelets jangling. Greta has never met anyone who can say as much with her eyebrows as Mary Foster, and right now, they're raised sky-high. "I know your mom really liked him."

This is not remotely true, but Greta appreciates it all the same.

Her parents met Luke only twice. The first time, at the New York City launch party for her debut album, she'd chickened out and introduced him only as her producer, worried that if they knew he was more than that, they'd hate him for a thousand different reasons: the cigarette tucked behind his ear and the sleeve of tattoos on both arms, the drawling Australian accent and the way he sneered whenever someone talked about a band he considered inferior.

"We've heard so much about you," her mom said that night, smiling gamely as she shook his hand. "And the album is wonderful. You two make beautiful music together."

Luke hadn't been able to help himself; he'd burst out laughing. Even now, Greta can picture the look on Conrad's face, the dawning disappointment as it all snapped into place.

The second time, things were more serious between them, and she brought Luke home to Columbus over the Fourth of July. For two days, he did everything right: he collected candy with her nieces at the town parade, helped her mom decorate the American flag cupcakes (adding an Australian one for good measure), and brought her dad a bottle of his favorite scotch. He even found a way to ask Conrad about his job selling ads for the Yellow Pages without seeming to imply that this line of work had perhaps outlived its usefulness.

On the last morning, she found him out on the patio, attempting to fix the broken barbecue, and as she watched him bend over it the way he usually stood over the sound board in the studio—tweaking and adjusting her songs until they became as close as they could to the way she heard them in her head—she was surprised that something so mundane could still be so attractive.

But afterward, as they sat waiting for the plane that would take them back to New York, he put his arm around her shoulders. "I can't wait to get home," he said, and when she murmured in agreement, he tipped his head back with a sigh. "If that were my life, I think I'd off myself."

This, of course, is the exact same thought Greta has every single time she goes home. It's the same thought that kept her picking at her guitar most nights in the freezing-cold garage when she was younger, the one that propelled her to a college two thousand miles away in southern California, then catapulted her straight to the opposite coast afterward.

It's what's driven her all these years, the fear of all that—of getting stuck, of standing still, of being ordinary. And it's what's kept her going, in spite of the wall that rose up between her and her dad, another brick for every aspect of her unconventional life, every decision that carried her farther from Ohio, from a nine-to-five and a mortgage and a white picket fence, from the way her brother's life has unfolded—which is to say, the way most lives unfold—first a steady job, then marriage, then parenthood, all of it sure-footed and predictable.

But to hear Luke say it—Luke, who drinks only out of mason jars and wears a knit hat even in the summer, who can light a cigarette in the wind and recite the lyrics to all of her songs—was too much.

"It's not so bad," she said, watching their plane appear out the window, inching toward the accordion-like jet bridge. It always struck her as extraordinary that the distance between Columbus and New York could be covered in just a couple short hours. Most of the time, it felt like the two places existed in entirely different universes.

Beside her, Luke sat up a little. "You can't be serious," he said, his accent getting thicker, as it always did when he said something snarky. "I can't even picture you living there when you were a kid. Never mind now."

"I'm not saying I'd want to—I'm just saying it's not so bad."

"What? The suburbs?"

"No," she said. "Coming home."

"There are fifteen thousand kilometers between me and *my* parents," he said with a smirk, "and that's still not enough."

She didn't know it then, but that was the first loose thread.

From across the table, Mary is still watching her expectantly.

"It wasn't meant to be," Greta tells her.

"Well, that," her dad says, "or you didn't want it to be."

"Conrad," Mary admonishes him in the exact same tone that Helen would've used, and Greta gives her a grateful smile. But it's not a surprise. And it's nothing new.

She turns to her dad, whose collar is wrinkled now that her mom isn't here to iron it for him. He's looking at her the same way he's been looking at her for twenty years: like she's a math problem he can't quite work out.

"What?" he says, like he isn't trying to pick the same fight they've had about a thousand times. It's not about Luke. It's not even really about her settling down, though that's part of it. It's that the life he wants for her is fundamentally different from the life she wants for herself, and music is the boat that's forever carrying her away from it.

"You didn't even like him," Greta says, and though her voice is light, there's something unmistakably steely underneath it.

"But *you* did," Conrad points out. "So I don't really understand what happened."

What happened, she wants to say, is that her mom died. What happened is that Helen went into a coma, and the world turned inside out.

But that's only part of it, of course. That's the cause.

Here's the effect:

Greta had been in the middle of a show at the time, a sixty-minute set at a music festival in Berlin, and when her brother kept calling and calling, Luke was the one to pick up her phone. By the time she'd finished playing, he'd booked her a flight to Columbus.

"Just me?" she asked, the shock of it coursing through her as she stood with him backstage afterward, still sweaty and jangly from the show, still trying to absorb the news.

He looked surprised by the question, which was ridiculous. They'd been together for two years by then, and this, she'd assumed, is what people do in situations like these; this is what it's supposed to mean to have a partner.

"Well," he said, running a hand through his hair. The next band had come on, and outside the tent, they could hear the dull roar of applause. "I mean, it's a family thing, right? I wasn't sure you'd want me there."

She stared at him. "So, what, you're just going back to New York?"

"No," he said, and at least he had the good sense to look embarrassed. "I figured as long as I'm here, I might as well stay for the rest of the festival."

That, she wants to say, is what happened.

Or, at least, that was the start of it.

Luke might have lit the match, but Greta was the one who burned everything to the ground a week later. She can't say that to her dad, though. So instead she says, "It's complicated."

Conrad raises an eyebrow. "Not really. It's the same thing that always happens. You date someone for a while, then get bored and break it off."

"It's not that simple, Dad."

"I'm sure it's not."

Greta swirls the wine in her glass, aware that they have an audience of four, each of whom is looking increasingly uncomfortable. "Life sometimes gets in the way."

"That's because your life isn't conducive to relationships." He picks up his menu and addresses the list of entrées. "They don't just *happen*. You have to make room for them."

She grits her teeth. "I like my life the way it is."

"As you should," Davis says from across the table, and when everyone turns to him, he shrugs. "Well, it's true. Her life is objectively pretty awesome."

In his twenties, Davis had played piano in a jazz trio, and he has a million stories about the old days in Chicago, late nights full of whisky and music with friends. She knows he loves his life now—he has a wife he adores and three grown kids who happen to be fantastic, and until a few weeks ago, when he officially retired, he was the neighborhood's favorite postman—but there's always a certain look he gets when they talk about Greta's career, something just south of envy and just north of wistful.

When the waiter arrives, they place their orders and hand over their menus, and Greta thinks it's over. But then Conrad, who has mostly been staring into his scotch glass, turns back to her.

"You know I only want what's best for you, right?" he asks, and he looks so old right then, so unhappy, that Greta almost says, *Right*. But she finds she can't.

"No. You want my life to look like Asher's."

"I want you to be happy."

"You want me to be settled," she says. "That's not the same thing."

Mary pulls back her chair and sets her napkin on the table. "You know what? I think we're gonna take a spin around the dance floor."

"Before dinner?" Davis asks with a frown.

"Yes," she says firmly, and the Blooms both stand up as well.

"Us too," Eleanor says, grabbing Todd's hand. "Time to cut a rug."

"It's a waltz," he says, but he follows her out to the dance floor anyway, leaving Greta and Conrad behind.

For a second, they just look at each other, and then at the now-empty table—the napkins strewn across bread plates, the lipstick-stained wine glasses—and Greta almost laughs. Instead, she clears her throat and says, "Look, I know you want me to be more like Asher, but—"

"That's not—"

"Come on," she says, more gently now. "Mom's not here to play referee anymore. The least we can do is be honest with each other."

He sighs. "You want me to be honest with you?"

"Yes," Greta says with some amount of effort.

"Okay." He swivels to face her more fully. The light behind him is soft and indistinct, and in the reflection from the window, she can see Davis twirling Mary on the dance floor. She forces herself to look back at Conrad, who has her same green eyes, her same inscrutable gaze. "You know your mom was your biggest cheerleader—"

"Dad," Greta says, her throat going thick, because even though she'd been the one to bring her up, it feels like he's cheating somehow, invoking her mother like this. "Don't."

He looks surprised. "Don't what?"

"This isn't about her," she says. "It's about you and me."

"That's my point," he says, shaking his head. "I know she understood this whole music thing better than me, but she was concerned about you too."

Greta works to keep her expression neutral. She doesn't want him to see how much this stings. She'd given up on him a long time ago, had accepted the fact that he didn't think much of her dreams. But her mom did. And that had always been enough.

"You don't know what you're talking about," she says.

"She was your biggest fan," he says, looking suddenly very faraway. "But she worried too. About you being alone and traveling so much and trying to stay afloat in an industry that's so uncertain. Maybe she covered it better than I do, but it isn't—it wasn't just me, okay? It was her too."

Greta sits very still, letting the words wash over her. After a few seconds, Conrad leans forward, the look on his face starting to slip.

"I'm sorry," he says. "I didn't mean to—"

"It's fine."

The song ends, and there's a smattering of applause from the diners. Conrad clears his throat. "We were never great without her, huh?"

"No," she says. "We weren't."

"It's even harder now."

She nods, surprised by how quickly her eyes have welled up. But it's true. Everything's harder now.

"I'm glad you came on this trip, though," he says, and in spite of herself, Greta laughs. Conrad tilts his head to one side. "What?"

"I was literally just thinking that I shouldn't have come."

"Well," he says with a shrug, "I'm glad you did."

"Are you?" she asks, looking at him carefully, but then the Fosters and the Blooms return to the table, still laughing from their adventures on the dance floor, and the waiter arrives with their salads, and the sky outside darkens another shade, and the ship sails on into the night, and it isn't until later that Greta realizes he never actually answered the question.

# Chapter Five

After dinner, Greta returns to her room, where she sits cross-legged on the bed, her guitar balanced on her knees. The others have gone to try their luck at the casino, but the thought of all those chiming slot machines is too much for her at the end of a day like today.

She holds a pick between her lips as she tunes the old wooden Martin. She rarely travels with this one; it's bulkier than the lean electric guitars she mainly uses when she performs. But she's had it forever, and there's a comfort to it, like a worn book, well used and well loved. She bought it in college, scraping together tips from her waitressing job at the local Olive Garden, every basket of breadsticks inching her closer. And though she now has literally dozens of guitars—most of them slim and sleek and powerful, more acrobatic and explosive in sound—she still finds herself reaching for this one often, each note vibrating through her like a memory.

She plays a single chord, the sound bright as a match in the small confines of the cabin. Then a few more, until she realizes she's veered into the beginning of "Astronomy." She lifts her hands abruptly, as if she's touched something hot, and the silence rushes back in like the tide.

It's more specter than song at this point. She'd started writing it on the flight back from Germany, still reeling from the news about her mom's aneurysm. She tried to sleep, but couldn't. She tried to drink, but her hands were shaking too badly. Out the window, the sky was completely black, and the absence of stars felt ominous. Her stomach churned.

She closed her eyes and thought about the glow-in-the-dark stars on her bedroom ceiling back home, the way her mom used to point up at them after reading her a story. The memory felt hopeful somehow, and she pulled out her notebook and began to write, trying to push back the darkness with each line, her own kind of prayer.

By the time the Atlantic was behind her, she had a full page of lyrics and the ghost of a melody. It was a song about charting your course and finding your way, but it was really—like all songs—about something more personal than that, about lying in bed with her mom when she was little, talking and dreaming and telling stories beneath those glow-in-the-dark stars.

It wasn't finished. But it had felt like the start of something.

She just didn't yet know what.

This time, when she begins to play, she's more deliberate. She picks out the opening notes of "Prologue," the first single off her upcoming album, the song she's meant to debut at Governors Ball next weekend. It's an entirely different sort of tune, fast-paced and full of heat, and even on an acoustic guitar, it fills the room.

She knows this is the way back, this song. It's her chance at redemption. But already it feels like a relic, something she wrote in a different lifetime, when her mom was still alive and Greta was still full of confidence.

There's a knock on the wall to her left, and she goes silent. She waits a few seconds before trying again, softly this time. But the next knock is more insistent. With a sigh, Greta sets the guitar on the bed beside her, grabs her mother's fleece from the hook on the back of the door, and steps out into the hallway, suddenly desperate for air.

Outside, the night is still suspended in twilight, everything misty and gray. Greta walks along the promenade deck until she finds a quiet spot. She leans out, her eyes watering from the wind. Far below, the ship kicks up a white froth, and the waves ripple out until they get lost in the fog. Tomorrow, they'll spend the whole day on this boat, stuck at sea until they reach Juneau the following morning. It feels like a long time to wait.

"All I keep thinking about is the *Titanic,*" someone says, and she glances down the railing to see the typewriter guy again. He's wearing a waterproof jacket, trim and green with a hood, and his brown hair is mussed from the wind.

"The ship or the movie?"

"Does it matter?" he asks with a smile. "Neither ended particularly well."

They're both quiet, peering out at the deepening sky. Greta is about to push off the rail and head inside when he looks her way again.

"This is kind of weird, isn't it?"

"What?"

He shrugs. "I don't know. Being out here like this. On a ship. At night. Just bobbing around in the middle of the water. There's something lonely about it."

"Is there?" she asks, and for some reason, this makes her think about the time she got a bad flu in her twenties and her mom flew out to take care of her. For three days, Helen made soup on the janky stove in Greta's tiny apartment, and they sat on the couch in pajamas and watched movies as the radiator hissed and the snow pinged against the window. One afternoon, when she thought Greta was sleeping, Helen called Conrad to check in, and in that foggy, thick-headed place between sleep and awake, Greta heard her lower her voice. "I know," she murmured. "It's times like this when I wish she had someone too."

Until that moment, it hadn't occurred to Greta to feel lonely.

She'd just returned after seven months of touring, opening for a band she'd admired since she was sixteen—the whole experience quite literally a dream come true—and in all those days of travel and nights onstage, all the quotidian acts of her life had been shed: regular phone calls to her parents, texts to friends, even the fling she'd been having at the time with Jason Foster. When she'd returned, her brain was still sparking and firing, overcharged by those months filled with fans and frenzy, and she'd spent the next few weeks in the same gray hoodie and leggings, moving from her notebook to her computer to her guitar in a burst of creative productivity. She'd never been happier.

But suddenly she could see things through her mom's eyes: how she'd come home to an empty apartment and had no one to take care of her when she got sick. It didn't matter that Greta hadn't actually asked Helen to come; she would've been fine ordering soup from the diner downstairs and resting up until she was better. And it didn't matter that she could afford a bigger apartment now if she wanted one; it was that this place she'd lived in for so many years felt like home. Her life wasn't this way by default; it was this way because she liked it this way.

She turns back to the guy with a shiver. His eyes are still on the water.

"I've been reading a lot about Herman Melville lately . . ." He pauses, glancing over at Greta uncertainly. "Melville was—"

" 'Bartleby, the Scrivener,' " she says, and his eyes light up.

"Wow," he says. "Most people go right for *Moby-Dick*."

She nods at the water. "Too obvious."

"Anyway," he says, looking pleased, "I was reading about when Melville first went to sea. He was only nineteen, which seems so young now, and he wound up on this merchant ship that sailed from New York to . . . actually, you know what?" He laughs. "This is the part where my six-year-old would tell me I need to recalculate."

"Recalculate?"

"Like on a GPS," he says sheepishly. "When you go down the wrong road, and it starts recalculating your route. I have a tendency to take the long way."

"That's not always a bad thing," she says, and he scratches at his beard, which is trim and flecked with gray at the edges. He's handsome in a deeply wholesome way, clean-cut and earnest, and though he can't be more than a few years older than her, he seems like an adult with a capital *A*, like someone who has his shit together, like the guys she sees in holiday photos from college friends she's mostly lost touch with because their lives are too different.

He walks over and sticks out a hand. "I'm Ben, by the way. Ben Wilder. As in Laura Ingalls."

In spite of herself, Greta laughs. "You must have sisters."

"Daughters," he says with a grin, and her eyes automatically flick to his hand. He's not wearing a wedding ring. "And you are?"

"Greta." She pauses, debating about the last name, then decides it doesn't matter. He won't know her. She can tell just by looking at him that he listens mostly to Dave Matthews and Bob Dylan. Maybe a little Phish in college. "James," she says finally.

"As in Bond," he says with a knowing nod.

"As in Bond," she agrees.

The lights above them flicker on as the sky settles into an approximation of darkness, and in the distance, they can hear the rise and fall of voices from one of the ship's many bars.

"You know," Ben says, "sailors in the British Royal Navy used to get a ration of rum for every day they were at sea. It was safer than the water. And good for morale."

"I bet."

"I think I'm gonna go for one. You're welcome to join."

She hesitates. But only for a second. "I should probably get back."

"Okay," he says with a smile. "Then I'll see you around, Bond."

"Have a good night, Laura Ingalls."

# SUNDAY

*Chapter Six*

Greta wakes in the dark, the only light coming from the glowing red numbers on the alarm clock, which reads 3:08 A.M. She's used to this moment of confusion, the first few seconds after sleep when she has to think hard to remember where she is, which hotel room in what time zone. But the absence of windows and the rolling of the ship beneath her makes this all the more disorienting. It's been twelve hours now, and this is the first time she's truly felt like she's at sea.

She reaches for her phone, squinting as the screen brightens, and sees she has a text from Luke: Got my jacket. Left the key.

That's it. No goodbye. No sign-off. Just: the end.

She doesn't really blame him. It had taken her weeks to even respond to his request for his favorite leather jacket, which he'd forgotten the day he came to pack up his things and which she'd been secretly hoping he might let her keep. For a while, she'd taken to wearing it around the apartment. It still smelled like his cigarettes.

Now she stares at his name on her screen, debating whether to simply delete the whole contact. But she doesn't. Instead, she toggles back and lets her finger hover over the entry for Jason Foster.

She hasn't heard from him since the day of the funeral, when she'd fled the reception downstairs and found him in her old bedroom, running a hand along her first guitar, the one her dad had bought all those years ago. They hadn't seen each other in a long time, almost two years, and it had never occurred to her that he'd come home for the service. As she watched his dark hands trace the curve of the instrument, moving slowly across the swirling mahogany, she felt goosebumps rise on her forearms. It was almost like he was touching her instead.

Greta's mom had died exactly twenty-four minutes before her plane hit the tarmac. After listening to the voicemail from Asher, she'd sat with her head pressed against the cool of the window, her heart clenching like a fist inside her chest, until a flight attendant laid a gentle hand on her shoulder, and she'd realized she was the last one on the plane.

At the moment, Luke was still in Germany. He'd tried to get a flight back when she told him, but a bad storm had swept in just after she left, grounding most transatlantic travel, and everything had been booked for days. Already, he'd missed the funeral, which her father had insisted on scheduling as quickly as possible, and it was becoming obvious that he was going to miss being there at all. It didn't matter that he'd sounded devastated when he called to break the news to her. She wasn't even really upset about this. There were other things, too many to count. Even so, she knew this would be the one she'd never forgive.

And now Jason was in her room. Jason Foster: the first boy she'd ever loved, and the man she returned to after every failed relationship.

They had rules about this sort of thing. They never officially dated, and they never used each other to cheat. There were no strings attached and no expectations. This was fun and satisfying, nothing more. And it worked for both of them: Greta, who was always traveling and could never seem to commit to anyone for the long haul, and Jason, who was always working and had never wanted anything permanent.

But now her boyfriend was stranded overseas, and her mother had just died, and everything was a mess.

And mostly, he was there, and Luke wasn't.

Neither said a word as they walked toward each other, but Greta remembers, in the fog of grief and exhaustion and shock, thinking how inevitable it felt right then. There was a moment to tell him about Luke—a moment to consider Luke, period—and then that moment passed, and Jason's arms were around her, and there was nothing more to be done about it.

Afterward, they lay in her old twin bed and stared up at the glow-in-the-dark stars. Jason let his head fall to the side, peering at her childhood bookshelf. He reached over to pull out a fraying paperback, and she put a hand on his arm.

"What?" he said, turning back to her with a lazy smile. "You worried I'm gonna find your diary? I bet it says 'Greta Foster' all over it."

She rolled her eyes. "You wish."

"Oh, come on," he teased. He had a new haircut, faded on the sides, that made him look younger, and something about seeing him here in her childhood bed—with that self-assured grin and those dimples that used to make her go wobbly—made her feel like time was elastic, like all her teenage fantasies were suddenly coming true. He tickled her hip, and she shivered. There was laughter in his voice when he whispered in her ear: "You wanted to marry me from the day the moving truck rolled up. Admit it."

Greta shook her head. "No way."

"Admit it."

"Fine," she said with a smile, relenting. "Maybe a little. But then I grew up."

He dropped his head back onto the pillow, looking up at the stars with a thoughtful expression. "Do you ever wonder where we'd be if . . ."

"What?"

"If we'd gotten together for real."

Greta looked over at him, too surprised to answer.

"Like, would we have ended up back here, do you think?"

"In Columbus?" she said. "No way."

He smiled. "I don't know. Sometimes I can see it. A little house in the neighborhood. Kids playing tag until dark, the way we always did. Family dinners. Barbecues out back. The whole deal."

She knew he was just musing, that on this of all weekends, the air was thick with nostalgia. But it was still jarring to hear. Jason was the only person Greta knew who had been equally anxious to get away from this place, this kind of life. In high school, he'd thrown himself into his work with a single-minded determination that had eventually carried him to Columbia, where instead of taking a breath, he'd redoubled his efforts, graduating at the top of his class. Later, he became the first Black CFO at his hedge fund, a position he'd worked twice as hard as his colleagues to get, all those smug white guys whose dads were clients or who played golf with people who were. But it wasn't just a job to him. And New York wasn't just a place to live. They were dreams he'd dreamed on the front stoop of the small yellow house next door to where they were lying in bed right now. And he'd gone and made them real.

"You would never leave the city," Greta said, still trying to get her head around the idea of it. "Would you?"

His brown eyes were intent on hers. "Maybe under the right circumstances," he said. "What about you?"

"I don't know," she told him, unsure whether they were talking about geography or something more. Her mind was a muddle, with the reception carrying on below and the plastic stars glowing above. She felt like kissing him and she felt like running away. She felt like crying and she felt like escaping. She didn't know what she felt. She hardly ever did.

"We should probably get back," she said eventually, and he looked disappointed but rose up onto his elbows anyway.

"You're probably right," he said with a nod.

They made their way downstairs one at a time, after smoothing shirts and straightening hair and unmussing everything that had been mussed. Greta was only a few steps into the kitchen when her dad waved her over. He was already talking to Jason, who gave her a knowing smile.

"Did you see who's here?" Conrad asked, clapping Jason on the shoulder. In only a few days without her mom, he already looked different—pale and grizzled—but she could tell he was trying to make an effort, to fill the role that Helen usually did when they had people over. "So nice of you to come in for this, son. I know it would've meant a lot to her."

"I wouldn't have missed it," Jason said with a solemn nod. "She was one of my favorite people."

"You're still in banking, right?" Conrad asked. "I know you two run in pretty different circles, but do you ever see each other in the city?"

"Not for a while," Jason said at the exact same moment Greta said, "Sometimes."

"I'm not nearly cool enough to hang out with a rock star on a regular basis," Jason continued, all dimples and charm. "I imagine there aren't a lot of suits at your shows."

Greta raised her eyebrows. "You'd know if you came to one."

"They're always sold out," he said with a grin.

"Lucky you know someone then."

Their eyes were locked now, and Greta nearly forgot her dad was standing there until he lifted his bottle of beer. "Oh," he said, turning to her. "Luke called a little while ago. He finally managed to get a flight, so he'll be here tomorrow morning."

Greta dropped her eyes to the floor, though she could feel Jason watching her. "Great," she managed to say, her voice very small, and then her dad headed off to help Asher with the food, and it was just the two of them again. She braced herself for whatever it was he might say, but he only reached out and took her hand in an overly formal way.

"I'm really sorry about your mom," he said, pressing her fingers tightly for a beat, and then he turned around and walked into the next room, leaving her alone in the kitchen.

That was the last time they spoke. For the rest of the day, he avoided her, and when Luke finally showed up the next morning—bleary-eyed from his long trip—Jason had already flown back to New York.

Greta sets her phone down, then picks it up again. It's after six in Ohio, which means her brother will be up with the kids. She starts to call him, then remembers she's at sea with limited service and types out a text instead: SOS. Twelve hours down. A million to go.

It only takes a few seconds for his reply to arrive: Four out of five of us have strep throat. Wanna trade?

Greta writes back, It's not easy being the favorite, which is what she says whenever he complains about his life, the life her dad so desperately wishes she had too. But her heart isn't really in it right now because, honestly, strep throat sounds only marginally worse than her own situation.

Another text comes through: How's Dad?

Same as always, she replies.

I'm glad you're there.

Me too, Greta types, then deletes it. The truth is, she's glad he has someone. But she suspects they both wish that someone wasn't her. Instead, she writes: Hope you guys feel better soon.

He signs off with a Bon voyage!, and Greta swings her feet off the bed. She sits there in the dark for a few minutes, listening to the sounds of the ship, and then she reaches for her guitar, hoping her neighbors are asleep this time.

Quietly, she begins to play, her fingers moving quickly from string to string. When she was younger, her teachers always tried to steer her back to the melody when she veered off course, not realizing that—for her—the experimentation was in fact the point. Even now, critics often struggle to describe exactly what her music is: indie or rock, pop or folk. The truth is, it's a little bit of all of them, and also nothing like any of them. It's a sound all her own.

Her eyelids begin to grow heavy again. *A lullaby,* she thinks, pressing her palm flat against the still-vibrating strings so that the music ends with a quiet thump. Then she places the guitar carefully into its case and crawls back under the covers.

When she wakes again, the clock says 9:21 A.M. She was supposed to meet her dad at the Overboard Buffet twenty minutes ago, so she ties her hair into a messy knot at the top of her head and dresses in a hurry, throwing on leggings and black boots and a jean jacket over the Pink Floyd T-shirt she slept in. Before leaving the room, she grabs a pair of sunglasses out of habit, slipping them on as she steps out into the hallway.

She rides the elevator up with a couple so old they both have to hang on to the gold bar that runs along the inside. The woman—who is small and stooped, with brown skin and deep wrinkles and a wispy halo of silvery hair—stares at her hard, then raises a finger to point at Greta's face. "You're very pale," she says with a frown.

Greta nods, because this is true enough. She takes after her mother, whose parents were both from Scotland. She has the same dark hair as Helen did, the same scattered freckles across the bridge of her nose, and the same pale complexion that's been described as porcelain in so many magazines, her brother jokes that people must think at least one of their ancestors was a toilet.

"Make sure you wear sunblock," the woman continues. "Just because the sky is gray doesn't mean it can't get you."

"Will do," Greta says as they come to a stop on the lido deck and the couple starts to shuffle out of the elevator. "Thanks for the tip."

"You don't want to look like me when you're eighty-nine," the woman calls back over her shoulder, and Greta smiles.

"I should be so lucky."

At the restaurant, she spots her dad and the rest of the crew across the buffet. They're sitting at a table in the corner beneath a painting of a grizzly bear, their plates already empty. Her dad holds up a champagne flute when he sees her, and Todd slides another in her direction as she pulls out a chair. He's already got his binoculars around his neck, ready for the day.

Greta frowns at the glass. "Isn't it a little early?"

"I thought you were a rock star," Davis teases, and when Greta takes a sip, she can feel it fizz all the way down her throat.

"What's the occasion?" she asks.

"Well," Mary says, beaming, "we got an email from Jason this morning."

"Which is an occasion in and of itself," Davis jokes, and Mary looks so excited she doesn't even bother to roll her eyes at this. Instead, she lets out a happy laugh.

"They got engaged last night!" she says, and when it's clear that Greta still isn't sure what's happening, Mary widens her eyes. "Jason and Olivia."

For a moment, Greta just stares at her. She's never even heard of Olivia. Beneath them, the ship lists, and she can feel the champagne sloshing around in her empty stomach. She has to concentrate to keep it from coming back up again.

"Wow," she says finally, trying to arrange her face into something resembling a smile. "That's . . . wow. Congrats. To both of you."

"Mother and father of the groom," Mary says, smiling at Davis, who grins back at her. "It has a nice ring to it."

"Speaking of rings," Eleanor says, her face brightening at the thought, "did they send a photo?"

"I couldn't get it to download," Mary tells her. "But apparently he bought it at a flea market, so who knows . . ."

"Well, she said yes," Conrad says. "Which is the important thing."

Mary lets out a happy sigh. "That's true. She said yes."

"How long have they been together?" Greta asks, trying to sound like a vaguely interested childhood friend rather than someone who has been sleeping with their son on and off for the past decade.

"Oh, must be about a year now," Davis says. "She's a nice girl. You'll like her."

"I'm just happy he's finally settled down," Mary says, and for once, Greta doesn't even care about the look Conrad gives her, which plainly suggests she might think about doing the same. She's too busy trying to get her head around it: Jason Foster is getting married.

For all her years of teenage pining, and all the chemistry they discovered later, she never really imagined herself with him in that way. Not for real. Jason works on the forty-second floor of a huge international bank. He wears suits every day and takes black cars to the office and always preferred to stay at his place, which is sleek and shiny and has white carpeting so pristine that Greta was afraid to drink red wine there. Her life—the small, cluttered apartment with its wilting plants, the months of travel and the late evenings in bars with random musicians, the nights she wakes up with a tune in her head and sets the room aglow with her phone screen as she tries to capture it—that's never been for him. They never would've worked.

Still, she feels a gut punch at the thought of him marrying someone else. It occurs to her that if they've been together for a year, that means he was surely with Olivia that day Greta found him in her old bedroom. She knows she's not above reproach herself; she was with someone too. But they were on the decline, whether or not Luke realized it yet. Jason, on the other hand, was ramping up to a proposal. And in the Horrible Person Olympics, doesn't that make him worse?

It's a particularly strange kind of loss, when something you don't think you even want gets taken away from you. Greta feels the sting of it, a dull hurt rising from someplace inside her she hadn't even known was there. She thinks maybe it's sadness, a tiny sort of grief; but if she's being really honest, it's probably something closer to embarrassment, or maybe even jealousy, though for what, she's not entirely sure. She doesn't want that life. Not now. And not with him. So then why should this news unsettle her so much?

Her dad is saying something to her, and she blinks at him. "What?"

"We're gonna hit the spa," he repeats, standing up. "We've all got appointments at ten."

"For what?" she asks, surprised. Her dad is a beer guy. A fishing guy. A sit-around-and-watch-baseball guy. Greta has never in her whole life known him to go to a spa; in fact, the idea of him walking around in a fluffy robe is about as strange as if he'd shown up to breakfast in a clown costume.

"Some kind of massage," he says, glancing over at Todd, who is wearing a brand-new hat with the logo of the cruise ship on it. "Is that what's happening? These guys made the appointments. I have no idea what I'm getting myself into."

"You'll love it," Eleanor assures him as she digs through her purse for a tube of cherry-red lipstick. "It's just what you need to relax and take your mind off things."

Conrad's smile freezes slightly, but he nods. "I'm hoping it'll help my back, anyway."

"Did you want to come?" Mary asks Greta. "We weren't sure. We figured you might want a break from all of us old folks."

"I'm okay, thanks. I'm gonna grab some breakfast, and then I can meet up with you later."

"Here," Conrad says, sliding a piece of paper over to her. It's a list of daily activities, and he's circled several of them in blue pen. "We've got the spa at ten, then lunch at the Admiral at noon, then there's a talk I want to see at two, and bingo at three—"

"Bingo?" Greta says skeptically.

He ignores this. "Then we're supposed to be passing some sea lions around six, so we'll head out to the promenade deck to catch that."

"And hopefully some marbled murrelets too," Todd adds with enthusiasm. "They're often found in these parts."

"And hopefully some marbled murrelets too," Conrad agrees in a slightly placating tone. In all the years they've been friends, Todd has had little success in recruiting the others to his favorite hobby. "Then dinner tonight at Portside, and the piano bar for a nightcap."

"Wow," Greta says, staring at the list. "That's quite the itinerary."

"You can come to as much or little as you want," he says, standing up from the table. "Totally up to you."

"Here." Mary hands her a booklet with the daily schedule of activities. "See what sounds good to you, and meet us wherever, okay?"

Greta nods. "Sure. Enjoy the spa."

When they're gone, she sits alone at the table with a cup of coffee, staring at the painting of the grizzly bear. One of its giant paws has a silvery fish pinned under it, the river streaming around them. The fish is wild-eyed and flailing, even in stillness, and Greta starts to feel queasy again. She forces herself to look away.

The booklet on the table is thick, with two neat staples along one side. She flips idly through the photos and descriptions of various events—the jugglers and magicians, hypnotists and mimes, lecturers and historians—until she recognizes a familiar face. Right there on page 11 is a picture of Benjamin Wilder, bestselling author and associate professor of history at Columbia University.

For some reason, this makes her laugh. He looks so serious in the photo, so professorial, with those thick-rimmed glasses and an expression of great concentration. Beneath the picture, there's a bio that's mostly about his internationally bestselling novel, *One Wild Song,* which apparently tells a fictional version of the story of Jack London, the author of *The Call of the Wild* and *White Fang,* among other works. She glances over at the itinerary her father had marked up and sees that the two o'clock lecture is called "Jack London: An Alaskan Perspective."

She hadn't been planning on joining them for much besides the sea lions. But when she stands up to go to the buffet, she tucks the booklet into the pocket of her jacket, just in case.

## Chapter Seven

If her dad is surprised to see Greta waiting at the door to the auditorium, he doesn't show it. He's still pink-faced from his morning at the spa, and the deep groove between his eyebrows—which has taken up residence in the months since her mom died—has all but disappeared.

"How was it?" Greta asks when he walks up. "Relaxing?"

"Actually, yes," he says, raising his arms in a stretch. He's wearing a navy golf jacket zipped up all the way, and his mostly white hair is still damp from the shower. Her eye is drawn, as it always is, to the hook-shaped scar on his chin, from a fight he'd broken up during his bartending days. When she was little, Greta used to trace it with her finger. Now she sees how much the map of his face is crowded with other lines too. "My back feels amazing," he says as he lowers his arms again. "What are you doing here?"

She holds up the itinerary. "You gave me your schedule."

"I know," he says, looking around at the crowd outside the auditorium. Beside them, there's a poster with the name of the talk and a picture of Ben's book, which features a snowy landscape and a distant team of sled dogs. "But you've never really been the lecture type."

"I only avoid lectures from *you*," she teases, and to her surprise, this makes him laugh. "Besides, we're stuck on the ship all day. What else am I gonna do?"

"You say that like it's a sailboat. They've got everything here.

Why don't you try the casino? Or go shopping at one of those stores in the atrium?"

Greta stares at him. "Is that what you think I like to do?"

"I have no idea what you like to do," he says. "Except play guitar."

"Well, I tried that already, and my neighbors weren't too pleased."

He rolls his eyes. "Please try not to get kicked off the ship, okay?"

"What could they even do?" she asks. "Send me off on a dinghy?"

"I don't know, but let's not find out."

Over his shoulder, she sees the Blooms and the Fosters, all looking equally refreshed, and when the doors open, they file into the auditorium behind a decent-sized crowd, pretty much all of them in their seventies.

Mary leans over to whisper to Greta as they take their seats. "Have you read it?" she asks, gesturing at the image of Ben's cover, which is being projected on a screen at the back of the stage. "We did it for book club. It's beautiful."

"I've never even read *Call of the Wild*," Greta says, her eyes wandering around the room, which is more than half full. This is where they hold the big shows at night, the dancers and comedians and magicians that pull in large crowds, so it's actually not a bad turnout, though already an elderly man is snoring behind her. It sounds like a buzz saw, but his companions either don't notice or aren't bothered by it.

A thought occurs to her, and she turns back to Mary. "When?" she asks with more urgency than intended. "When did you read it for book club?"

At first, Mary looks confused. But then it clicks and she gives Greta's hand a sympathetic pat. "Your mom loved it too," she says with a smile.

When Ben walks out, Greta sits forward. He's wearing a tweed blazer with a blue-and-white checkered shirt underneath, and he spreads his arms wide and grins at the audience.

"Wow," he says, looking delighted by the size of the crowd. "I guess we have a lot of Jack London buffs on this ship, huh?"

The audience chuckles at this.

"How many people here have read *The Call of the Wild*?" Ben asks, and quite a few hands go up. His eyes comb the theater, and when he notices Greta, he pauses for a second, looking surprised. She half-raises her hand, deciding she must've at least seen the movie at some point. Mary gives her a sideways look, and Greta shrugs.

"How about *White Fang*?" Ben asks, pulling his eyes away from her, and Greta lowers her hand as several new ones go up. "Okay, great. That's not bad. But I have a feeling I'm about to stump you all. Who here has read *The Cruise of the Dazzler*?"

There's a ripple of laughter when people twist around to see that there are no longer any raised hands. Ben stares at them in mock astonishment.

"C'mon, folks. That was one of his first novels. *The Cruise of the Dazzler*. Very important for our purposes here today, since you should all know that I'm planning to be the dazzler of this cruise."

On the other side of her, Eleanor lets out a bark of a laugh. "Corny but cute," she says, leaning in to whisper to Greta. "Just my type."

Ben introduces himself but he doesn't linger on his own story. Instead, he moves right into talking about Jack London's perilous journey through Alaska at the height of the Klondike gold rush, and all the writing that came out of those long wintry months in the Yukon. Greta had expected it to be kind of boring, listening to him discuss the importance of the stories in a historical context and the problematic aspects in a modern one. But it's not.

He's not Billy Joel at the Garden; he's not Springsteen at Asbury Park. But he's a good speaker, and he brings the past to life in a way that keeps everyone's attention. Which is no easy feat, given that it's probably nap time for half the audience.

When it's time for questions, he calls on a woman in the front row who is waving her hand so hard it looks like she's trying to hail a cab. "How long did it take you to write your book?" she asks, then sits back in her seat, satisfied.

"Oh," Ben says mildly. He adjusts his glasses, then gives her a smile. "Well, I suppose you could say it took most of my life, since I've been thinking about Jack London since I was a kid. But as for the actual writing, maybe a couple years. I had done a lot of the research already, just from a lifetime of interest."

"But it's fiction," says a man sitting a few rows down. "So that's got to be harder. You had to make the story exciting too."

Greta finds it amusing that so many of the questions about his process are similar to the ones she's asked again and again in interviews, and she can tell that his answers—like hers—are somewhat canned at this point. But still, everyone is leaning forward with genuine interest, waiting to hear what he has to say, and it occurs to her that they must have read the book. All of them. For some reason, this comes as a surprise.

When the talk is over, her dad starts to head out along with the Fosters and the Blooms. "Don't want to be late for bingo," Mary says as she scoots past Greta's knees. "You coming?"

Greta glances at her dad, trying to gauge whether he'd like her to, but to her relief, he's already walked off with Davis and Todd.

"Don't worry," Mary says. "We'll keep an eye on him."

She's about to get up and follow them out, already wondering how she's going to fill the rest of the day, when she sees Ben still standing in the front, talking to a small crowd that's gathered to ask him more questions. His jacket is off and his sleeves are rolled up, and he looks utterly delighted to be discussing his favorite subject. It occurs to Greta that he might be the only other person on this entire ship that isn't on their way to either bingo or the kiddie pool right now, and so she stays behind, propping her feet up on the back of the seat in front of her.

When the last person finally leaves, he gathers his papers and swings a messenger bag over his head. He's halfway up the aisle when he notices Greta still there in the back, and his face brightens.

"Hi," he says, moving along the row to sit one seat away.

She smiles. "You were pretty good up there."

"Wasn't my first rodeo," he says, but he looks pleased. "Did you stick around to ask more questions? I'm not sure I would've pegged you for a Jack London fan."

"I'm not," she says so quickly that he laughs.

"Not *yet.*"

"I think I was the only one in the whole room who hasn't read your book."

He waves this away with a grin. "It's highly overrated."

"I'm sure it's not."

"Well, then clearly you're also the only person who didn't read the *Times* review," he says, his brown eyes dancing. "They called it 'overblown and self-important.'"

Greta laughs. "Trust me, I've seen worse."

"It's okay—so did Jack London."

"You must really like the guy," she says, "to spend that much time with him."

He nods. "I always thought I'd write a new biography, but most of that ground has been covered, and I realized I was less interested in the facts than the story. So I decided to make it a novel." He looks around at the auditorium. "I didn't expect any of this, though."

"How could you?" Greta says with feeling. "You hope for it, maybe. But the odds are always so long. It's like winning the lottery."

"Exactly," he says, clearly relieved to be understood. "I spent two years chipping away at the book, mainly just to amuse myself. When I was done, I showed it to a friend in the English department, and he slipped it to his agent, and everything happened pretty fast from there. All this stuff is still really weird to me. Interviews, book tours, festivals . . ."

"Cruise ships."

"No, I was definitely counting on the cruise ships. I mean, why else would you write a book?" He smiles, then shakes his head. "I shouldn't joke. I'm actually sort of embarrassingly excited to be here. I've never been to Alaska before."

"Really? Not even a research trip?"

"Nope. I woke up every morning at four o'clock to write, and worked until my kids were awake. There definitely wasn't time for a research trip. Or money. But now I'm finally on my way." He pauses and looks at her sideways. "So what about you?"

"What about me?" she asks, peering up at the ceiling.

"What do you do when you're not cruising?"

"I'm a musician."

"No way," he says, raising his eyebrows. "What do you play?"

"Guitar, mostly."

"Right! I remember now." He mimes carrying a case, and she realizes it was only yesterday that she'd seen him with his typewriter. "And you do it for real?"

She knows what he's asking: whether it's a job or a hobby. It's what most people ask when she delivers this piece of information. It used to bother her, especially when she was younger and still grasping for a sense of legitimacy. But now there's a kind of satisfaction to it, well-earned after so many years of working and hoping and striving, of playing in front of crowds of eleven people in basement bars and opening for bands with far less talent and far more fans. There were successes along the way, of course, and a fairly steady sense of momentum, but Greta didn't truly break through until a few years ago, and it's different when it happens in your thirties, when you've got more than a decade of effort under your belt. So to her, this is what *making it* feels like: it's not the albums or the crowds or the money. It's getting to say—clearly and straightforwardly, without asterisks or qualifications—that yes, in fact, this is what she does. She's a musician. Simple as that.

Over the years, she's gotten all manner of condescending responses: *I'd love to get to play guitar all day* and *Man, wouldn't it be nice to do something fun instead of work* and *Wow, you can really support yourself doing that?* The fans, of course, are different, and there are more of them every day. But she'll never fully understand why skepticism is most people's first reaction. Maybe it's jealousy. Or maybe it's something deeper than that, a kind of resentment for having the audacity to be living her dream when theirs had to be left behind.

But when she answers Ben, he looks slightly awestruck.

"Wow," he says. "That's . . . possibly the coolest thing I've ever heard."

Greta smiles at this. A few seconds go by before she realizes they're both just sitting there, as if waiting for something.

Finally, he clears his throat. "So, um, were you sticking around because you had a question?"

"Yes," Greta says, standing up. "Did you want to get that drink now?"

## Chapter Eight

As they walk out of the auditorium, Ben stops to take a picture of a grand-looking staircase that winds down toward a lower level. A minute later, he pauses again, snapping a shot of a random sculpture of a sea otter.

Greta looks at him sideways. "Have you been commissioned to photograph the entire boat?"

He laughs. "They're for my kids. I'd prefer to send postcards, but they're way too impatient for that." He takes one more of the view out the window, the stripe of blue water and the spruce trees behind it. Then he slips the phone back into his pocket. "Oh, and it's a ship."

Greta shrugs. "Same thing."

"Not really," he says. "Ships have at least two decks above the waterline. This has eleven. Plus it weighs a lot more than five hundred tons. And its only form of propulsion is an engine, so . . ."

She gives him an incredulous look.

"Sorry, I'm a nerd," he says at the exact same time she says, "You're such a nerd."

They cross the lido deck, where the smell of chlorine is thick against the fogged-up windows and a water aerobics class is underway, dozens of swim caps bobbing in the turquoise water. As they walk out into the atrium—a bustling area full of shops and restaurants, as if they're not at sea at all but rather in a suburban mall somewhere—Preeti, the girl from yesterday, comes wandering out of an art gallery. Her face lights up when she sees Greta, and she yanks out her earbuds and hurries over.

"Hi," she says, giving Ben a cursory glance, then turning back to Greta. She holds up her phone. "I told my friend Caroline that I met you, but she doesn't believe me. Do you think we could take a selfie so I could send it to her as proof?"

"Sure," Greta says, glancing over at Ben, who looks understandably baffled by this.

He nods at the phone in Preeti's hand. "Want me to take it?"

"Um, no thank you," she says, narrowing her eyes at him. "I mean, it's a selfie, so . . ."

"So we've got it," Greta says, trying not to laugh at the look on his face. Preeti punches a few buttons, then holds the phone out, and Greta bends so their faces are close together. She gives a practiced smile just before the flash goes off, then straightens again.

"Proof," she says as they examine the photo. Greta's eyes look greener in the light, and her dark hair is wavy and loose. She's not wearing any makeup, and her face is characteristically pale. Beside her, Preeti is grinning and flashing a peace sign.

"I was always trying to get her to listen to your stuff," Preeti says as she sends it off, "but she's basically only into, like, Taylor Swift—which is fine, if that's your thing—but after that video of you went viral, she finally . . ." She stops, and her eyes, which have been on her phone, flick up to meet Greta's with a slightly panicked expression. "Sorry, I didn't mean—"

"It's fine," Greta says lightly, though her face is warm. She shouldn't feel as thrown as she does. Just because she's on a boat in the middle of nowhere doesn't mean anything has changed. It doesn't mean people aren't still talking about it. But this is the first time anyone she doesn't know—anyone outside her team—

has talked about it to *her*. And now, suddenly, here it is. Right out in the open.

Preeti's eyes are still wide. "I wasn't—"

"I know," Greta says, trying not to look at either one of them: Preeti, who is mortified, and Ben, who is deeply confused. "It's fine. Don't worry about it."

"Okay," Preeti says after a moment. She looks like she wants to say more, but instead she holds up the phone a little awkwardly. "Well, thanks for the selfie."

"Of course," Greta says in a too-bright voice. "I'll see you around, okay?"

When she's gone, Greta begins to walk again, and Ben trots to catch up to her. "What was that about?"

"Nothing," she says, shaking her head. "Which bar do you want to try?"

He's still looking at her sideways. "So you're, like, someone people know."

"Don't be too impressed. I'm pretty sure she's the only one on this whole ship."

"Yeah, but you have *fans*."

"So do you," Greta says as she heads toward the first bar she sees, which—inexplicably—has a tropical island theme. There's a Jimmy Buffett song drifting from inside, and the entrance is lined with fake palm trees. She starts to head in but turns when she realizes Ben isn't following her. "What?"

"Who are you, really?"

"I told you," she says. "I'm a musician."

"Like a pop star or something?"

She frowns. "Do I look like a pop star to you?"

"I guess not."

"Like I said, I play the guitar," she says with a shrug, but something about the encounter with Preeti has made her wobbly. She thinks about Gov Ball next weekend, and her hand closes around the phone in her pocket. She feels a sudden urge to call her manager, Howie, and tell him to forget the whole thing. That she's not ready yet. That it's too risky to go back out there before she is.

But she hasn't even told him she's on this trip. She hasn't told anyone: not her publicist, not the label, not her agent, not even her best friend, Yara, a keyboardist who is out touring with Bruce Springsteen and would understand better than anyone why she's avoiding them all.

For several days now, there's been a steady drumbeat of emails and text messages about the festival and the launch of the new single. The subject lines include requests for local radio appearances and sit-downs with music journalists. Strategies for how to frame what happened in March and "reset her image." Suggested talking points and timelines.

Greta hasn't read any of it.

It's so unlike her. She's not usually the stereotypical version of a rock star her dad seems to think she is: consumed by the lifestyle and leaving the business part to others. She cares too much for that. She writes her own tracks and handles her own licensing, shows up early for sound check and spends hours and hours in the studio. When she's onstage, it's supposed to look effortless. Not just the way she plays—the massive guitar riffs and thrilling crescendos—but also the way she appears to the audience: powerful, incendiary, captivating. All those things are true. But they're fueled by a relentless work ethic and a deep desire to keep getting better, to keep making music, to keep people listening and showing up and buying albums.

Now, of course, that's all gone out the window. Both the image and the work ethic.

Now all she wants to do is get a drink and pretend none of this is happening.

Inside, they find seats at the bar. There are brightly colored flowers everywhere, and the bartenders are wearing Hawaiian shirts. A blue surfboard leans up against the wall.

"All very Alaskan," Ben says once they've ordered their drinks: a margarita for him and a strawberry daiquiri for her, because what else do you order in a place like this?

"Yeah," Greta says, looking around, "this is definitely getting me in the mood to visit a frozen tundra."

Ben looks amused. "It's hardly a tundra. We're going to be seeing some of the most interesting landscapes in Alaska. In the world, really."

Their drinks arrive, and she plucks the small paper umbrella out of hers. "You've clearly done your homework."

"You haven't?"

"This was sort of a last-minute decision for me."

"A last-minute Alaskan cruise?"

Greta hesitates a second, debating whether to be honest, then says, "It was supposed to be my mom here with my dad and their friends—not me." She takes a sip of her daiquiri, which is much too sweet. When she lifts her eyes again, Ben's smile has fallen. "It's okay," she says quickly, even though it's not. Not at all. "It happened a few months ago."

"That's not very long."

"No," she agrees, "it's not."

He taps a finger against his glass. She can see the faint line where his wedding band had once been.

"It's nice you can be with your dad," he says, and she nods.

"They'd been planning this trip for ages, and he still wanted to come. So my brother asked me to keep him company."

"Why you?"

She shrugs. "Because he has three kids and a day job."

"And you . . ."

"Have very few daily responsibilities and a zillion frequent-flier miles." She takes a long swig of her drink. "It's fine. I wouldn't even mind it, honestly, if it didn't mean a whole week with my dad."

"You guys don't get along?"

"Not really."

"Why not?"

"Because I don't have three kids and a day job."

He stares at her. "Seriously?"

"That's part of it."

"What's the other part?"

"Let's just say I'm not exactly the favorite."

Ben opens his mouth to say something, then closes it again.

"What?"

"Nothing," he says. "It's just . . . I have so many questions for you. I'm not sure what to ask first. I don't want to overwhelm you."

Greta smiles. "I'm not easily overwhelmed."

"Okay. So your dad—"

"Wait," she says, lifting her glass, which is now empty. "I do need another drink first. In fact, I may need several."

"Fair enough."

She swivels in her seat, facing him more fully. Their knees are almost touching, but not quite. "Do you have another lecture today?" she asks, and he shakes his head. "So you don't have anywhere else to be?"

"No," he says. "Why?"

"I think we should get drunk then."

Ben laughs. "I don't think so."

"Why not?"

"I'm here for work." He glances around as if someone might overhear them. "I'm representing Columbia."

"And, what, you're worried someone might approach you with a question about *The Call of the Wild* that you'll be too shit-faced to answer?"

His expression shifts, and he leans forward, eyes glinting. "Dude. I could drink a whole case of beer and still be able to tell you every detail of Jack London's life."

Greta motions for the bartender to bring them another round. "Prove it," she says.

# Chapter Nine

Somewhere around their third or fourth drink, Greta runs to the bathroom, and when she gets back, Ben is staring at her with a strange expression.

"What?" she asks, and he holds up his phone.

"I just looked you up."

"Uh-oh," she says in a playful voice, though every muscle in her body has gone tight. "That sounds ominous."

She searches for traces of pity—some sign that he's seen the video—but instead his expression is full of wonder. "You're kind of a big deal," he says, holding out his phone, as if she's asked for proof. On the screen, there's a picture from a *Rolling Stone* shoot she did when the first album came out. She's wearing a sleek black dress, and her dark hair is piled high on her head, and something about the makeup or the lighting makes her look like she's all angles. Her eyes are huge, greener than they should be, and there's a challenge in them.

He obviously hasn't gotten very far in his googling. This is the photo most often used of her, the first to come up in any search. But looking at it now, all Greta can see is how nervous she was underneath, how much she was sweating beneath the heat of those lights, the slight irritation around the corners of her mouth, a result of the photographer's repeated pleas for her to look at him without looking at him, whatever that was supposed to mean.

"You're kind of a big deal too," she says as she settles back onto the stool beside him.

Ben shakes his head. "It's not the same."

"Of course it is. You're a bestselling author. And you get to do what you love."

"I don't love it," he says with a shrug. "Not the way you do."

She raises her eyebrows. "How do you know? You just met me."

"I watched you play," he admits, nodding at his phone, which is now resting on the table between them. Even with a beard, he can't hide his blush.

"You did?"

"Yeah, just for a few seconds. But you're really good."

She begins to wave this away as she so often does, like it's no big deal, like it hardly even matters. But then she changes her mind and nods. "Thank you."

The bartender returns, and they order another round, and some appetizers too. It's nearly five now, and the bar is crowded all around them. It's almost alarmingly easy to forget they're on a ship off the coast of Alaska, and the fact of it seems stranger and stranger to Greta every time she remembers.

"So how did you get started?" Ben asks, leaning an elbow on the bar. "Is this what you always wanted to do? Do you play any other instruments?"

"Ben," she says.

"Yeah?"

"You don't have to interview me."

"What if I want to interview you?" He's smiling a little, his eyes trained on hers.

She takes a long sip of her drink. "You don't love it? Really?"

"What?"

"Writing."

He shakes his head. "I'm not one of those people who's been making up stories since they were a kid. I kind of backed into it."

"By being a professor?"

"By being a huge nerd."

She laughs. "Those aren't the same thing?"

"Very funny," he says, narrowing his eyes at her.

"But you'll write more?"

He shrugs. "I'm under contract for another one, but I'm having a hard time getting started."

"What's it about?"

"Herman Melville."

"Right," she says. "Whales."

"Among other things."

"So what's the issue? He's just not Jack London?"

She expects him to laugh again, but he doesn't. Instead, he looks somber. "I don't know. Maybe. I mean, I got my first copy of *Call of the Wild* at an estate sale when I was ten. My parents were buying a rocking chair, and when the guy found me reading it in a corner, he told me to keep it. I must've read that thing a hundred times. I loved it so much I wrote my college essay on Jack London, how I wish I had his spirit of adventure, how I'd never been more than fifty miles from my family's farm and was ready to make my own way in the world. Turned out to be my ticket out of there." He runs a hand over his beard, his eyes on the window behind them, where a layer of fog sits lightly atop the water. "When people talk about the way books can shape you, it always makes me laugh, because yeah, of course they do. But with me, it isn't a metaphor. My life would quite literally be completely different if I hadn't found my way to that book. Or, I guess, if that book hadn't found its way to me."

Greta smiles. "Nothing like your first love."

"Well, it turned out to be a lot more durable than my actual first love," he says morosely, then forces a laugh. "Sorry, it's still kind of new. Being separated. Though I guess the two things are wrapped up together, in a way. I started working on *Wild Song* just after we got married, and it came out about six months ago, right as everything was falling apart." He stares into his glass. "Anyway, now that story is over, and it's time to start another one. I guess I'm just having a hard time turning the page."

Greta isn't sure if they're talking about his books or his marriage now. "It can be tough to move on," she says. "You pour so much of yourself into that first one, and then you're supposed to do it all over again, just like that. There's a reason they say seconds are cursed."

He gives her a blank look.

"You know, the sophomore slump: how so many artists have these brilliant debuts and then their next try falls completely flat."

"Did yours?"

She takes a swig of her drink. "We'll see. It comes out in July."

"Wow," he says. "Well, I'm sure it'll be great."

Greta nods, fighting an impulse to tell him the whole story. Over the last three months, she's been almost acrobatic in her efforts to avoid the subject. But there's something about talking to a complete stranger—someone she'll never see again after this week—that almost makes her want to open up. Almost.

"Sometimes," he says, picking at the edge of his coaster, "I'm not sure I have another one in me."

She frowns at him. "You could quit? Just like that?"

"I like teaching. And being around people. Writing is lonely. It's different than playing music."

"That can be lonely too," she admits. "I'm on the road a lot."

"Yeah, but you have a band."

"Not a set one. Just musicians coming in and out on different tours."

"Well, you have fans."

"So do you," she says. "It's still lonely."

They look at each other for a long moment. The floor sways beneath her, and Greta's not sure if it's the alcohol or the ship. A new song comes on, and she lifts her eyes to the ceiling, searching for the speakers. When she looks back at Ben, he's still watching her.

"Can I ask you a question?" he says, but he doesn't wait for her answer. "Do you want all those things? That your dad wants for you?"

Greta shifts in her seat. It's been a long time since anyone has asked her that, a long time since she's let someone into this part of her life.

"I don't know," she says eventually. "Sometimes I think . . . maybe. I know I don't have forever. But I also love my life. The freedom of it. And I like being selfish. I know how that sounds, but I like that I can spend a whole weekend working on a new song if I want to. I like being on the road two hundred days a year. And being able to throw a few things in a bag and head out the door without anyone hassling me about my schedule. It's nice not to have too many strings attached sometimes." She gives him an impatient look. "I realize how that makes me sound. And I know most people don't feel that way. Most people want security. They want someone to be there for them. A partner."

"And you don't?"

"I don't know," she says. "I mean, it's not like I haven't had relationships. And some of them have been really great. But I don't mind it—being on my own. Sometimes I even kind of love it."

Ben nods. "Nothing wrong with that."

She swirls the little paper umbrella around in her glass. "I do wonder if I'll feel differently about it all later, and then it will be too late. I don't want it now." She gives him a hard look, as if he were about to argue otherwise. "But I hate wondering whether

Future Greta will be pissed at Current Greta for not having my shit together, you know?"

He laughs. "I'm still too pissed at Past Ben for some of the stuff he did to worry too much about Future Ben at the moment."

"Do you miss it?"

"What?"

"Being married, having a partner, a home."

He runs a finger along the edge of his glass. "I miss my girls."

"Tell me about them."

The look that passes across his face is so genuine, so sweetly earnest, that Greta feels like she knows everything about what kind of father he is before he even says a word. "Well, Avery is six, and Hannah is four," he says, reaching for his phone, presumably to show her some pictures. But then he changes his mind and pulls his hand away again. "Avery is obsessed with unicorns and books and ninjas, and Hannah is obsessed with whatever Avery is obsessed with."

"Sounds like they have good taste."

"They do," he says with a smile. "They're pretty great. I mean, don't get me wrong—they can be a lot too. But they're both such funny, ridiculous, amazing little humans." He shrugs. "It's pretty cool."

"And their mom?" Greta keeps her face neutral as she says this. She's not sure why, exactly. It can't be that she's interested in Ben, because he's exactly the opposite of everything she ever looks for in a guy. He's like the cardboard-cutout version of who she might've ended up with if her life had followed all the usual paths: the type of person you build a future with, the kind of future that includes engagement rings and mortgage statements, summer vacations and pregnancy tests, baby registries and preschool applications—all the things that make Greta feel sweaty and claustrophobic.

But there's something undeniably charming about him too,

and Greta is aware that she's spending as much energy wondering why she's still talking to him as she usually does coming up with an excuse to leave in these situations.

"She's . . ." Ben begins, shifting in his seat. Everything about him has tensed up, from his shoulders to his jaw. "We're not . . . I don't know. We officially separated about six months ago. She stayed with the girls in New Jersey, and I moved back into the city. But things were bad long before that." He rubs at his beard and blows out a sigh. "We met in high school."

"Ah," Greta says, as if this explains everything.

"I mean, we broke up for a couple years in college, so it's not like she's the only—" He stops and shakes his head, then starts again. "When you've known someone that long, the way you are together sort of sets, like paint drying or cement hardening. It doesn't leave a lot of room for change. And then you have kids, and that's the best part in some ways, but it's also the hardest, and it brings all these other issues to the surface, things that were easier to ignore before there were a couple of little people who depended on you, and it breaks your heart to think of ruining your family just because you're not as happy as you think you *could* be, so you keep at it. But it turns out there are other ways to ruin things too, slower ways, and . . ." He looks up at Greta. "God, sorry. I don't mean to treat you like a therapist."

"You're not," she says. "It's fine."

"Anyway, we're separated now. And things are better. But harder too."

"Is it the kind of separation that's a prologue to divorce?" she asks. "Or the kind that's more of a break?"

"Honestly? I have no idea."

Greta nods. "What do you want it to be?"

"Honestly?" Ben says again, giving her a weary smile. "I have no idea."

An announcement comes over the loudspeaker that they're

nearing the colony of sea lions and so they finish their drinks and then wind their way through the ship, both a little unsteady. When they pass the open entrance to the jazz club, Ben stops abruptly.

"Look," he says, taking a few steps in, surveying the empty seats and the quiet stage. A row of colorful electric guitars hangs above the rest of the equipment, and Greta stares at them longingly; it's like spotting an old friend in a sea of unfamiliar faces. "You should play something."

She shakes her head. "I can't just take one."

"C'mon," he says. "That's not very rock 'n' roll of you."

"I guess I'm not feeling very rock 'n' roll these days," she says with a rueful smile.

They make it out to the starboard deck, where they both stand blinking into the sudden daylight. Earlier this morning, everything had been misty and pale, the silvery water stretching as far as Greta could see. But now they've come across a different landscape altogether, motionless blue water flanked by hulking gray mountains. The passage is dotted with small chunks of floating ice, and there's an eerie stillness to the place, the rush of the wind making the world seem full of static.

All at once, Greta feels astonishingly sober. She looks around for her dad and the rest of the group but doesn't see them in the crowds lined up along the rails.

"Wow," Ben says quietly, almost reverently, and she follows his gaze.

Ahead, there's a cluster of hunched gray rocks, and when the ship glides close enough, a collective murmur goes up from the passengers gathered on the deck. At first, the sea lions are nothing more than a series of brown shapes, dozens of them, maybe even more. But soon they can see each one distinctly, their pointed noses and powerful flippers. Most of them are sleeping, or at least lounging, their bodies a series of commas and dashes across the rocks. Others lift their heads to yawn or let out a roar, and a few slip into the water with a splash.

Greta glances over at Ben, who is staring in awe. She has a feeling that he'd look the same way even if he were sober, but for her, everything has taken on a slightly surreal quality.

"Last year I had this speaking gig in San Francisco," he says, "and we decided to take the kids along. I had the whole thing planned out. Golden Gate Bridge, Lombard Street, Alcatraz, the works. But it all went off the rails when we got to Pier 39. They took one look at those sea lions and refused to leave. They were completely transfixed. We stayed there for hours, just watching them sleep in the sun. It was a good day."

Greta smiles, but she's thinking back on her own childhood vacations, which were mostly spent camping up in Michigan. Asher would complain about the bugs and Greta would moan about the weight of her backpack; Helen, who had grown up traveling to Europe, would wrinkle her nose at the pot of beans over the portable stove; and Conrad would grumble as he struggled to set up the tent on his own. But later, they'd all sit around the fire, hands sticky from the s'mores, faces flickering in the dark, and there was a warmth to it that Greta would carry back with her to the old patched-up tent, where the four of them slept in a row, she and Asher wedged between their parents. Sometimes, Conrad would reach over the top of their heads for Helen's hand, and Greta would fall asleep like that, the knot of their hands like a crown above her as the wind rattled the sides of the little tent.

The sea lions begin to slip from view, the sound of their roars growing distant. Around them, the crowd drifts back inside the ship. But Greta and Ben stay there at the railing, watching the mountains glide by, unable to tear themselves away.

"We should go in," he says eventually, and she realizes she's shivering. "Want to get one last drink to warm up?"

Before she can answer, Greta spots her dad walking over, a woolen hat pulled low over his forehead. Automatically, she finds herself standing up straighter, like a teenager again, about to get busted for drinking in the middle of the day.

"Hi," she says a little too brightly, and Conrad gives her a suspicious look. He glances from her to Ben, and Greta shakes her head. "Sorry, this is Ben Wilder."

"Yeah, I know," Conrad says. "I saw his lecture this afternoon. With you."

Greta nods. "Right. Well, there was more I wanted to know, so . . ."

"You're brushing up on all things Jack London," he says, his eyes landing on Ben with a hint of amusement. "I guess there are worse ways to spend the day."

"Not according to my students," Ben says cheerfully.

Conrad turns back to Greta. "You saw the sea lions?"

"Yup," she says. "They were amazing."

"What else have you been up to?"

She shrugs. "We checked out one of the bars."

"Really," he says in mock astonishment, and it's so unexpected that Greta laughs.

"Drinking rum is good for morale when you're on a boat," she informs him, as beside her, Ben gives a professorial nod. "So I've heard."

"Can't argue with that," Conrad says. "Though it's not a boat. It's a ship."

"See," Ben says, turning to Greta with a grin. "Told you so."

For a second the words hang there between them, harmless and mundane. And then Conrad's face clouds over as they register. *Shit*, Greta thinks as she watches him. It only takes a second. Just like that, his eyes drop to the wooden deck and his shoulders tense. If you didn't know any better, you'd think he was just moody, the way the warmth has gone out of his eyes when he glances up again. You'd think he was unpredictable.

But Greta knows better.

Her head is still moving too slow, but her heart picks up speed.

"So what are you doing the rest of the day?" she asks him, trying and failing to sound casual, to gloss over it, like a middle schooler whose friends are mad at her and who is desperately trying to make it okay.

His voice, when he answers, is cool: "I already gave you the itinerary."

"Right," Greta says, blinking fast. "I'm not sure I'll make it for dinner, so maybe I'll just plan to meet you for breakfast tomorrow?"

Conrad is still stone-faced. "Whatever you want," he says, and then, as he starts to walk off, he adds, "We'll either see you or we won't."

When he's gone, Ben lets out a low whistle. "So that's your dad."

Greta manages a nod.

"You must be ready for that drink now."

But she's not. Suddenly, she's exhausted. And all she wants is to be alone.

"I think I'm gonna head back, actually," she tells Ben, already walking in the direction of the wooden doors.

"Sure," he says, trailing after her. "I should probably do the same. I've still got some final essays to grade." She gives him a skeptical look, and he laughs. "After a few cups of coffee."

Inside, they pass the couple she saw in the elevator this morning, the woman shuffling down the hall one tiny step at a time. "No sunburn," she says, looking delighted.

"No sunburn," Greta calls out as they pass her.

Ben looks at her with amusement. "Another fan of yours?"

"Something like that," she says.

There's a large crowd waiting for the elevators, everyone talking excitedly about the sea lions. Without discussing it, Greta and Ben turn and start climbing the red-carpeted staircase.

"So can I ask . . ." he says, looking sideways at her. "What was that back there?"

Greta sighs. "You know that game Taboo, where you try to avoid saying a certain word or phrase?"

"Yeah."

"Well, you said it."

"Me?" he asks, surprised. "What was it?"

"Told you so."

He frowns. "You told me . . . not to say it?"

"No, that's it. That's the phrase."

"I'm confused."

"It's the title of one of my songs," she says, breathing harder as they round another flight of stairs. "My first big hit."

"Ah," he says, understanding passing over his face. "And it's about your dad."

"Yes."

"I gather it's not a love song."

"Not exactly."

He nods. "How bad was it?"

"The song or the fallout?"

"The fallout," he says. "I assume the song is great."

"It is," she says with a smile, and decides to leave it at that.

She stops walking when they reach the seventh-floor landing. Ben does too.

"This is me," she says, nodding down the endless hall of doors.

When they turn to face each other, she realizes how tall he is, and without quite meaning to, she thinks about the logistics of kissing him, whether standing on her toes would be enough, or whether he'd have to meet her partway. It's true he's gotten more attractive with each drink—the easy smile, the warmth in his eyes, the way he sits forward when she talks, like he's not only listening but absorbing everything she says—but it makes no sense because he's still technically married and she's still technically a mess, and the only reason this is even crossing her mind is because they're both drunk and alone in the middle of nowhere. In the real world, on dry land, in the light of day, they'd be completely wrong for each other.

As she stares at his lips, she finds herself thinking of Jason, then of Luke, then of Ben's wife back home with his two daughters. The boat is tilting beneath her feet, and it's hard to tell what's alcohol and what's the ocean, what's real and what's not. She puts a hand on the wall to steady herself, and Ben looks startled by the movement. Something flickers in his eyes, but she's not sure what it is. He clears his throat.

"I think," he says slowly, "that Future Ben would be really mad at Current Ben if he didn't ask if we could hang out again."

Greta feels a wave of relief, and then, before she can fully examine this, a rush of pleasure. She gives him a bleary nod. "I'll be around."

"Good," he says, taking a few steps backward. "Then I'll find you."

"Thanks," she says, already heading down the hall, and though she knows this is the wrong thing to say, the response not quite matching up to the statement, it's also true. She'd like very much to be found.

# MONDAY

# Chapter Ten

Sometime after midnight, the cabin phone rings. Greta's muddled brain is so convinced it's the alarm clock that by the time she knocks that to the floor—the red numbers blinking off, the windowless room going inky black—the ringing has stopped.

It starts again a few seconds later, and she picks up this time.

"I've been quarantined," says the voice on the other end, and it takes Greta a few seconds to formulate a question.

"What?"

"Quarantined," he repeats. "In my room."

"Why? What happened? Are you okay?"

Her dad sighs heavily. "My stomach has been funny, so I called to see if I could get a refund on the cannery tour tomorrow, and apparently the cruise ship people panic when passengers don't feel well so—"

"The cannery . . . ?"

"In Juneau," he says impatiently. "We're supposed to— You know what? Never mind. The point is that I've been quarantined."

The ship rocks steeply from side to side, and Greta squeezes her eyes shut, thinking that she shouldn't have had so much to drink yesterday.

"You're sick?" she asks, feeling a little queasy herself.

Conrad lets out a grunt. "I'm fine. You toss your cookies a couple times and they treat you like Patient Zero. Never mind that the goddamn ship is rolling around like we're in the Bermuda Triangle. I swear I—"

"So you're not allowed to leave your room?"

"No."

"For how long?"

"At least another eighteen hours."

"Jesus."

"I know."

They both go quiet for a second, and then Greta forces herself to say, "Do you want me to come over there?"

"Nobody's allowed in," he says without bothering to hide his exasperation. "That's the whole point of a quarantine."

She tries not to let the relief creep into her voice. "Okay, well, do you need anything?"

"I'll be fine," he says. "Can you tell the others I won't make the tour tomorrow? You can take my place if you want. It's the cannery and then a ride on the tram."

"Oh," Greta says, and her voice goes up an octave, "yeah. Maybe I'll—"

"You don't have to," he says gruffly.

Again there's a pause. The room is so black it almost feels like she's floating. She grips the phone harder, remembering how she used to creep out into the backyard after their fights, sitting on the old childhood swing set until it was too dark to see. They fought about everything then: about her grades, about her sneaking out, about the fact that she cared about the guitar more than math or science, more than anything, really.

Even then she missed the days when Conrad used to stand at the entrance of the garage and watch her play, a silhouette against the setting sun. But she was no longer an eight-year-old kid with a too-big guitar, her tongue stuck out in concentration. She was twelve, and then thirteen, and then fourteen, perpetually clad in flannel and scuffed Converses, already chafing against the great injustice of growing up on the outskirts of Columbus, where nothing ever happened. By then, her father had already seen enough to know that he would lose her to music, that she would choose that over everything else, and the great big spotlight of his attention had swiveled to Asher, who was a kicker on the high school football team and tried hard in math, who wore an Ohio University sweatshirt and dreamed of all the same things Conrad had once dreamed of, all the things he'd never had: college, opportunity, getting a leg up in the world.

The summer she turned fifteen, Greta saw an ad for a guitarist in the record store where she hung out after bagging groceries, and when she showed up to audition, everyone else was older, eighteen and nineteen and twenty. They looked at her with condescending smirks until she started to play; then they immediately offered her the spot. Practice started every night at nine, which was her weekday curfew, so she perfected the art of sneaking out and back in again. But sometimes she got caught, and when she did, there was always another fight, one more in a series of many, so many that she grew numb to them, so many it became hard to care what he thought.

By the time she was a junior, her bandmates had all gone off to college, which was fine. They had never really played any gigs, just practiced in a kid named Topher's basement, and Greta was better than they were anyway. But she kept sneaking out all the same. Kept hiding cigarettes in her bedroom. Kept hitching rides downtown whenever a band she liked was performing at one of the music venues. And so the fights continued. Helen did her best to play referee, to absorb or deflect whatever bitterness flowed between the two of them, but even so Greta would usually find herself in the cool of the backyard afterward, sitting on that swing set, sometimes stewing, sometimes crying, sometimes just giving herself the space to wonder what it would be like to live a different sort of life, in a different sort of place, with a different sort of father.

Every once in a while, he'd come out and join her. He never apologized or explained himself, even though Greta suspected her mom had sent him out there to do just that. He was much too stubborn. And so was she. Instead, he'd just lower himself onto the swing beside her, the beam creaking above them, and for a long time, they would sit there together in the dark, gazing up at the wash of stars.

They'd always been better with silence.

"I feel bad," Greta says eventually, the phone pressed hard against her ear, "that you're going to miss Juneau."

Conrad's voice, when he answers, is softer. "Me too."

"I'll check in on you when I get back."

"You can't—"

"Quarantine," she says. "I know. I meant I'll call or something."

"Oh," he says. "Okay."

In the deep, deep dark, she finds herself nodding. "Okay."

And then he hangs up.

She falls asleep again immediately, into the kind of hard, dreamless sleep that usually follows a show. When she wakes, she fumbles around for her phone on the table, and sees that it's almost nine.

The buffet is on the lido deck, and it's crowded this morning. A couple of kids run past wearing powdery doughnuts like rings on their fingers, and an attendant pushing an elderly man in a wheelchair tries to fight his way past the line for coffee. The tables are arranged along the perimeter of the ship, pressed up against the windows, and Greta spots Mary and Eleanor sitting at one of them, their heads bent over a phone.

For a second, she pauses, struck by the sight of them together like that, thinking about how her mom should be there too. These women had been as much Helen's family as Greta and Asher and Conrad, the three of them trading gardening secrets and tips on asking for a raise, organizing meals when one of them was sick, and throwing parties for every occasion. They spent summers in each other's backyards and winters at each other's kitchen tables. They were friends—best friends—but they were also family.

And now there are only two of them.

When Greta walks up to the table, Eleanor beams at her. "Mary was showing me some pictures of the proposal," she says, turning the phone around. Greta doesn't have time to prepare herself; just like that, she's looking at a picture of Jason, down on one knee, grinning up at a beautiful Asian woman who looks like she's straight out of a J.Crew catalog.

"He did it in Central Park," Mary says proudly. "She was shocked."

*Who isn't?* Greta wants to say, but she doesn't.

Years ago, she and Jason were at a bar in the East Village when a guy—through sleight of hand or maybe something more technical—made a ring appear in the token slot of a Skee-Ball machine. Right there on the beer-soaked floor, he dropped to one knee and the girl burst into tears. Jason had turned to Greta and rolled his eyes.

"What?" she asked. "What would *you* do?"

"I wouldn't," he said simply.

It was one of the things they had in common, this aversion to commitment, to knitting your life to someone else's. When she used to stay over at his place, he would pointedly move the toothpaste back where it belonged after she used it. When they woke up in the morning, he would go about his routine as if she weren't there. And that was fine with Greta, who did the same on the rare occasions when he slept at her place. They were two independent people who wanted it all: someone in their bed at night and also out of it first thing in the morning.

Until now, apparently.

"Wow," Greta says, peering closer at the picture, searching for signs of Jason's unhappiness like an FBI agent examining a hostage video. But there's nothing. He looks overjoyed to be perched on a rock in Central Park, proposing to a woman he allegedly loves.

"What does she do?" she finds herself asking.

"She's a vet," Mary says, still smiling at the photo.

"Oh," Greta says, surprised. "That's amazing. Where did she serve?"

Both women laugh. "No, no," Mary says. "A veterinarian. She treated his puppy, which is how they met."

"He has a puppy?" Greta says, picturing the white carpets in his sleek high-rise apartment. "Since when?"

Mary frowns. "Maybe a year or so?"

"Don't you two ever see each other?" Eleanor asks. "The Big Apple can't be *that* big."

"Bigger than you think," Greta says morosely.

Davis and Todd return then, plates heaped with pancakes. They make an odd pair: Todd, skinny and pale and so like a stereotype of an insurance adjuster that it's almost weird that he *is* one, and Davis, broad-shouldered and athletic, with a personality even bigger than his stature.

"Hey, kid," Davis says as he slides awkwardly into a too-small chair. "Heard your dad spent the night getting acquainted with the bathroom floor."

"You talked to him?"

He nods as he pours syrup over his pancakes. "He's in rough shape."

"He didn't sound that bad last night. Just annoyed."

"Well, he's that too," Davis says. "But he'll be fine."

"We decided it wasn't the food," Eleanor says, watching carefully as Todd shoves a forkful of eggs into his mouth, "since the rest of us are still okay."

"He probably picked up some sort of bug before we got on," Mary agrees. "Hopefully it'll be quick."

Underneath the table, Greta sends him a quick text: Doing okay?

Conrad replies immediately with a deeply sarcastic super.

"You taking his spot today?" Davis asks, and Greta looks up again. "We're gonna watch them stuff some salmon into a can."

"Then they're gonna hoist us up Mount Roberts," Todd says, pushing a brochure across the table to Greta. It shows a red box of a tram strung up on a cable, rising steeply up the side of a tree-covered mountain. "I'm hoping we might spot a sooty grouse up there."

"That sounds like a drink," Eleanor says. "Some sort of wintry cocktail."

"I think it's a whisky," Davis offers.

Mary shakes her head. "That's Famous Grouse."

"Who says the sooty grouse isn't also famous?" Eleanor asks with a grin, and Todd rolls his eyes at all of them.

"It is," he says. "At least in the Pacific Coast Ranges."

Greta is busy examining the pictures of the tram. She doesn't know if she can spend the whole day with them. Not just because Davis will be asking the tour guide a thousand questions and Mary will be trying to make Greta feel included and Eleanor will be forcing them all to take silly group photos at the top and Todd will be wandering around making bird noises.

It's because they were supposed to be doing all this with her mom.

Mary seems to read her mind. "No pressure at all," she says. "We have an extra spot on the one-twenty tender if you're interested." She nudges a different brochure in her direction. "But if not, you definitely won't be bored in Juneau."

"Thanks," Greta says with a grateful smile, taking it with her as she heads over to the buffet.

While waiting in line for an omelet, she leafs through the various tour options: whale watching and helicopter rides and dog-sledding. When she flips to a photo of the Mendenhall Glacier, white and craggy and hulking, she realizes she's seen it before: on her mother's calendar back in Ohio.

She glances up again, her heart fluttering.

Over the heads of the other diners, the windows are specked with rain, everything beyond wreathed in haze. She looks back down at the picture. It's impossible to grasp the scope of the thing; she knows it must be huge, but in the photo, it looks like nothing more than a patch of snow caught between two mountains.

Still, all at once, she's desperate to see it.

## Chapter Eleven

Even once she's standing on the wooden slats of the boardwalk, Greta can still feel the waves beneath her feet. This is the first time in two days she's been on solid ground. The air smells of damp pine needles and the promise of rain, and a low fog hangs over the port of Juneau, a smattering of brightly colored clapboard shops and restaurants with a steep mountain rising into the mist behind them. She zips her waterproof jacket, another one taken from her mom's closet. Conrad had unceremoniously handed them both to her when they'd met at the airport that first morning in Vancouver, assuming—correctly—that she hadn't packed properly for a trip like this.

She turns in a small circle, trying to figure out what's next. Around her, other passengers walk with purpose, clutching tickets and itineraries, eager to begin their adventures. She spots a row of small wooden stalls, each one with a sign for a different activity: mountain biking, helicopter rides, float planes. There's one that says MENDENHALL GLACIER, and she walks over. The guy in the window—who has blond dreads and a bored expression—looks up from his phone. "Bike, dogsled, or kayak?"

She shakes her head. "I just want to see the glacier."

"Right," he says slowly. "By bike, dogsled, or kayak?"

She blinks at him. "Can't I just . . . walk?"

"Too far," he says, returning to his phone.

"No, I meant once I get there."

He points a finger out the window and to the left. "There's a city bus over there. It'll drop you at the visitors' center. Next one should be here any minute."

When she turns around, Ben is standing there.

"Hi," he says with a sheepish grin.

"Hi," she says, then gestures over her shoulder at the window. "Mendenhall?"

"Thirteen point six miles long. Has retreated one point seven-five miles since 1929. Has a lake with its own ecosystem." He stops when he sees her face. "Not what you were asking."

"No," she says. "I was just wondering if you're going too."

"Oh," he says, his eyebrows rising above his glasses. He glances at the guy with the dreads, who is now cleaning his fingernails with the corner of a credit card, then back at Greta. "Yeah. I am."

"By bike, dogsled, or kayak?"

He looks bewildered. "What?"

"Never mind. There's a bus stop over there."

They buy tickets at an ancient-looking machine, then wait on the corner beneath the gauzy rain as the bus pulls up. Inside, it smells like mildew, and Greta half-expects to find wads of gum tacked to the ceiling, like in the school buses she rode as a kid. The olive green seats are nearly filled, so there's no choice but to share—they slide into the only empty one, first Greta, then Ben, who has to angle his long legs into the aisle.

As they bump along through downtown Juneau and out onto the highway that runs along the water, they're unable to avoid leaning into each other every time there's a turn. "Sorry," Greta mutters at one point, gripping the back of the seat in front of them, but then they veer left and it's Ben's turn to apologize, and after a while, it all becomes a little funny.

They're deposited in the gravel parking lot of a welcome center, near a sign that outlines various hikes to the glacier. It's raining harder now, and though they're both wearing waterproof jackets, they don't have umbrellas. Rain drips off Greta's eyelashes and the tip of her nose, and her shoes—a worn pair of Vans—are already taking in water.

Ben—who is of course wearing hiking boots—has produced a guidebook from his jacket pocket. He's reading it intently even as the pages grow more and more damp.

"There's a lookout point at the visitors' center over there, or else you can hike down to the river for a closer view, or . . ." He glances up at Greta, and for an awkward beat, they stare at each other, trying to gauge whether they're doing this together or not. The wind picks up, blowing the rain sideways, and Greta glances off toward the trailhead.

"Let's hike," she says, already starting to walk, and Ben tries to hide his surprise as he hurries after her, tucking the guidebook into his pocket.

It's not long before the glacier comes into view, and they both stop. From a distance, it might be mistaken for a thick layer of snow, winding between two mountains like a great frozen river. But they're close enough now to see the jagged places where the ice has broken off and the way its edges are tipped with an other-worldly shade of blue. Greta feels something inside her go still at the sight. It looks just like the photo on her mom's calendar.

They gaze at it for a long time, as the rain comes down and the clouds drift overhead, as people stream past them, snapping photos and posing for selfies. On impulse, Greta reaches for her phone, but then decides against it. There's no way a picture could capture this.

"Wow," Ben says, turning to her. His hair is plastered to his head and he's starting to shiver, but his eyes are bright. "We're in Alaska."

Greta can't help smiling at the wonder in his voice. "We're in Alaska."

They continue down the muddy trail toward the lake that separates them from the glacier, the rain pinging off their jackets. In the distance, the brilliant orange of a kayak cuts through the mist, and a pair of hawks fly in low circles overhead.

"So," Ben says as they inch their way down a small slope, their shoes—Ben's perfectly functional, Greta's wholly inadequate—slipping in the mud. "The rest of your crew wasn't up for this?"

"My dad's not feeling well," she tells him, "and the others went to a cannery."

"That sounds . . ." He searches for the right word. "Gross."

Greta pauses to lift a muck-covered sneaker. "Unlike this."

"They're family friends? The others?"

"Yeah, I've known them all since I was a kid. My parents met Eleanor and Todd after their daughter bit my brother in kindergarten, and Mary and Davis have lived next door since I was in middle school." She pushes back the branch of a tree, dousing them both with water, but they're too soaked for it to matter. "My mom—she really loved them. This whole trip was her idea. She was always coming up with activities for the group: bowling and apple picking and Super Bowl parties, stuff like that. Every Christmas, she'd get everyone together and make us go caroling in the neighborhood."

"Even your dad?"

"Even my dad," Greta says with a smile. "He was always grumpy about it, but I think there was a part of him that secretly loved it. Or maybe it's just that he loved my mom." This last part comes out thickly, but Ben doesn't seem to notice. "Besides, if it weren't for her, he'd have just sat at home and watched baseball all the time."

Ben glances back at her, and Greta bites her lip, realizing what she's said.

*If it weren't for her.*

The glacier comes into view again, a narrow slice of it between trees. Ben drops back, falling into step beside her, the fabric of their jackets whistling each time their shoulders brush against each other.

"How's he doing with all of it?" he asks.

"Okay, I guess." She steps to the side to let some other hikers pass. When they're gone, she says, "This is the first time I've seen him since the funeral."

Ben turns to stare at her. "You haven't seen him in three months?"

"I told you, we're not very close."

"Yeah, but . . . he must be so sad."

"So am I," she says, and it comes out more bitterly than she meant it.

"Well, he must be lonely."

"He's got my brother."

"Have you ever tried talking to him about all this?" Ben asks, clearly unable to get his head around it.

"He's not that kind of dad."

"How do you know unless you try?"

"Come on," she says with a wry smile. "I was a kid who carried around a notebook full of terrible song lyrics. You think I wasn't pouring my heart out to my parents every chance I got?"

He laughs. "Fair enough."

"Whenever we argued, I'd write these ridiculously long notes that explained all my feelings—trust me, I had a lot of them—and slip them under their bedroom door. You haven't seen melodramatic until you've seen a twelve-year-old's handwritten rebuttal to her parents' decision not to let her go to Casey Huang's first coed party."

"I'm suddenly dreading the tween years," he says with a grin.

"They always worked on my mom. She'd come in later that night and crawl into bed with me and we'd talk it all through. But my dad never even bothered to read them."

Ben looks shocked. "He didn't?"

Greta shakes her head. "This one time, he opened their bedroom door just as I was slipping the envelope underneath. My mom was still downstairs, so it was just him, and I could tell he was still furious with me. I'd borrowed their credit card to get a CD—"

"Which one?"

"The new Sleater-Kinney. Obviously."

He laughs. "Obviously."

"Anyway, he asked if I'd come to apologize, and I told him everything I had to say was in that letter, which was of course about how my allowance should be higher so that I could buy CDs for myself. But he just picked it up off the floor and ripped it to pieces."

"That's awful," Ben says with real feeling. "No wonder you wrote that song."

"What do you mean?"

He shrugs. "You had to find another way to make him listen."

Greta stops and looks at him, amazed to be so effortlessly understood. Above them, the birds are chirping, and a single column of sunlight works its way through the trees. The glacier looks enormous from here, dramatic in the mist. They both turn to gaze at it for a moment, then begin to walk again.

"You know," Ben says, his boots making sucking noises in the mud as he follows her, "when Emily first got pregnant, I was really scared. I'd just finished my PhD, and was teaching a full course load, and working on the book, and I would've been more than happy to just keep going like that. I bet you'll understand this more than most people, but I have a tendency to get lost in my work and forget about everything else."

Ahead of him, Greta tilts her head to one side to show that she's listening.

"Even when we got engaged, it was only because we went to

nine weddings that summer and then got into a fight on the drive home from the last one because we'd apparently been together longer than any of those couples and I still hadn't gotten around to proposing."

"Why not?" she asks, letting him catch up to her.

"Honestly? It never occurred to me."

Greta smiles. "So how long did it take you to do it?"

"I asked her right then," he says with a laugh. "We were hungover and stuck in traffic, coming back into the city from the Hamptons. She pulled over to the side of the road and made me at least get out of the car and onto one knee."

"And she said yes?"

"She said yes," he tells her. "But the kid thing—that felt different to me. Bigger. Scarier. We weren't even really trying, so it caught me completely off guard. The day we found out, I made a list of things I wanted to be as a dad. Honest. Supportive. Kind. And then Avery came along and it was all crying and dirty diapers and middle-of-the-night feedings, and there's not really any time to think about a bunch of adjectives when you're covered in spit-up." He glances over at her. "The truth is, being a parent is mostly just reacting. Sometimes you get it right and sometimes you don't. You give what you can. And at the end of the day, most of it is just being there."

Greta opens her mouth to speak, but before she can, Ben hurries on: "Look, I realize we just met, and I don't know much about your dad. It's entirely possible he's the world's biggest jerk. But he could also be a guy who's mostly just been reacting his whole life, trying his best and maybe not always getting it right. The important thing is that it seems like he wants to be there right now. And he clearly wants you to be here too."

"Except," Greta says, "it was my brother who suggested I come."

Ben smiles like a lawyer about to rest his case. "But if your dad really didn't want you on this ship, I doubt you'd actually be here."

This hadn't ever occurred to Greta. When she'd finally called Conrad to suggest joining him—a few days after she'd promised Asher she would—he'd been quick to dismiss the offer. "I don't need a babysitter," he'd said, much to her relief, and her half-hearted insistence had done little to change his mind.

But the next day, she woke up feeling guilty. It was something about the way he'd answered the phone, his voice less gruff than usual, more plaintive. She pulled up the website for the cruise line to see if they still had any available cabins, and when she saw that they did, she sighed. The second time her dad picked up, she didn't ask him. "I'm all booked," she said, and a few beats passed before he replied: "Okay."

She and Ben continue to walk in silence, Greta deep in thought as they trudge up a slope leading back to the visitors' center. After a while, the rain starts up again, falling in fat drops now, and Ben glances over at her apologetically.

"We should've turned back sooner," he says, squinting at the sky. "Sorry."

"It's okay," she says. "I don't mind walking."

"Me neither. That's my favorite thing about being back in the city, actually. I can wander for hours."

"Me too. Especially when I'm writing. It helps me think."

"Same. Where do you live?"

"East Village."

He nods, as if he expected as much. "I bet you're one of those people who never goes above Fourteenth Street."

"Depends on what's above Fourteenth Street," she says, and he smiles. "Remember that huge storm in February? The one where they shut down the subway? I walked all the way up to Central Park in that. Took me ages. There was a foot and a half of snow by the time I got there, and I had to take a cab back home because I couldn't feel my toes. But I worked out a whole song that day."

Ben is looking at her with a strange expression. "So did I."

She frowns at him. "You wrote a song?"

"No," he says. "I trekked down to Central Park in that storm."

"You did?"

He nods. "I love walking in the snow."

"Me too," she says. "The streets get so quiet."

"And it feels like the city is all yours."

She shakes her head. "I can't believe you were there too."

"It was pretty surreal," he says with a faraway look, and she knows exactly what he's talking about: the way the swirling snow had started to quiet just as it got dark, how—after hours of wind and noise—the world felt suddenly like the volume had been turned down. The lampposts were capped in white and gave off an otherworldly glow, and everyone she passed moved slowly through the heavy drifts, as if in a dream. It's so strange to think now that one of them could've been Ben.

"Imagine if we'd run into each other," he says as if he can read her thoughts.

"I don't know. It's a pretty big park."

"Yeah, but that's the thing about New York. It's always bringing people together at unexpected moments. That's part of its magic. I once ran into my best friend from second grade in the middle of the Great Lawn."

She smiles. "Well, I was all the way down near Central Park South."

"And I was all the way up near the top," he says with a shrug. "Ships in the night, I guess."

"Ships in the night," she agrees.

## Chapter Twelve

They ride the bus back to Juneau in their wet clothes, then linger on the boardwalk, watching the floatplanes take off from the harbor. It's only five P.M., which means they still have four hours until their ship leaves. Ben attempts to leaf through his guidebook again, but the pages are so soggy it's nearly impossible to turn them. The rain starts coming down harder, and they give up entirely.

"Let's go find a bar," he says, and they head up one of the main streets.

They pass up the first couple of places because they're too crowded with tourists. The third one is emptier and looks straight out of an old western, with a fireplace in the corner and wood-paneled walls, antique mirrors with blurry reflections, and a bartender with a mustache so long it curls at the edges.

They order a couple of beers and carry their glasses to a table in the corner. It's small and a little wobbly but close enough to the fire that Greta can feel the warmth starting to creep back from the outside in, first in her fingers and toes, then her arms and legs.

"What would you be doing on a normal Monday afternoon?" Ben asks as the door opens and a large group of men in fishing gear walk in, bringing the smell of rain and the sound of laughter.

"There's no such thing for me," she says with a smile. "That's the best part."

"Okay, but . . . what if you were in New York right now?"

Greta considers this. "Is it five o'clock in New York too?"

Ben waves a hand. "Sure."

"I could be home writing, I guess," she tells him. "Or out somewhere getting an early bite, if I have a show. Or maybe at the studio, depending on where I am in the process."

"You have a studio?"

"I rent one. When I'm not on the road." She takes a sip of her beer and tilts her head at him. "What would you be doing at five o'clock on a Monday in New York?"

His eyes drift to the tin ceiling, the rusty light fixtures that look like they've been there since the 1800s. "Well," he says. "Six months ago, I would've been hurrying through the end of my European history seminar so that I could make the five thirty-two from Penn Station and get home in time for dinner with the girls."

"And now?"

"Now," he says with a rueful smile, "I'm usually driving my students nuts by going fifteen minutes over, then heading back to my depressingly bare faculty apartment and drinking a few fingers of Glenfiddich while I attempt to write something half as good as my last book."

"Does the whisky help?"

"With the writing?" he asks with a laugh. "Or with everything else?"

She gives him a long look. "You know, when I'm stuck on a song, it usually has more to do with my life than my creative process."

"Well, my life is a total mess right now, so I guess I should probably stop blaming Herman Melville."

"I'm sure he deserves at least some of it. I mean, the guy hunted whales, right?"

"We all have our faults," Ben says with a sardonic smile. "I certainly have mine."

Greta studies him over the rim of her glass. "You seem pretty okay to me."

"You should talk to my wife then. She'd probably have a few things to say about it."

"Hard pass," Greta says, but he doesn't smile. She watches him spin his glass in a slow circle on the scarred wooden table. "What does she think of you being all the way up here in Alaska right now?"

He shrugs. "She's used to the travel at this point. When the book came out, there was only supposed to be a five-day tour. But then it started to take off, which meant more cities and more speaking engagements."

"And she didn't mind?"

"No, she did," he says, his shoulders tightening. "She blamed it for a lot of our problems at first. Even though they started long before that. We'd been growing apart for years, ever since the kids were born. But sometimes it's harder to see that up close."

"And easier when you're out on the road."

He nods. "It's like that feeling of getting off a long flight and taking your first breath of fresh air. You were okay on the plane. You could breathe just fine. And you could survive like that for a pretty long time if you had to. But once you're off, you realize you wouldn't want to live that way forever. Not if you had a choice. I think being away did that for me. It helped me realize I hadn't breathed—*really* breathed—in a very long time."

"I get that," Greta says. "I've been there too."

"You have?"

"I mean, not married," she says. "But a lot of the guys I've dated thought it was cool at first when I went out on the road. They worked in advertising or tech or had jobs I honestly can't even remember because they were so boring. But it meant they had normal schedules, normal lives. And after a while, it started to wear on them that I was always on the move. You miss a lot in this life. Weddings. Birthdays. Anniversaries. It's hard to make relationships work. Friendships too. Most of mine have slipped away over the years. My friend Yara is a musician too, so it works with her. But with others, not so much . . ." She trails off and takes a sip of her beer. "Which is why I now tend to date people who are already in the business."

Ben lifts his eyebrows. "Oh, are you . . . ?"

"No," she says. "Not at the moment."

"Right," he says, trying and failing not to look pleased. "Right."

Suddenly, Greta's face feels too warm from the fire. She picks up her glass but realizes it's empty. Ben shoots to his feet, pushing his chair back hastily.

"Another round?" he asks, then walks off without waiting for an answer.

As she watches, he leans over the bar to order, then notices the giant stuffed head of a grizzly bear and pulls out his phone to take a selfie with it. Greta is thinking it might be the most unself-consciously dorky thing she's ever seen when he raises an index finger and takes a second one pretending to be picking the bear's nose.

She closes her eyes and scrubs at her face, wondering if he's seen the video by now. Because that's what you do, isn't it, when you meet someone random like this? You go digging for information. Fifteen minutes of searching this morning, and Greta already knew Ben's middle name (Robert), his hometown (McCall, Idaho), and his alma mater (Colgate). She found a picture of him at a faculty dinner with his wife, who is tall and blond and pretty, if a bit generic-looking, and read several interviews he did when the book came out, where he mostly talked about Jack London but also mentioned how much he loves Dave Matthews (she knew it!), how he eats exactly eight almonds for a snack while he writes (because of course he does), and how he wanted to be an explorer when he grew up. The biggest scandal she could find was a prank involving a swimming pool and a pair of swans during his senior year of college.

A similar search for Greta is fairly quick to yield evidence of her meltdown—not just the video but dozens of articles too—and she's weighing the odds that Ben is someone with a moral objection to Google-stalking when a text from her manager, Howie, pops up on her phone: Where the hell are you?

She stares at it for a moment, then writes: Alaska.

I'm serious.

So am I.

You're in Alaska?

She takes a selfie with the bar and the bear and a half dozen men in plaid shirts in the background, then sends it to him.

That looks like Brooklyn, he writes back.

Trust me, it's Juneau.

Please tell me you'll be back in New York tomorrow.

She winces, then writes: Saturday.

You're killing me.

Sorry. It's a slow boat.

You're on a boat?

A ship, actually, she replies. It's a long story. I'm with my dad.

Oh. Wow.

Yeah.

Okay, well, just so you're aware, everyone here is going to lose their shit over this.

Greta bites her lip. I know you'll handle it.

I'll try. But I need you to promise me you'll show up on Sunday.

I will.

I don't mean physically, he says. You have to knock it out of the fucking park.

Her stomach does a little flip. But before she can respond, Howie writes back again.

And you better spring for the good wifi package, because we might need to do some remote interviews.

Thanks, Howie, she writes, but her heart quickens.

All of a sudden, Sunday seems incredibly soon.

A bottle of beer comes sliding across the table, and she looks up to see Ben sitting down across from her again. "You okay?" he asks with a frown, and she nods as she slips her phone back into her jacket pocket.

"Fine." Behind her, a group of men are talking about the day's kayaking adventure, roaring with laughter as they recount how one of them managed to flip over three times. "Don't take this the wrong way," she says to Ben, "but you seem like the kind of guy who would've had something planned for today."

"Why would I take that the wrong way?"

"I don't know. You seem sort of . . ."

"Boring?" he says. "Normal?"

Greta shakes her head. "I didn't say that."

"You didn't have to," he says. "Look, maybe I don't play in a band or go to cool parties or smoke a lot of marijuana." He pronounces this last word so deliberately that it's a struggle for Greta to keep a straight face. "I'm a dad, you know? And a professor. I like to read. I nerd out over history, and I collect random facts the way most dudes collect—I don't know, beer cans? Sports memorabilia? I don't even know what most dudes collect. And I actually like doing laundry. I've got a whole system to color-code my calendar, and I set an alarm clock even on mornings when I don't have to work . . ." He trails off with a frown. "And I don't really know why I'm telling you all this except that you make me feel kind of insecure."

"Why?" she asks.

"Because I think I might be one of those normal guys with normal lives that you were talking about, and sometimes I wish I weren't. And because you're so much cooler than me. Which, I realize, makes me sound like I'm in high school, but that's sort of how you make me feel. Like I'm the yearbook editor and you're the girl in the grunge band that plays all the parties I never get invited to."

Greta laughs. "Can I tell you something?"

"Yeah."

"I set an alarm clock too."

He raises his eyebrows. "You do?"

"Otherwise I'd never get anything done."

He takes a sip of his beer, but she can see the edges of a smile around it. "I did have plans, you know. I was supposed to go fishing today. I signed up months ago."

"You did?"

He nods. "As soon as I booked the cruise. The salmon are just starting to run this time of year, and I wanted to make sure I had a spot."

Greta stares at him. "Why didn't you say anything?"

"Because," he says with a shrug, "I decided I'd rather see a glacier with you."

She smiles at him, and he smiles back at her, and she can't help feeling a little unmoored, sitting here in this far-flung bar on the edge of Alaska, a million miles away from whatever she'd normally be doing at five o'clock on a Monday in New York City. In the opposite corner, three old men in flannel shirts have picked up a couple of banjos and a tambourine and begun to play, and it's intoxicating, all of it, the bright sound of the instruments and the quivering light from the fire, the smells of mud and hops and the laughter and voices all around them. Greta sits back and closes her eyes as she listens, and when she opens them again, Ben is watching her with a more serious expression. Something about it makes her feel dizzy.

When they finally leave—their table cluttered with empty bottles and plates greasy from the fish and chips they'd ordered—the air outside feels almost medicinal. All that had been fuzzy goes suddenly sharp, and they stand beneath the old wooden sign like two divers who have just made their way to the surface.

It's after eight, but dusk is only just beginning to push in at the edges of the sky. The streets are still busy, filled with tourists carrying plastic bags of souvenirs, hurrying in the direction of the ships. A few local kids are smoking cigarettes on a bench, and a man locks the door to a wooden crab shack.

Greta and Ben make their way along the pier, not quite walking in a straight line.

He looks at her sideways. "That was fun."

"It was," she agrees.

"Like, really fun." He stops and scratches at his chin. He looks handsome right then, even with his ridiculously practical hiking boots and the still-soggy guidebook sticking out of the pocket of his rain jacket. "The most fun I've had in a while. Which must sound pathetic."

She smiles. "I had a good time too."

"It's only eight-fifteen," he says, glancing at his watch. "The night is still young."

She nods toward the end of the boardwalk. "We have to catch the last tender."

Ben tips his head back and peers at the sky. *"Love me tender,"* he warbles a little too loudly, a little bit drunkenly, *"love me sweet."*

An older couple looks over reproachfully as they walk by, but Ben doesn't notice. He's still singing off-key, turning in an uneven circle, and when he stops, he's only a few inches from Greta. Part of her wants to roll her eyes at him, while another part of her— a part she's too drunk to fully examine right now—wants nothing more than to kiss him.

He squints at her, his eyes taking a second to focus.

"Hi," he says with a bleary grin.

She laughs. "Hi."

The air is thick with brine, and the way he's looking at her makes her head light. He frowns and takes a small step closer.

"Hi," he says again, though this time, his face is serious.

"Hi," she says, her heart beating a bit too fast.

There's a flower petal in his hair, small and pink and inexplicable, but just as she reaches for it, just as he leans toward her, they're both startled by the sudden sound of a duck quacking. They draw back, each looking around with equally puzzled expressions, until something registers on Ben's face and he lets out a laugh.

Greta watches in confusion as he fishes the phone from his pocket. "*That's* your ringtone?"

"What do you have against ducks?" he says with a grin. By now, the quacking has stopped, but as soon as he focuses on the screen, his face falls.

"Shit," he says, sounding instantly sober.

"What?"

"It's my wife . . . my ex-wife . . . my . . ." He looks completely lost. "Maybe I should . . . you know . . ."

"Of course," Greta says, watching as he punches a button. But instead of the blond woman whose picture she saw online, a small round face appears on the screen. Even at a glance, Greta can see that she looks like Ben: the inquisitive brown eyes and the gently sloping nose. She sits up anxiously, jostling the phone, her hair mussed from sleep.

"Daddy," she says with a grin, revealing a huge gap where her front teeth should be. "Guess what just happened?"

Ben laughs. "I can't believe it," he says as he turns slightly away from Greta. "You're keeping the tooth fairy pretty busy these days."

Greta walks up the boardwalk a little way to give him some

privacy. She checks her own phone and finds a text from Asher: Have you killed each other yet?

No, she writes back, but that's only because he's locked up in his room. She pauses, then adds: (I swear I didn't do it.)

Yeah, Asher responds. He woke me up at 4 am to tell me after I'd been up all night with the twins.

It's tough being the favorite, she writes, and he sends her back an eye roll emoji.

There's also a text from Mary, a few hours old and in the kind of punctuation-free jumble that's all her own: back on board will be in dining room at 7 join us if you want hope you had a good day!!!

When Greta looks up again, it's to see Ben standing alone on the boardwalk, the phone now at his side. He's staring out at the water with an unreadable expression.

"Everything okay?" she asks, walking back over.

He nods, though he looks distracted. "Avery lost a tooth in the middle of the night and wanted to tell me about it."

"That's sweet," Greta says, and Ben glances over like he forgot she was there.

"I hate missing stuff like that," he says quietly. "It's happening so much more these days, between the travel and the separation, and sometimes I don't know whether it's . . ." He stops and shakes his head. "Sorry. You don't need to hear about this."

"I don't mind," Greta says, and he offers a small smile. But still, she can feel it: the way the air has gone out of the night.

Neither says anything for what feels like a long time. Instead, they both look off toward the ship, which is sitting out in the bay, checkered with lights. A moment ago, it had looked sparkly in the evening mist. But now the fog has thickened, making everything dull and distant.

"We should probably get back," Greta says eventually, and Ben nods.

This time, they leave space between them as they walk, carrying the awkward silence with them onto the motorboat and across the small stretch of darkening water, over the gangway and into the ship's elevator, all the way up to the sixth floor, where Ben steps off ahead of her and—just before disappearing—manages only a quiet, disappointingly formal *good night*.

# Chapter Thirteen

It takes several minutes for the door to open, and when it does, Greta finds herself face-to-face with a version of her dad she's never seen before.

She stares at him. "Are you okay?"

"Do I look okay?" he asks, staring back.

He does not. His face is pale and his hair is greasy and he's wearing a set of wrinkled gray pajamas. Even from the hallway, the room feels humid and stuffy, and it has a slightly sour smell to it.

Greta peers around him to where the curtains are pulled shut in the back. "Why don't you open the door to get some fresh air?"

Conrad gives her a weary look. "I don't have the energy to stand here explaining to you why I don't have the energy to do anything beyond make it to the bathroom and back."

"I'll do it," she says, moving past him into the room. She tries to hold her breath in a way that isn't obvious as she yanks back the thick beige curtains and pushes open the door to the veranda. The night air rushes in, bringing a welcome chill. Greta stands there inhaling it for a moment, still a little drunk, then turns to see her dad crawling back into the bed.

"Much better," she says as she begins straightening up the rest of the room. There are towels strewn everywhere, and three empty cans of ginger ale on the small table by the couch.

"You're not supposed to be in here," Conrad says with his eyes closed. "Don't touch anything."

"Has anyone been in to check on you?"

"A cleaning crew," he mutters. "And a nurse."

"And?"

"Nobody else is sick," he says. "So it's not the food."

"Good," she says, and when he opens one eye, she shrugs. "Well, for the rest of us anyway."

He groans and tugs the covers up to his neck. "You have to go. I'm still quarantined."

"For how much longer?" she asks, pulling out the desk chair and sitting down beside the bed.

"Twenty-four hours after the last time I . . ." he trails off. "You know."

"Right," she says. "How long has it been now?"

He struggles to free his arm from the sheets and checks his watch. "Two."

"So twenty-two more hours?"

"Thank god I spent all those paychecks on a math tutor," he says, and then shifts around under the covers and lets out a sigh. "This is awful."

"At least we're at sea tomorrow."

"Trust me, the only thing worse than having the stomach flu is having the stomach flu on a ship," he says. "These waves are killing me."

"I only meant that hopefully you won't have to miss another stop."

"It's Glacier Bay next," he says, his voice pained. "Do you know how long we've—" He stops abruptly. "Do you know how long I've been looking forward to seeing it?"

"Worst-case scenario," she says, motioning to the window, "at least you've got a balcony."

He closes his eyes again. "It's not the same. I wanted to go up to the crow's nest and see what the view is like. I wanted to hear the lectures from the geologists and naturalists. I wanted to take pictures with Davis and Mary and Todd and Eleanor."

"Dad," Greta says gently. "You'll still get to see the glaciers."

"You don't even know which ones we're seeing. I bet you haven't read anything about them."

"I like to be surprised," she says, unzipping her rain jacket. Conrad looks alarmed to see her settling in. He opens his mouth, but before he can say the word *quarantine*, she shakes her head. "It's fine. I have a hardy constitution."

He snorts. "You have the constitution of a Dickensian orphan."

"Hey," she says, but she can't help laughing. "They're your genes."

"Don't blame me. I'm not usually this pale. That's all your mother."

Greta notices that he's shivering and gets up to close the balcony door. It's after nine now, and the ship's engines are beginning to whir to life again. Across the water, the mountains are turning to silhouettes. She leaves the door open a crack, unable to part with the fresh air entirely.

"Is there anything you need?" she asks. "Did they give you medicine? Something bland to eat?"

"No food," he mumbles into the pillow. "Please don't even say the word."

Greta sits down again. "Do you want a book? Or a movie?"

"No, no," he says, and then: "I just . . . I really miss your mom."

"I know," she says quietly.

The ship moves over a swell, and she leans back in the chair and looks around the room, awash in yellowy light. On the wall, there's a painting of a log cabin covered in snow. Conrad's breathing grows steady, so steady it's hard to tell whether he's still awake.

"What would she do?" Greta wonders after a minute, not entirely sure whether she's asking him or talking to herself. She doesn't expect an answer, but he shifts beneath the blanket and his head appears again.

"She would've told you to go," he says. "So you don't get sick too."

"No, I meant—"

"I know what you meant." His voice is harsher now. "But she's not here, so what good does it do to think about it?"

Greta's heart cracks a little at this. She closes her eyes, trying to picture her mother, and the image that surfaces is of Helen in the front row at one of her shows, bright-eyed and loose-limbed and grinning. Conrad has only seen Greta play once in the last ten years: at her album-release party, which he came to under protest, less than thrilled about missing a work conference. Afterward, when she asked what he thought, he shrugged. "It was pretty good," he said. "As these things go."

But Helen—she didn't just love seeing her daughter perform, she loved the actual shows too. She always had, ever since the days of middle school talent shows and gigs at local restaurants. The first real performance she saw was years ago, before the EP, before the album, before anything really, when Greta flew her out for a short set at a small but enthusiastic venue in Seattle. At the time, Helen was still a school nurse and kept delightedly telling everyone—taxi drivers and waiters, hotel clerks and other musicians—that she was on spring break. Greta had picked her up from the airport and suggested they go shopping for something more concert appropriate, something where she wouldn't stand out so much in the crowd. But of course, Helen insisted on wearing her usual khaki pants and cardigan and loafers.

"I don't mind sticking out, honey," she said cheerfully. "That way, you'll be able to spot me."

The crowd wasn't huge that night, maybe a couple hundred people. But as soon as she stepped onto the stage, Greta saw that her mom was right. There she was, right up front, with her thin glasses and short gray hair and sensible shoes, beaming amid a sea of college kids and hipsters dressed mostly in black. When their eyes met, Helen smiled and lifted a small white sign. Greta was in the middle of a complicated riff, but when the song came to an end, she took a few steps forward and squinted at it, trying to make out the words.

GRETA'S MOM, it said in simple block lettering.

She laughed, her heart lifting at the sight. Then she stepped back behind the microphone. "My mother is here tonight, ladies and gentlemen," she said. "You can't miss her. She's the one with the sign."

From the audience, Helen beamed, and the delighted fans clapped and snapped pictures, one of which went semi-viral on Twitter the next morning: this tiny woman in argyle in the middle of a packed club, proudly clutching her sign and beaming at her daughter up on the stage. The internet loved it, and for a week afterward, Howie fielded a surprising number of requests for interviews with "the rock-star mom." When Helen declined because she "needed to finish this month's book club pick," Howie sent Greta a screenshot of her reply with the caption Your mom is a trip.

After that, it became a tradition. Every now and then, whenever Helen had some time off from school and wasn't already enlisted for grandkid duty, Greta would arrange for her to come out to a performance, and Helen would show up with her homemade sign. It traveled to Minneapolis and Orlando, Denver and Los Angeles, Houston and Nashville. In Cleveland, someone spilled a beer on it, and when Helen made a new one, she was sure to laminate it this time. The fans couldn't get enough.

In March, when Greta touched down in Columbus only to discover that she was too late—that her mom had died while she was in the air—she went straight home. Conrad and Asher were still at the hospital, dealing with all the paperwork—fumbling through the unhappy logistics of death—and so the house was empty. Upstairs, she switched on the light in her mom's small walk-in closet and closed the door. Then she lay down on the floor and curled up in a ball, the way she used to as a kid when the world felt like too much.

She didn't cry; already she felt too hollowed out for that, numb from the top of her head to the very tips of her toes. Instead, she pressed her face to the wooden floor, her heart loud in her ears. Her mom was everywhere here—in the neatly folded sweaters and the scarves her dad used to get her for Christmas. The closet still smelled of her perfume, and Greta rolled onto her back and breathed in and out, in and out, her eyes roving around until they landed on a high shelf, on the spine of a book she'd never seen before.

When she hauled herself off the floor to reach for it, she realized it was a scrapbook, bristling with photographs and yellowed newspaper clippings. She opened it up randomly to find her very first mention in *Rolling Stone,* then flipped backward and came face-to-face with a picture from the eighth-grade talent show, her hair wild and her arm a blur.

She sat down again, the book in her lap. It was all there, everything: a paragraph in the *Village Voice* about her first gig in New York City, a photo of the two of them backstage before a show in Chicago, even her first guitar pick, fastened neatly to the page with two pieces of tape, and a small handwritten label beneath it, like an exhibit at a museum. There were clippings and ticket stubs, photos and articles, all the flotsam and jetsam her mom had collected over the years, a whole career in one book. And there, in the very back—pressed between the pages and all ready for the next show—was the sign.

GRETA'S MOM.

She sat there holding it for a long time, surprised that such a simple piece of laminated paper could shatter her so completely. And then a door opened downstairs, and the house filled with voices, and she tucked it back between the pages of the scrapbook and peeled herself off the floor.

Now the ship groans beneath them, rolling from side to side. Greta stands and walks over to where the door is ajar, the room suddenly too warm again. She inhales deeply, wishing for the first time in a while that she had a cigarette.

"She should be here," she says, scanning the blue-black water. "She was the one who took care of everybody. I'm not good at this stuff."

Conrad lifts his head to watch her with feverish eyes. "Neither am I."

"I know," she says, amused. "Remember when Asher broke his wrist playing hockey and you didn't believe him?"

"I wouldn't exactly put it that way."

"You told him to walk it off," she reminds him as she returns to the chair by his bed. "You only took him to the doctor later because Mom made you."

"It was just a stress fracture."

"He says it still hurts when it rains."

"Good thing it wasn't you."

"Why?"

He looks at her as if it should be obvious. "Because how could you play the way you do with a bad wrist?"

Greta blinks at him, not used to this version of her dad.

"What?" he asks with a frown.

"Nothing. It's just . . . that almost sounded like a compliment."

He lets out a little grunt. "You know how good you are."

"I do," she says with a smile. "I've just never heard *you* say it."

"That's not true. Remember your eighth-grade talent show?"

"You'll be happy to know I've improved a bit since then."

He turns onto his back, eyes on the ceiling. "I've never understood how you could move your hands that fast. You certainly didn't get it from me."

"Hey, I've seen you chop an onion," she jokes, but he looks thoughtful.

"I used to do card tricks, you know."

This is such a wildly unexpected thing for him to say that Greta can't help laughing. But right away, his face darkens, and she presses her lips together again.

"I'm serious," he says, as if he isn't always. "I knew a lot of tricks when I was younger. But I never really had the hands for it." He holds his up, examining the wrinkles and veins. "I could shuffle okay. But sleight of hand was never my strong suit."

"Maybe you should've invested in a rabbit and a hat."

"I probably would've, if I'd had the money. I really loved it."

She shakes her head. "I can't believe you never told me this before."

"I was a kid with a hobby," he says, giving her a curious look. "But I moved on. Most people do."

This last part hits just the way it's meant to, and Greta can't help marveling how even when he's sick, his aim is impeccable. Before she can say anything in response, he lurches for the garbage can and retches into it, then wipes his mouth with a towel. When he lies back again, his face is pale and a little sweaty. Greta grabs a water bottle off the desk and hands it to him. It takes him too long to untwist the plastic cap.

"Dad," she begins, watching his throat bob up and down as he takes a sip. Some of it dribbles down the front of his pajamas. "Maybe you should—"

"Did I ever tell you about the first time I laid eyes on your mother?"

*Of course,* she wants to say. *Only about a million times.*

But she feels sorry for him right then. She thinks of the guy who refused to read her letters, the one who was later forced to hear her lyrics—who could never *unhear* them—and he seems like an entirely different person from the one desperately missing his wife, heartsick and lonely and stuck in bed on a trip they were meant to be taking together.

Which is how she finds herself saying, "Tell me again."

"I used to cut the grass for her parents," he says with a distant smile. "They had this huge house and an even bigger yard. It would take me hours to get through it. I'd seen their daughter around, obviously. She was a couple years younger than me, probably sixteen at the time, and she was beautiful, the most beautiful girl I'd ever seen. Totally out of my league."

*Not as it turned out,* her mother would always say at this point in the story, and the empty space where her voice should be feels so stark right now—like a missing line in a play, a forgotten note in a song—that Greta almost says it herself.

"I was always daydreaming about what I'd say if I got to talk to her," he finally goes on, "even though I was just this poor kid with a terrible haircut from the wrong side of town, sweaty and covered in grass clippings. Then one day it finally happened, and you know what brilliant thing I said to her when I got my big chance?"

Greta smiles. "You sneezed."

"I did," he says with a laugh. "And then I said, 'Pollen.' That's it. Just . . . 'Pollen.'"

"It was a good line," Greta teases him, "as it turned out."

But his smile fades, replaced by a worried expression, and he twists sideways and reaches for the garbage can again. For a few seconds, he holds it there in front of his face. But the moment passes. He sets it down again, relieved, and leans back against the pillows.

"Maybe you should rest," Greta says, but he ignores this.

"I didn't see her again for years," he continues. "She went off to Vanderbilt, and I went off to the war, and when I got back, I started bartending at this place called—"

"The Fat Owl," Greta said.

Conrad nods. "Anyway, one night she walks in with her boyfriend, some preppy guy she met at school. I get them some drinks, and they sit at the bar, and he starts explaining the rules of baseball to her in this really condescending way while she doodles on a napkin, and the whole time I'm thinking: *This guy? Really?*"

"So then he goes to the bathroom . . ." Greta prompts, because this is taking longer than usual, and her eyelids are getting heavy.

"I'm wiping down the bar, and she's still drawing on the napkin, and without even looking up, she goes, 'How's the pollen count today?' I just about fell over. That was it for me. Our eyes met. I asked what was on the napkin and she showed me a picture of a penguin, and I said I could do even better." He squeezes his eyes shut and laughs hoarsely. "I don't know what came over me. But I wrote down my phone number."

"Bold move."

"It was," he says, looking satisfied, and when their eyes meet, the warmth between them is real. For a second, Greta is reminded that they have at least one thing in common: they both loved her mother more than anything. He scratches at his chin, his eyes filled with amusement. "And it worked. A few weeks later, she came back to the bar, and that time, she was alone."

"And the rest is history," Greta says, which is meant to make him smile, but somehow it has the opposite effect. Instead, his face goes slack.

"Yeah, well, I guess it's all history now," he says, and to Greta's horror, there are tears in the corners of his eyes. He shakes his head. "We were supposed to be doing this part together."

"What part?"

"Winding down."

"Dad, come on. You're only seventy."

He looks as if this makes it worse, and she knows he's thinking about all the lonely years that could still be ahead of him. He wipes an arm roughly across his face, then makes a show of arranging his pillows and pulling up his blankets. "Anyway, you should get going."

"Dad."

"I'm fine."

She bites her lip. "Are you sure you don't—"

"You're not supposed to be here," he says with such finality that Greta has no choice but to scrape back the chair. For a second, she stands over him, and he does look old, but also somehow very young too, his pajamas a bit too big, his hair sticking up in the back. She remembers when she was a kid, the way he'd poke his head into the garage to tell her it was time for dinner. Sometimes she wouldn't hear him over the sound of the guitar, and then she'd look up to find him looming there, solid and immovable, filling up all that space in the doorway.

She puts her jacket back on, then walks over to the door. "Lights on or off?" she asks, a hand on the switch, and he mumbles something she doesn't hear. She flicks off the light and lingers there another few seconds, listening to the sound of his breathing. After a moment, she opens the door to the hallway, letting in a wedge of fluorescent light.

Just as she's about to walk out, she hears him say, "Good night."

"Good night," she says, closing the door behind her.

# TUESDAY

## Chapter Fourteen

In the morning, the sky is a brilliant blue, so sunlit and dazzling that people can talk of little else at the breakfast buffet.

"Perfect glacier weather," says the cruise director over the loudspeaker.

"Not a single cloud," marvels Todd, squinting at the windows.

"Such a shame your dad is missing this," says Mary as she squirrels away a banana for him.

"Don't forget your sunscreen," says the old lady when she passes Greta at the coffee machine.

"Wouldn't dream of it," Greta calls back.

It'll be hours before they reach Glacier Bay, but already there's an air of anticipation on the ship. While they eat, Davis and Todd indulge their newfound fascination with the cannery industry, swapping stats like they're talking about baseball. Eleanor takes the opportunity to nudge a flyer for the variety show in Greta's direction.

"In case you change your mind," she says with a wink. "Todd and I will be ballroom dancing. We've been taking lessons the last couple years."

"Wow," Greta says, wondering if the Fosters ever get tired of hanging out with so many white people. She turns to Mary with a little grin. "Are you guys ballroom dancing too?"

"My feet would never be the same," Mary says, nodding at Davis across the table. "But we'll do something, I'm sure."

"We'd love to see you up there," Eleanor says, looking at Greta hopefully. "And it might be a nice chance to—"

"No thanks." Greta makes an effort to keep her voice light, though she feels a twinge of annoyance at Eleanor's persistence. She pushes the flyer back across the table. "But I'll be there to cheer you guys on."

At the next table, a chorus of "Happy Birthday" breaks out. They look over to see a small, stooped Hispanic man surrounded by his extended family, all of them beaming as they watch him blow out the candle that's sticking out of his pancakes. Tied to his chair, there's a huge bunch of colorful helium balloons, and Mary turns to Greta with a smile.

"Your dad used to do that for your mom," she says, and Greta is frowning, trying to remember balloons of any kind, when Mary adds, "At school."

Years ago, Mary had taught third grade at the same elementary school where Helen worked as a nurse. Not long after, she went back for her master's in education and became a principal in the next district. But for a brief time, the two of them worked in the same small building together, carpooling every morning and afternoon, sharing lunches and trading gossip.

"You didn't know?" Mary says. "Every single birthday, he'd show up at the door to her office with all these balloons. The kids loved it."

"I had no idea," Greta says, though it's not really a surprise. She remembers watching her parents dance at their fifteenth-anniversary party, the two of them pressed together under the fairy lights in the backyard. "Gross," Asher had said, making a face as he watched them kiss. He was eleven then, and firmly against such displays of affection. But Greta couldn't take her eyes off them, the way they looked at each other, like each thought they were the luckier one.

"He used to come have lunch with her every Friday too," Mary says. "They'd meet in the cafeteria, and all the kids would make kissy faces and say, 'Mrs. James has a *boyfriend*.' And your dad, he'd just grin at them and say, 'She sure does.'"

Greta shakes her head in disbelief. "Every Friday?"

"Every Friday. By the time he got all the way across town, he could only stay for fifteen or twenty minutes. But he never missed it. Not once in all those years."

"They never said."

"They called it date night," Davis says with a grin. "I always told him he could do better than pizza day with a bunch of second graders, but it made your mom so happy."

They all fall silent. Mary reaches for Davis's hand and gives it a squeeze. Todd puts an arm around Eleanor, who leans into him. And at the other end of the table, Greta sits alone, turning over the stories and memories, the small joys and rituals of a shared life.

After a moment, Davis pushes back his chair. "We don't want to be late for trivia," he says, picking up his tray. "Gotta defend our title from yesterday."

"Come with us," Eleanor says to Greta. "It'll be good fun."

"The prizes are great," Todd tells her, pulling a pen from his pocket. It has a little cruise ship on the top.

Greta smiles. "Maybe another day."

"You sure?" Davis asks. "We could use some help with the music category."

This isn't true. Davis knows everything there is to know about music. But she can tell they're trying to make her feel included, which is sweet.

"When in doubt," Greta tells them, "go with the Rolling Stones."

As she walks out of the dining room, she spots Ben at the far end of the buffet, balancing a tray filled with a fairly ridiculous collection of bowls and cups. When he sees her, he stops abruptly, standing frozen in the middle of the breakfast rush. Then, looking flustered, he turns and hurries off in the other direction.

Greta blinks. There's a part of her that can't help feeling a little stung. But the other part is examining this one with something like bemusement. Because it was always a ridiculous idea, wasn't it? What was she supposed to do with a bookish college professor anyway? A guy who wears dad jeans and spent the last however many years in the suburbs of New Jersey?

For a fleeting moment, she imagines what it would be like to plunk him down in the middle of her life, the late-night writing sessions and the long months on the road, the interviews with eager reporters in local cafés and the high-powered performances that hardly leave energy for anything else. It's difficult even to picture him at one of her shows, amid the strobe lights and thumping bass, the sweaty, swaying, shouting crowd. It would be like bringing a puppy to a mosh pit.

Whatever this is, it's got to be chalked up to boredom. After all, she's stuck on this ship in the middle of nowhere with thousands of gray-haired tourists and screaming children. Her dad is holed up in his room, responding to her texts one word at a time—How are you feeling? Fine. Do you need anything? No—and the cell service is too spotty to call anyone else, even if the only person she wants to call right now didn't happen to be dead.

There's something uniquely awful about feeling lonely when you're trapped on a ship and surrounded by this many people. Greta moves through them like a salmon swimming upstream—past the shuffleboard court and the empty taco bar, the crowd waiting outside the auditorium for a wildlife lecture—feeling a clawing restlessness.

But there's no escape—not today—so instead she heads for her room, where she grabs a notebook and a pen. Back outside, she finds a wooden lounge chair on the promenade deck and settles in, watching the mountains slip past, each one bigger and more snow-covered than the last.

She uncaps her pen and stares at the blank page.

She grabs one of the scratchy plaid blankets and pulls it over her legs.

She squints at the slanted sun, hard and bright in the crystal air.

Two women in puffy vests power walk past her, and then again a few minutes later, and again after that. Each time, they pause their conversation to smile at her, and Greta nods back.

The blank page stares up at her.

It's not that this part is ever easy. But she's never second-guessed herself the way she's been doing the last few months.

She tries to remember the last good writing day she had, and realizes it was back in February, a few weeks before her trip to Germany. She and Luke had rented an old farmhouse upstate for a long weekend. They explored the little towns along the Hudson, poking around thrift shops and hiking to half-frozen waterfalls. The last night, they cooked in the ramshackle kitchen, a feast of roast chicken from the butcher, fresh vegetables from the general store, and a growler of beer from a local brewery. Afterward, they turned on a movie and curled up in front of the fire together, but Greta found she couldn't concentrate.

"Go ahead," Luke said as he watched her fidget, tapping her fingers against the remote, bobbing her leg.

"What?" she asked, and he laughed.

"I know you want to write."

She didn't bother to deny it, just gave him a kiss on the cheek before heading upstairs. It was something about the coziness of the house, the frost outside on the fields, the deep contentment of a weekend away. It should've relaxed her; instead it only made her eager to write.

Later, when Luke came upstairs, he crawled into the creaky bed beside her, resting his chin on her shoulder to read what she'd written.

"Beautiful," he murmured, his eyes fixed on hers, and she didn't know if he was talking about her or the lyrics, but it didn't matter, because he kissed her then, and they fell back on the pillows, and the notebook went tumbling onto the floor with a gentle thud.

Her phone dings, and she sets down her pen, grateful for the distraction. She sees it's a text from Howie: I got you the week off. But in exchange, you need to sit down with the Times after your set. And they'll want to ask about what happened. It's time to get it over with. Okay?

Greta hesitates, then writes, Okay.

Also, Cleo says they want approval over the set list.

Greta frowns at her phone. Cleo is her A&R person at the label, a tiny but formidable Black woman from Quebec who has a habit of breaking into French whenever she's annoyed or upset. Even if she hadn't been the one to discover Greta during a bar set in Red Hook one snowy night, she still would've been one of the coolest people Greta has ever met. But in the whole time they've worked together, she's never requested anything like this before.

Howie answers her question before she can ask it: They're livestreaming the set, remember?

Yeah, but why? she asks.

Because of everything, he writes, which of course means: all those months of delaying the album, all those weeks of lost publicity. This had been the solution. A live recording of her return to the stage. A way to break out the new single. And a path back for her, assuming she can stick the landing.

No, she writes. Why do they want approval?

I think they're afraid you might take another swing at "Astronomy." There's a pause, and then he adds: Don't shoot the messenger.

Greta closes her eyes for a second. It hadn't even occurred to her to try the song again. There's too much at stake. She knows this, and clearly Cleo and everyone else at the label does too. They want her to move on. To stick to a script. And that's fine with Greta. She's as anxious as anyone to leave this all behind her.

Fine, she writes back to Howie.

You'll be ready, he replies, right?

She looks out at the water, which is dotted with floating chunks of ice, each one reflected back on itself in the stillness. Around them, the water looks like glass. When she glances back down at her phone, she's not sure what to say.

She's always felt ready. Every single time she's stepped onstage. Every time she's held a guitar and closed her eyes and played that first note. That was the reward for pushing through thousands of hours of practice, and for all the rest of it too, the small indignities and constant rejections that piled up along the way: playing to near-empty rooms and waiting for calls that never came; being dismissed by agents and managers and execs; being told by pretty much everyone that it was too much of a long shot, this dream of hers, as if dreams were meant to be reasonable.

None of that had ever mattered. Not really. Because at her core, she had an unshakable faith in herself—and, even more than that, in her music.

But then, on an unseasonably cold night in March—exactly one week after her mom died and one day after she broke up with Luke—everything fell apart.

Six minutes. That's how long she was onstage at the Brooklyn Academy of Music.

As it turns out, it takes a lot less time to derail a career than it does to build one.

The performance had been planned long before the bottom fell out of her life, a single song as part of a charity concert to raise money for arts education. If she'd been in a frame of mind to do anything at the time, she might've tried to bow out. But she wasn't. And so she didn't.

It was a risk to play something so new. The whole of "Astronomy" was written on three crumpled notebook pages, notes and lyrics she'd scribbled blearily on that long flight home from Germany, then practiced only a handful of times since.

She knew it wasn't right yet. Not just because it had been written so hastily. But because it was a song about love and hope and memory, a wish more than anything else. There was nothing in there—nothing at all—about the grief that had opened up beneath her like a black hole the moment the plane had landed. And in some ways that made the song feel like a lie. But it was a lie she still wanted to live inside for as long as she could.

There was more to write. But that would mean saying goodbye.

And she wasn't ready to do that yet.

Still, what else could she have possibly played that night? What else could've meant half as much?

She was okay at first. Her throat was thick as she moved through the opening, her voice brittle as she began to sing. But music had always been her refuge. It was a place to go when the world was dark, a reliable shelter in any storm. She could walk this tightrope, then go back home to her apartment, crawl under the covers, and close her eyes again.

But as she made it to the end of the chorus, she noticed the sign in the audience, held up by a solemn-looking white guy with a beard, who stood swaying beside his equally solemn girlfriend.

It said: GOODBYE, GRETA'S MOM.

Up until then, she hadn't cried. Not at the wake or the funeral or on the floor of her mom's closet. She hadn't cried on the trip

back to New York, though she'd felt like she was leaving her actual bones behind, or when she'd broken up with Luke the next
morning. She knew it was something she could outrun for only so
long, that the dam would burst eventually. She just didn't expect
it to happen on a stage in Brooklyn with nearly three thousand
upturned faces holding what seemed like three thousand phones
with cameras in them.

But staring at that sign, she felt like a balloon with a pinhole,
all the air slowly seeping out of her. The oddest part was how
aware she was, how her thoughts matched up so precisely with
what her body was doing. *Now my legs are going slack,* she
thought as her foot came off the pedal. *And now my fingers are
frozen,* she thought as the pick fell onto the stage.

Simple. Mechanical. Inevitable.

Behind her, the two backup musicians—Atsuko on the drums
and Nate on the keys—continued to play even after Greta had
stopped, bent forward like someone who'd been punched in the
stomach, all those eyes tracking her as she tried to catch her
breath. She didn't even know she was crying at first, not until she
felt a tear travel down the bridge of her nose, and by then, Atsuko
and Nate had stopped too, and it was silent in a way that no music
venue should ever be, in a way that felt wholly and entirely wrong.
A murmur broke out, and she knew they were still with her, the
audience, sympathetic and concerned and maybe even a little
touched to see someone being so real, a little excited to bear witness to such a raw display of authenticity.

But then something shifted, and as she continued to cry, as the
silence yawned between them, she could feel it going on too long,
could feel it stretching out painfully, so she forced herself up to
the microphone again, hoping to summon an inner strength that
was surely there—because wasn't it always there in moments like
these, if you dug deep enough?—and she started again, playing
without a pick, singing without breath, and what came out was

so scratchy and out of tune that she couldn't even pretend to keep it up. There was another silence, less forgiving this time, and she opened her mouth to apologize but found she couldn't even do that.

The crowd stared at her, and she stared back at them.

Then, without another word, she simply turned and walked off the stage, feeling the heat of all those cameras following her.

Howie insists it wasn't as bad as she thinks.

But it was. She knows, because she's seen the video. It's everywhere.

What was hardest to swallow wasn't the fact that she'd melted down in front of a large crowd or even that the footage had spread so far and wide. Given the circumstances, it was an acceptable sort of failure, one wrought by grief, and most of the articles about it said as much.

The part that knocked her totally off-balance was the pity that came along with it. Pity for her collapse, for her moment of weakness, for her vulnerability.

And pity for the song itself, which was the worst part of all.

*Rolling Stone* called it "maudlin and sentimental—at least what could be heard of it." *Pitchfork* said it was "more nursery rhyme than song, a saccharine ballad out of step with James's usual vibe." *New York* magazine was blunter, dubbing the whole thing "an utter disaster from top to bottom."

Greta had always come to the stage from a place of power. It was where she felt most confident and in control. A thick skin is a requirement in this line of work, especially as a female musician— a female guitarist, no less—and she had long since learned how to take criticism. She has no problem dealing with heckling. She can brush off insults and disapproval and snark.

But the tidal wave of sympathy—not just for her situation, or even the performance, but for the song itself—was what really flattened her.

The label was furious. They were in the middle of a rollout for her second album, which they'd been promising would be even more explosive and exciting than her first. And then she went and stood up onstage and cried her way through an overly sentimental ballad, which was now the top result when you searched for Greta James.

They wanted her to do another show right away. A chance to quickly wipe the slate clean and move on. But Howie—who had flown overnight from L.A. to New York and shown up at Greta's apartment the next morning with coffee and bagels—convinced them it would be better to take a pause, even just for a week. That week, of course, had turned into a month. And then another. Soon, everything had to be pushed back: the single, the album, the tour, all the publicity. Even so, it took a long time for Greta to begin paying attention again, to start to worry about any of it— not because the other, greater loss had faded but because she knew if she lost this too, she might never recover at all.

Now she looks at her phone again, trying to imagine being back onstage, singing a brand-new song, all of the execs hoping for a fresh start, all of her fans looking for a story to tell, all of it in concert with the embarrassment and doubt that have been beating like twin drums underneath her grief, that constant fist around her heart.

She knows it's time. It's past time. It's possibly even too late.

But still, she's not sure she's ready.

One of the strangest things about death is that it doesn't mean you stop hearing someone's voice in your head, and right now, Greta knows exactly what her mom would say.

*You'll be fine. You're ready. You've got this.*

But she's not here to say it.

And so Greta attempts to do it for herself.

I'll be fine, she writes to Howie. I'm ready. I've got this.

She's just not sure she believes it.

## Chapter Fifteen

Greta is standing at the rail, mesmerized by the tiny icebergs floating past in the tranquil water, when Mary appears at her side. She's wearing a red coat, and her knit hat is pulled tight over her short black hair.

"The bad news," she says, leaning her elbows on the railing beside Greta, "is that we lost our trivia title. The good news is that we got the one about the Rolling Stones."

Greta laughs. "Happy to help."

"I checked on your dad." Mary rubs her hands together. "He seems a lot better."

"Did he yell at you about the quarantine too?"

"Honestly," she says, "I'd be more worried about him if he hadn't."

"I feel bad he's stuck in his room," Greta says. "I can't even blame him for being grumpy for once."

"Go easy on him. He's having a hard time."

"We all are."

Mary gives her an appraising look. "I'm glad you're getting a little break this week."

"I've been on a break for a while now, actually."

"I know. I saw the video."

"You and about two million other people," Greta says, turning to her with an attempt at a smile. But it falters when she sees the look on Mary's face, which is so tender it makes her want to cry.

"For what it's worth, I thought the song was beautiful."

"That's only because you miss her too."

"Maybe," she says, looking thoughtful. "Will you ever play it again?"

"I've been explicitly instructed not to," she says, then shrugs. "It's not finished anyway. It's something I started writing on the plane. Before I knew . . ." Her voice breaks. "Anyway, even if it hadn't ruined my entire career, it's not really a fit for my shows."

"What do you mean?"

"It's just not my brand, a song like that."

Mary rolls her eyes. "What ever happened to just writing what you're feeling?"

"You *saw* what happened," Greta says ruefully. "I think it's better if I leave that particular chapter behind for now."

"That chapter," Mary says gently, "will be with you for a while. Whether you want it to be or not. Sometimes the only way out is through."

"That sounds like something my mom would say."

Mary smiles. "I'll take that as a compliment."

For a few seconds, they both gaze out as the first glacier comes into view, a brilliant white against the blue-green water.

"She would've loved this," Mary says, then shakes her head. "I still can't believe she's gone."

"I know."

"Sometimes I find myself looking out the window for her when I'm doing the dishes. Or reaching for my phone to call her when something funny happens. It's like my brain knows but my body doesn't."

"My body knows," Greta says, and it's a struggle to keep her voice even. "I feel it everywhere. In my heart. My lungs. My bones."

Mary slips an arm around her shoulders and gives her a squeeze.

"I know she wasn't perfect," Greta says. "She could be so frustrating and stubborn, and she was such a sore loser when we played board games. And she never stepped in enough when my dad was being a jerk. She could have, and she didn't, because she loved him too and I think she felt like it was her job to be neutral. But that's not how it's supposed to work, especially not when one person is clearly so wrong. And it always hurt, that she was more silent than I wanted her to be, even though I never said it. Even though I never told her." She pauses for a second, rocking back on the rail, then shakes her head. "Also, she made the worst coffee. Like, seriously bad. And she had no street smarts. She'd come to New York and act like she was in a musical, like the whole world was singing along with her. And . . . she left me. She left all of us, but it feels like she left me most of all, and I know that's completely self-centered, but it's how I feel. I hate that she's gone. I just really, really hate it."

The ship is moving slowly now, barely disturbing the water. Everything around them is still, as if they've drifted into a painting.

"And this isn't helping anything," Greta says, blinking back tears, "being here. I should be in New York right now, doing press for the festival, trying to salvage my career."

Mary leans on the rail beside her. "You're here for your dad."

"He doesn't even care."

"He does. He's just not great at showing it."

Greta gives her a skeptical look.

"I know the pair of you have had your issues," Mary says, eyebrows raised, "but you know what your mom used to always say, right? That you were two peas in a pod."

"She did not."

"She did. Whenever you were at each other's throats, she'd complain about how stubborn you both could be, how neither of you would ever give an inch. How totally alike you were."

"No," Greta says, "it's Asher that—"

"Asher's made similar choices, and his life might look like your dad's," Mary points out with a smile. "But deep down, at the core of who you both are, I think your mom was right. Two peas in a pod."

"Some pod," Greta says, frowning out at the ripples of water.

She thinks of their conversation last night, tries to picture her dad as that hopeful young guy behind a bar, tries to picture him as anything other than what he is now—an obstinate ad salesman, conventional down to his toes—but her imagination fails her.

"I'm not saying he can't be difficult sometimes," Mary says. "But underneath all that, he wants what's best for you."

"He wants what *he* thinks is best for me. There's a difference."

"Fair enough," she says with a nod. "But that's also part of the deal. You think I haven't been praying for Jason to get married for years now?"

Greta knows she's meant to laugh at this, but she can't manage it.

"I honestly wasn't sure it would ever happen," Mary says. "I used to complain about it to your mom all the time. We spent so many of our morning walks coming up with schemes to get the two of you together."

"You did?" Greta says, looking over again, incredulous.

"Our two globe-trotting, work-obsessed, commitment-phobic New Yorkers," Mary says with a grin. "We figured if we couldn't pawn you off on anyone else, maybe we could at least get the pair of you together." She laughs at Greta's expression. "Sorry. It was out of love."

"I didn't know she cared so much about that."

"She just wanted you to be happy. She also understood that that was only one version of it." Mary reaches out and puts a hand over Greta's. "She was ridiculously proud of you. You know that, right?"

Greta manages to nod, but honestly, she's not so sure anymore. Her mom taught her that no matter what she did with her life, she should do it wholeheartedly. That she should try hard and work harder, dream big and care deeply. But for the first time in her life, she feels like she's in full retreat.

Mary tugs her hat down over her ears and nods toward the doors of the ship. "I should go. I promised the others I'd meet them. But you should come with us to the musical tonight. It's supposed to be great. Almost as good as Broadway."

Greta raises her eyebrows.

"Well, maybe off Broadway," Mary says, and they both glance out at the snow and ice. "*Way* off Broadway. But you should come. We're going to the early show."

"Yeah, okay," Greta says, thinking she has nothing else to do tonight but sit alone in her windowless room not playing the guitar. "As long as there's no chorus line."

Mary laughs. "No promises."

Soon the glacier is upon them, and the deck begins to fill with people. The voice of a geologist crackles over the speakers, but otherwise, everything is hushed. Greta thinks about her dad alone on his balcony somewhere above, taking it all in.

"Wow," says a little boy beside her, and she follows his gaze. This close, she can see how absolutely huge the glacier is, a solid block stretching across the space between mountains. The front of it is jagged and craggy, a shade of blue so unreal it's like someone has taken a spray can to it. Everything is still except for the seagulls that circle the ship looking for table scraps, and though the sun has come out, the world still smells of winter.

Greta draws in a breath, thinking: *There will never be a way to describe this.*

And then: *She would've loved it.*

There's a sound like gunfire, a loud crack that echoes out across the quiet bay, and a few people point frantically to the left side of the glacier. When her eyes find the spot, all Greta can see is the aftermath: a splash that breaks the stillness of the water. But a second later, another slab of ice shears off the side and goes crashing down, a mini-avalanche, the sound of it reaching them seconds later.

"That noise you're hearing," says the geologist, "is the calving of the ice. Or white thunder."

"White thunder," the boy repeats with a kind of quiet reverence.

Greta stares at the place where the ice disappeared, thinking how beautiful it is, all of it—the dreamlike mountains and cerulean sky, the clouds reflected in the bay—and how sad too, to see something so magnificent crumbling before their very eyes.

She pushes off the rail and heads inside.

# Chapter Sixteen

Greta is on her way to the auditorium that evening when she gets a text from Asher.

I heard you stopped by to see Dad last night. He seemed glad. It's been a tough start to the trip.

She pauses on the red-carpeted staircase, thinking of the way his face had looked so drawn and pale. I know, she replies. I feel bad for him.

Not exactly what he was picturing.

Well, she writes, that ship had already sailed. So to speak.

A few beats go by before Asher responds: When people ask what it's like to have a rock star as a sister, it takes a great deal of restraint not to tell them what a dork you are.

Don't worry, she writes. When people ask me what it's like to have a bank manager for a brother, it's the first thing I mention.

He sends back an emoji with its tongue sticking out.

Outside the theater, a crowd has gathered, everyone eager to get in and find good seats for the eight o'clock show. For a second, Greta considers doing a U-turn and walking straight back to her room. Or escaping to one of the outer decks and disappearing under a blanket again. Anything but ninety minutes of cruise ship entertainment. But then Davis Foster—towering over everyone else—spots her and lifts a hand.

"You all look nice," she says when she reaches her unlikely

crew, all three of them dressed up for the night. "What's the occasion?"

"No occasion," says Davis, tugging at his sports coat. "Just a totally arbitrary dress code for the dining room."

"Gala attire," Eleanor says with shining eyes. She's wearing a sparkly black dress, and her hair is curled at the ends. "Todd already scarpered off to get out of his suit."

Davis gives his wife—who looks elegant in an emerald-green dress—a mutinous look. "Lucky him."

Mary shakes her head. "A couple more hours won't kill you."

"No, but a couple hours of musical theater might," Davis says cheerfully.

The ship, which had been steady all afternoon as they lingered in the bay, has now begun to roil again. Even after only a few days on board, Greta can feel it like a metronome inside her; she's begun shifting her weight from one foot to the other almost without realizing it.

Eleanor stumbles forward a step. "How on earth is anyone meant to dance in this?"

"That's their whole job," Mary says. "They're obviously trained for it, which means they can handle—"

The ship lurches hard to the left, and someone crashes into Greta from behind, shoving her straight into Davis, who laughs as he helps right her again.

"Guess we know how *you'd* do onstage in this," he jokes. But Greta isn't listening. When she turns to see who nearly managed to take her out, she finds herself face-to-face with Ben. He looks as surprised as she is, and there's an awkward beat as they stare at each other.

Eleanor Bloom is the first to speak: "Jack London!"

Ben glances over at her. He's wearing the same tweed jacket as the day of his lecture, elbow patches and all, and his hair has been neatly combed. On his red tie, there are tiny embroidered dinosaurs.

"My friends call me Ben," he says after a moment, an effort at humor that collapses entirely when he turns to Greta, straight-faced and serious. "Sorry about that. Guess I still don't quite have my sea legs."

"Gets a lot harder after dinner," Davis says, miming a drink, then shrugs in response to Mary's look. "At least for me."

Ben steals a glance at Greta. He looks like he's about to say something, but she beats him to it. "Everything work out with the tooth fairy?"

He gives her a pained look. "Yes. Thanks."

The doors are open now, and people are starting to file into the theater, hurrying to get the best seats.

"You going to the show?" Davis asks Ben, who—much to Greta's surprise—nods.

"You are?" she can't help asking. "Why?"

Eleanor and Mary both snap their mouths into thin, disapproving lines, a couple of substitute moms mindful of her manners. But she ignores them.

"I like musical theater," Ben says stiffly.

"Yeah, but . . . on a boat?"

"It's a ship," he says, and she rolls her eyes.

"I bet you five bucks one of the dancers bites it."

"Greta!" Mary says, looking shocked.

But Davis laughs. "I'd take that money," he says to Ben, who doesn't seem to hear him. His eyes are locked on Greta's. He looks like he's trying very hard not to be amused.

After a moment, he clears his throat. "I should probably . . ."

"Yeah," Greta says. "Enjoy the show."

"You too," he says, then nods at the others and heads inside.

"Goodness," says Eleanor once he's gone. "What did you do to him?"

Inside the auditorium, they find a row of seats toward the back. Greta goes in first, then Eleanor, then Mary, then Davis, who takes the aisle since his legs are so long. A minute later, Todd appears with his field guide tucked under one arm.

"Ah, go on," Eleanor says, rolling her eyes at him as Greta shifts over to make room. "You brought a book?"

He shrugs. "Just in case."

"In case of what? A mystery bird decides to join us?"

"You never know," he says with a grin.

Around them, people chatter excitedly. There's another show at ten, so this one is filled with the early-to-bed crowd. In the back, there's a fleet of walkers and wheelchairs, and about two seconds after sitting down, the man directly in front of Greta pops up and tells his wife that he needs to use the bathroom one more time before the show starts. This spurs three others around him to do the same.

Just before the lights dim, Greta spots Ben. He's sitting a couple rows in front of her but off to the side, so that when he turns to scan the audience, their eyes meet. He looks away again immediately, but she can see the effort it takes in the tensing of his shoulders, and something about that lifts her spirits.

"Here we go," Eleanor whispers as the first notes of music begin to play, and Greta has a sudden memory of seeing *The Nutcracker* with the three of them—her mom and Mary and Eleanor—when she was about twelve. The Blooms' daughter, Brigid, was old enough to more convincingly refuse, and the rest of the kids—Asher, Jason, and Jason's two older brothers—would never be caught dead at the ballet. So it was only Greta who sat glumly at the end of the row, tugging at the collar of the dress she hadn't wanted to wear.

When the lights went down, her mom leaned close. "Just you wait," she whispered. "It'll be magical."

It wasn't. At least not for Greta. The music was pretty and the dancing was fine, but by the start of the second act, Greta's knee was bobbing impatiently and she was wishing she were anywhere else.

The moment the lights came up, the audience burst into applause, and to her surprise, she looked over to see that her mom was crying. And not just a few tears. Her cheeks were wet and her eyes were red; she looked completely undone by the performance.

"Are you okay?" Greta asked, half mortified and half incredulous.

Her mom smiled as she dug through her purse for a tissue. "I'm *wonderful*," she said with such emotion that Greta couldn't help puzzling over what she'd missed. It wasn't that she'd never thought of her mother as having feelings. She'd seen her cry over other things, too many things to count: holiday commercials and tragedies on the news and even the birds that came to the feeder she put up in their backyard. But something about the ballet had peeled her back in the way certain songs sometimes did to Greta, leaving her raw and exposed. The music might've been different— "Dance of the Sugar Plum Fairy" instead of "Smells like Teen Spirit"—but the expression on her face was the same, and this struck Greta as strange and revelatory, that they could be so similar and so different all at once.

Now the first few dancers come rocketing onto the stage with all the force of a cannon, a blur of sequins and tap shoes and too-bright smiles. Already, the whole thing is slightly ridiculous. The costumes are over-the-top, and of the six performers, at least two are immediately off-key. But there's a lot of enthusiasm on that stage—a *lot* of enthusiasm—and Greta appreciates the effort that requires, so she decides to keep an open mind.

That is, until one of the guys takes a spill.

It isn't entirely his fault. The ship pulls hard to one side with a rolling motion that seems to ripple through the audience. But the dancers are in the middle of a number involving a complicated bit

of footwork, so it hits them even harder. The first guy—an ener-
getic man in some sort of satin tux—careens into the second guy,
who barely manages to stay upright. It's too late, however, for his
friend, who—wobbly-legged as a baby deer—takes a tumble.

The audience gasps, but the other dancers keep up their furious pace. On the floor, the guy in the tux—uninjured and
unbowed—struggles to his feet again, and the crowd goes wild.

This is when Greta notices that Ben is watching her.

And this time, when she looks back at him, he doesn't look
away.

She waits for him to grin or nod or give a sheepish shrug, something to acknowledge the bet she offered him. But he doesn't.

Even in the dark, there's something magnetic about his gaze.
Just like that, she forgets all about the shaky dancers and the performance that's continuing gamely up onstage. Just like that, the
rest of the audience disappears, and it's only the two of them.

There's the kind of magic her mom was talking about at *The
Nutcracker*, and the kind her dad was talking about last night.
And then there's this: two people in the dark, watching each other
like there's a string pulled taut between them.

She's not surprised when he stands up to leave. She's already
doing the same.

To get out of the row, she has to squeeze past Eleanor and
Todd, then Mary and finally Davis. The two women give her quiz-
zical looks, but the one Davis shoots her is plainly jealous.

By the time she gets up the aisle and pushes open the double
doors at the back, Ben is already waiting in the empty hallway.
When he steps toward her, she's still not entirely sure what will
happen, and there's a thrill to this that makes her heart beat fast.
Later, she'll try to remember who kissed who, but it's impossible
to tell. One second there's a space between them, and then suddenly there's not; suddenly his arms are around her and her hands
are on the back of his neck and their bodies are pressed close to-

gether. His beard is rough against her face but his lips are soft, and he tastes of whisky, and whatever this is—this current running between them—it's electric enough to make her forget where they are, floating on this strange, overstuffed ship in the gathering dark of a cold Alaskan night.

When they pull back again, Greta feels a little dizzy. She glances up at Ben, who is looking at her with wonder, his brown eyes full of warmth.

"I've been wanting to do that since last night," she tells him, and he smiles.

"I've been wanting to do that since the first moment I saw you."

Then he takes her hand, and together, they hurry down the long hallway.

# WEDNESDAY

# Chapter Seventeen

They're still awake at three A.M. when light starts to filter in around the edges of the curtains.

"I feel kind of cheated," Ben says, turning onto his side so that his face is only inches from Greta's. "When you finally get to stay up all night talking to a girl you like, the night isn't supposed to end this early."

"Just think of it this way," she says with a grin. "We're that much closer to morning sex."

"That definitely helps," he says, looking at her the way he's been looking at her all night—his face serious, his eyes intent on hers—and brushes a strand of her hair away from her forehead so gently that it makes her shiver.

"Are you cold?" he asks, already throwing back the covers and getting out of bed. He's wearing only a pair of boxers covered in tiny penguins with scarves, and in the gray light of the room, she can see the muscles in his back as he fumbles through a drawer. He tosses her a gray sweatshirt that says COLUMBIA across the front. It's frayed at the cuffs and impossibly soft and it smells just like him.

"Can I ask you a question?" she says as she pulls it over her head. When she emerges again, he's wearing a T-shirt with the name of the cruise ship emblazoned on it.

"Where did I buy this?" he asks as he climbs back into bed and pulls her close.

"No—well, yes. I mean, I was going to ask about the penguins, but now I kind of want to know how many times you've been to the gift shop."

"Only twice," he says, and when she gives him a look, he shrugs. "Fine. Four times. But once was because I forgot my toothbrush. And as for the penguins, they felt thematically—if not scientifically—appropriate."

She nods at his tie, which she'd tugged off the moment they crashed into the room, and which is now draped over his type-writer. "How do you explain the dinosaurs?"

"Who doesn't like dinosaurs?"

"Asteroids?" she suggests, which makes him laugh. He kisses her, and the kiss ripples all the way down to her toes.

"I knew it," he says when they break apart again.

"Knew what?"

"That you were a nerd at heart."

Later, they open the curtains to watch the sun come up over the white-tipped mountains, the buttery light streaming in. Ben's arms are around her, his beard scratchy against the back of her neck, their legs entwined. It's strange to lie in bed while the land-scape scrolls by, to be entirely still as the world comes to them.

"You're so lucky you have a window," she says, turning around to face him. He frowns at this, and she runs a finger over the lines on his forehead. Then—unable to help herself—she takes his face in her hands and kisses him.

"Wait," he says, pulling back again, "you don't?"

"Nope. There's the beige wall with a picture of a bear, the beige wall with a picture of a mountain, the beige wall with a door to the bathroom, and the beige wall with the suspicious red stain."

"Jeez," he says, blinking at her.

"Don't worry. I'm pretty sure it's just wine."

"No, I mean—that must be so claustrophobic."

"It's not ideal."

"Then why—"

"Because," she says, the words more clipped than intended, "by the time I booked, that was all they had left."

Ben looks stricken. "Right. Your mom. I'm so sorry—"

"It's okay," Greta says, but he finds her hand underneath the covers anyway. The gesture makes her throat tight. "Let's talk about something else."

"Penguins?"

"Do you know anything about penguins?" she asks, managing a small smile. "Because I've got nothing."

"How about dinosaurs then? Hannah went through a big dino phase last year, so I have a lot of good facts. Jokes too." He clears his throat. "What does a triceratops sit on?"

"What?"

"Its tricera-bottom."

She groans. "I refuse to dignify that with a laugh."

"Yeah, but you kind of want to," he says, lying back on his pillow with a satisfied grin. "I can tell."

For a moment, she studies his face, the fine wrinkles around the corners of his eyes, the hint of gray in his beard, silvery in the early light. "I bet you're a really good dad," she says, and he looks surprised.

"I try to be. It's harder now, obviously. But they're awesome, and they deserve a great dad." He hesitates, then asks, "What about you? Are you a kid person?"

Greta thinks of her nieces, a whirling scrum of tears and laughter and affection. Sometimes, when she's visiting, she tries to imagine what it would be like if they were hers, if she were the one responsible not just for the day-to-day stuff—the changing of diapers and the negotiations over vegetables, the carpools and pajamas and bedtime stories—but also the larger work of shaping little human beings, making sure they value the things you do, like empathy and kindness and equality, while still having minds of their own; basically doing everything you can to keep them from turning into assholes one day.

It seems like an impossible job, being a parent, and a sad one too, watching them pinwheel further and further away and out into the world, so much more interesting and complicated than you imagined they might be, like a song that starts out as one thing and ends up something else—not necessarily better or worse, but different. And entirely out of your control.

"They're okay," she says to Ben.

"I know everyone says this, but it's different when you have your own."

Greta nods, noncommittal. "Yup. Everyone says that."

"That's because it's true. Honestly. Other people's kids are total monsters. They have sticky hands and snotty noses and they're really, really loud."

"And yours aren't?"

He shrugs. "They are. But somehow it's cuter when they're *your* sticky, snot-nosed, noisy little monsters."

"I get it," Greta says. "I have three nieces, so it's not like I've never spent any time with kids."

"How old are they?"

"The twins are five and the little one is three."

"Wow."

"I know. My brother and sister-in-law have their hands full."

"What are their names?"

"Asher and Zoe."

"No, the kids."

Greta hesitates. "Don't laugh."

"Why would I laugh?"

"Violet, Posey, and Marigold."

Ben raises his eyebrows. "Oh. Wow."

"Zoe owns a flower shop," she says by way of explanation.

"But the girls are honestly great. They're so silly and unself-conscious, and they give the best hugs. And they're always asking if they can be in my band."

"What do they play?"

"Right now? They mostly just bang on whatever's around."

"Sounds promising."

"It is," she says, absently rolling up the edge of the sheet, then letting it unfurl again. "The thing is, I love them. I really do. But even when I'm with them, I don't feel like I'm missing out on that. At least not right now." She shrugs. "I like my life too much."

"What about marriage?" Ben asks. "Can you ever see that for yourself?"

He's doing what they all do: pacing the perimeter, trying to locate the outer edges of her feelings on the subject. Greta doesn't mind; she's never tried to hide who she is. Once, she met up for drinks with a guy she'd broken up with the year before, and while they sat at the bar, he kept trying to look at her left hand.

"What?" she finally asked, annoyed, and he gave a sheepish shrug.

"Just trying to see if you're wearing an engagement ring," he admitted.

Greta was twenty-eight at the time, and though her friends had started to get engaged—through a series of increasingly over-the-top proposals that would've mortified her—nothing could've been further from her mind. When she laughed at the idea of it, the guy looked first confused, then maybe a little relieved, like he'd dodged a bullet of some sort.

It's not that Greta doesn't want any of that—marriage, children, the whole complicated circus—it's that she doesn't *need* it. Not the way so many other people seem to. If she were to stumble across someone perfect for her, if she found herself wanting to be with him more than she wants to be flexible, more than she wants to be on the road—then that would be great. Of course it would.

But if it never happens? She'd be okay with that version of her life too. And that's what makes people so uneasy.

"Maybe," she tells Ben. "If the conditions were right."

He looks amused. "Isn't that the case with anyone getting married?"

"I have a lot of conditions," she says with a grin. She expects him to laugh, but he looks troubled. Underneath the covers, he untangles his hand from hers, sitting up.

"Listen, I'm really sorry about yesterday," he says. "When my daughter called . . . I didn't mean to be so weird."

Greta sits up too. "It's not like I don't know you have a family."

"I know. I think I just— It's like I forgot about my real life for a second. And then Avery called, and everything came crashing back, and I felt so guilty."

"For being away?"

"For being with you," he says, rubbing his bleary eyes beneath his glasses. "This is all such new territory for me, and I feel like I'm having some sort of identity crisis. I know I'm always going to be this responsible suburban dad, and I love being that. I do. But I'm also supposed to be using this time to see if there are other ways to be happy, other ways to live, and then the minute I let myself off the hook long enough to actually flirt with someone, it felt like the universe was saying, *Not so fast, Ben.*"

Greta raises her eyebrows. "That was flirting?"

"I didn't say I was good at it," he says with a rueful smile.

"You seem way too practical to believe in karma."

"Maybe it's just the guilt then. But it's frustrating, because there's no reason I should feel guilty about this. We're allowed to see other people. It was part of the deal. And meeting you . . ." He looks suddenly nervous. "Don't read too much into this, because it'll sound way more intense than it actually is . . ."

She rests her chin on her knees. "Okay."

"It's the best thing that's happened to me in a while," he says, looking at her in a way that makes her face feel warm.

She waits a second for the alarm to set in, dependable and familiar.

But to her surprise, it doesn't.

"And not just because you're so much cooler than me," he continues, still serious. "Or because my seventeen-year-old self would be freaking out that I'm in bed with a rock star right now. Though he definitely would. It's because you know exactly who you are. And you have no idea how refreshing that is."

"It's possible," Greta says, "that you might be giving me a bit more credit than I deserve. I have no idea who I am. Especially right now. I'm a complete mess."

"Everyone's a mess," Ben says with a shrug. "But you do it with style."

She laughs. "Thanks. I think."

"Listen, I'm very aware of how all this sounds," he says, sitting forward. "So please don't panic or anything. It's not like I don't know what this is."

"I'm not panicking," Greta says. "Do I look like I'm panicking?"

"No," he says. "You look beautiful."

She shakes her head, smiling in spite of herself. "Okay, that's too much now. Take it down a notch, Wilder."

He laughs and holds up both hands. "Sorry. My point is that I know this isn't real life. So I don't want you to think I'm getting carried away or anything."

Greta glances out the window. At the foot of one of the mountains, there's a small cabin, the first they've seen in miles, and it looks so lonely there—so stark and windswept and forlorn—that it gives her a chill. She slides out of bed, picking her way past the piles of their clothes—thrown off so hastily only a few hours before—and pulls the curtains shut again, erasing the stamp of light on the bed, returning the room to a dusky gray.

When she turns around, Ben is watching her with an unreadable expression. They gaze at each other across the small space for a moment, and then he lifts the corner of the blanket.

*Real life,* she thinks, the words pounding through her head as she burrows back under the covers. Her father believes her whole adulthood has been an exercise in avoiding it: dodging anything too permanent, running from whatever might ground her. But what she's tried to do is the exact opposite: she's tried to live a dream. And maybe it's possible for those things to coexist; maybe you can bend your life into some combination of the two. Or maybe you can't. Maybe you have to trade one for the other at some point along the way. Maybe it's not that different from growing up.

"There's this quote from Jack London," Ben says, then pauses. "Well, some academics question whether the words can truly be sourced to him, because it actually came from—"

"Ben?"

"Yeah?"

"Just give me the quote."

"Right," he says. "It goes, 'The proper function of a man is to live, not to exist.'"

They're both quiet, letting the words rattle around inside them for a minute.

"For a long time, it's felt like I've just been existing," Ben says eventually. "And now—I don't know. Maybe it's Alaska. Or the fact that I've stepped away from my life for a bit. But something feels different." Behind him, the edges of the curtains are golden now as the sun continues its invisible rise. He presses his palm against his chest, looking at her solemnly. "I can feel my heart beating, you know?"

Before she can think better of it, Greta reaches out and puts a hand on top of his, imagining for a second that she can feel it too, the steady thumping of his heart. But really, what she's feeling is her own.

"I know," she says.

## Chapter Eighteen

Greta doesn't remember falling asleep, but when she wakes, it's to the mad buzzing of her phone on the bedside table. Beside her, Ben is snoring so loudly it almost seems like an act, like an impression of someone pretending to snore. But it continues uninterrupted even as she wriggles out from under his arm to grab the phone.

There are several texts from her dad, each one more impatient than the last:

Ready to go?
Where are you?
You're not answering your door.
You better not still be sleeping.
I guess I'll meet you down there.
Disembarkation point at 10.
Wear something warm.
And waterproof.
I hope you didn't forget.
Where the hell are you?
Hello?

She looks at the time and sees that it's 10:07 and knows he must be furious by now, though she can't for the life of her remember what they were supposed to be doing today. She types out a quick text: On my way! Am I too late?

The response comes right away: I lied. It leaves at 10:30. Hurry up.

Greta slips out of bed and grabs her jeans off the floor, looking around for a pen and paper as she pulls them on. She writes a quick note to Ben: *Not panicking, just going to meet my dad—see you later.* Then she gathers the rest of her clothes and heads out the door, still barefoot and wearing his oversized Columbia sweatshirt.

The first person she sees, of course, is the old lady. This time, though, she doesn't say anything about sunscreen. She just raises her eyebrows and gives Greta an appraising look.

"Hope he was cute," she says as they pass in the narrow hallway, and then, a second later, she turns around and adds, "Or she!"

Greta laughs and hurries down to the staircase, hoping she won't run into anyone she actually knows. In her room, she throws on the pair of waterproof hiking pants her dad made her buy—for what, she wishes she could remember—and grabs a Dodgers cap that once belonged to another, more distant ex-boyfriend. She's tempted to leave Ben's sweatshirt on but switches it out for one of her own. Then she grabs her mom's rain jacket and heads out.

"Where's the disembarkation point?" she asks the first staff member she sees, a red-haired kid who can't be more than eighteen and fixes her with such a long look that she suspects he knows who she is. She tugs the baseball cap lower as he gives her directions.

By the time she finds her way there, it's 10:32, and Conrad looks deeply annoyed. There's a group of about twenty people waiting in the same area, their outfits—which range from winter coats to puffy vests to fleeces—not doing much to give away the day's plan.

"You're late," Conrad says as she walks up, his face stern beneath his hat, which has the logo of a random golf course on it.

"Only by two minutes."

"Thirty-two," he says. "If we're being technical."

"Well, we're on vacation," she says. "So we're not."

"You weren't in your room."

"Yeah, I was up early," she says quickly, hoping there are no pillow lines on her face. "So I thought I'd grab some breakfast."

Her stomach growls, and they stare at each other for a second.

"Anyway," Greta says, anxious to change the subject, "how are you feeling?"

"Fine," he says brusquely, like it's a ridiculous question to be asking. He still looks a little pale, but nothing like the last time she saw him. In spite of his grouchiness, she can tell he's happy to be getting off the ship. "I guess it was just a twenty-four-hour bug."

"Where's everyone else?"

"Gone fishing."

Greta scans the waiting area, looking pointedly at the many people in outdoor gear. "And we're not?"

"No, we're—" He stops, exasperated. "You didn't read the itinerary I sent you?"

"I'm a little behind on my correspondence."

"This is the day we're supposed to—" He stops abruptly, a hand on his coat pocket, looking unsure how to proceed. Finally, he says, "We're going on a wilderness safari."

"What's a wilderness safari?"

He sweeps an arm around as if this should be obvious. "It's— a whole thing. We go out on a boat to this island and look at the wildlife, then canoe down a river and hike to a glacier."

"So why aren't the rest of them coming?"

"I told you," he says. "They went fishing."

"Right, but—"

"Because," he says so loudly that a couple in matching red jackets look over. Conrad lowers his voice a bit. "Because your mom picked this one out. Just for the two of us."

The memory has a force to it: Helen at the kitchen table back in Ohio, humming Christmas carols under her breath as she flipped through the pages of a brochure. "Do you think your dad would like to do a scenic railroad tour?" she'd asked Greta, who was sitting across from her, trying to catch up on the emails that had piled up while she was on the road. Outside, small flakes of snow were pinging against the windows, and the smell of sugar cookies—which Helen had spent the afternoon baking with the twins—made the room feel cozy and warm.

Greta looked up from her computer. "Is it a tour *of* a train or *by* a train?" she said. "Because . . . neither."

"How about a zip line?"

"Seriously? Dad?"

Helen sighed. "I want to plan something for the two of us. I'm so glad the Fosters are coming, and I'm still working on the Blooms too, but it's not very romantic if we're with the group the whole time. How about a wilderness safari?"

She held up another brochure, this one with a picture of an orange canoe and a handsome young guide holding a paddle, and she looked so hopeful right then that Greta wanted to say, *You know you'll be on it with* Dad, *right? Not that guy?* But in an impressive display of restraint, she simply said, "I think that's the one."

"I think so too," Helen said, looking pleased. "There's a hike and a glacier and a canoe trip. Also a picnic lunch in a field of wild strawberries. You know how much your dad loves strawberries."

"I know," Greta said. "It all sounds very romantic."

Helen laughed. "You'd be surprised how romantic he can be."

"The guy who gives you a new pair of mittens every Christmas?"

"Lucky for him," she said with a grin, "I happen to find mittens extremely romantic."

Now Greta stares at Conrad, her heart sinking. Because this was supposed to be their day. Instead she's here, and Helen isn't, and somehow—somehow—they have to find a way to get through this without her.

"Dad," she begins, but before she can say anything more, a ruddy-cheeked man in knee-high fishing boots and a knit cap appears in the doorway, his arms spread wide.

"Hey there, I'm Captain Martinez," he bellows, "and if you're here for the wilderness safari, you're in the right place. We're gonna start by loading you guys onto the boat out there, but let me make sure we have everyone first."

As he begins the roll call, Greta can feel Conrad tensing up. It's rare to be feeling the same thing at the same time as him, but she knows they're both silently pleading for the captain not to call out her mother's name.

When he says, "James, party of two," she relaxes a little. But beside her, Conrad's face is still stony. Greta would like to think it's because he's wrestling with his own private grief over what the day could've been. What it should've been. But mostly, she suspects, it's the same sinking realization she's having right now: that they're about to spend an entire day together. Just the two of them.

"Okay, team," says Captain Martinez when he's done checking off names. He surveys the ragtag crew and nods. "Let's do this."

Without looking at her, Conrad starts to follow the group toward the exit, a door at the side of the ship that opens to a metal ramp. Greta trails after him, already exhausted by the day, which has barely begun. But she feels better the moment she steps outside. The town of Haines is spread before them like a postcard, a scattered collection of boxy buildings, bright red and white beneath a dazzling blue sky, all of it tucked beneath a line of jagged mountains. It feels like walking off a ship in the 1800s, arriving in this hardscrabble, windswept town, half sleepy and half wild. Like something out of a story about the gold rush, she thinks. And then she realizes that the story is probably *The Call of the Wild,* and that Ben will love this place with such exuberant, openhearted enthusiasm that she almost wishes she could be there when he wakes up to see it.

There are no tenders today; the ship has docked right up against a floating wooden pier, and the metal ramp clanks as they make their way down to it. Beneath the shadow of their towering ship—which must hold at least as many people as this town— a few smaller tour boats are lined up. Greta and Conrad follow the captain over to theirs, filing on behind the rest of the group and taking their seats along the benches inside. Beneath them, the boat creaks and sways.

Everyone seems way more prepared than Greta; there's the gray-haired couple with their floppy-brimmed hats and water bottles, the woman with a fancy camera around her neck and a waterproof case for her phone, the couple around her own age wearing so much khaki it looks like they thought they were going on an African safari instead.

Once everyone is on board, the captain gives a safety talk, pointing out life preservers and first aid kits, and then he rattles off a list of activities for the day. Greta is only half-listening, hypnotized by the rhythm of the water as it laps up against the wooden pilings of the dock. But then the word *picnic* breaks through the hum, and she looks up again.

"Strawberries," she says softly, just as the captain says, "There's a strawberry field at the edge of the island, and you're welcome to pick as many as you'd like. But watch out for the foxes, since they like them too."

Conrad glances at her. "I thought you didn't read the itinerary."

"I didn't."

"Then how'd you know that?"

She wants to say it. She almost does.

But the word *Mom* gets lodged in her throat.

Instead she says, "I must've heard about it somewhere."

The boat peels off from the dock, kicking up a wake as they steer away from the shore. Around them, everything feels saturated with color—the unnatural blue of the sky, the brilliant green of the water, the shocking white of the snow—like a knob has been turned up on the world. Greta closes her eyes, feeling the flecks of water on her face as they pick up speed. Beside her, Conrad sighs and then, in a voice so quiet she almost misses it, he says, "I love strawberries."

## Chapter Nineteen

They don't dock so much as run aground, the boat grinding up against a gravel beach on a remote spit of land. One by one, the captain helps them down, and Greta spins in a circle, her sneakers crunching on the rocks as she takes it all in: the rows of mountains with their sugary peaks and the bristle of spruce trees ahead. Woven between them, the glacier is a shock of white. From a distance, it almost looks like it's in motion, the way it curves and flows like water, as if at any moment it might come bearing down on them. But, of course, the opposite is true. Inch by inch, it's retreating. Eventually, all this will disappear.

A rusty school bus is parked across a field, painted green and beige like it's trying to blend in. Three rugged young white guys in wellies and baseball caps—two of them sporting thick beards—wait for them near the door.

"I haven't been on a school bus in fifty years," Conrad says, squinting at it. "My back hurts already."

"Come on, old man," Greta says cheerfully, and they make their way up toward the bus, their shoes squelching in the mud.

The ride is as bumpy as feared, and everyone flashes nervous smiles as they slide around in the seats. At the front, one of the bearded guides—who introduces himself as Tank—explains what they'll be doing up top: a hike to a river, then a canoe ride down an inlet, then a walk up to the base of the glacier.

The wheels spin and the bus lurches as the driver shifts gears, urging the bulky vehicle up the muddy road. Pine trees scrape at the windows, and Conrad winces every time they're jolted forward.

Greta rests her head against the back of the seat. "This reminds me of the summer you made me go to camp."

"Which you hated."

"I didn't *hate* it," she says. "I was just having an existential crisis."

"At ten?" He shakes his head. "Asher loved that place."

"Yeah, well, I'm not Asher."

"No, that's true." He says it thoughtfully, as if it's only now occurring to him. "You were always better with a guitar than a fishing rod."

"Hey, I caught a few that summer," she says, and Conrad gives her a skeptical look. "Okay, I caught Timmy Milikin." She grins at the memory. "Seriously. I snagged the back of his shirt."

"On purpose?"

Greta laughs. "What must you think of me?"

"I don't know sometimes," he says, but he says it almost fondly. "I really don't know."

They're dropped off at a wooden pavilion in the middle of the forest. Inside, there are rows of life jackets, wellies, and paddles, which the guides begin to pass out.

"Here," Conrad says, lifting his phone as soon as Greta manages to get everything on. The life jacket is too snug and the boots are too big and—automatically, instinctively—she holds the paddle like a guitar. He snaps a picture. "What do you think they'd pay me for this at *Rolling Stone*?"

She makes a face at him.

When everyone is fully kitted out, they fall in line behind Tank, who leads them down a wooded path strewn with pine needles. Greta follows Conrad, thinking again about that summer at camp, how all the other kids had seemed like caricatures of hearty midwesterners, aggressively enthusiastic about kayaking and woodworking. They traded friendship bracelets and sang songs and played Red Rover with cheerful abandon while Greta— scrawny and pale and preternaturally self-assured—faked illness after illness so she could lie in the cool of the nurse's office with her headphones on, listening to "Wonderwall" on repeat. She was ten and miserable and though she still didn't fully understand why yet, still didn't totally grasp who she might turn out to be, she knew for sure it wasn't someone who enjoyed shooting arrows at targets.

Ahead of her, Conrad trips over an exposed root, just managing to catch himself.

"You okay?" Greta asks, and he nods without looking back at her. But she can see that he's already puffing, one hand clutching his paddle, the other his coat pocket.

She knows he's always loved this stuff. He grew up on the outskirts of Columbus, in a house much too small for eight of them. There was barely enough money for food, never mind camping. But one summer, his best friend invited him up to Mohican State Park with his family, and for one glorious week, Conrad learned how to pitch a tent and tie knots and rub two sticks together to start a fire. It made him feel a million miles away from his own life, which was exactly what he was looking for, and they invited him back the next summer, and the one after that, until it became a tradition, the brightest spot in every year.

As soon as Asher and Greta were old enough to walk, he had them marching through the swampy ravines near their house on Sunday mornings. For years, he led Asher's Boy Scout troop, and he gave each of his kids a Swiss Army knife when they turned ten. It always baffled him that Greta could spend a beautiful day in the dusty garage, messing around with amps and pedals, when there were trails to explore and ponds to fish.

"You're an indoor cat," Asher once said, as if that explained everything. "And I'm a golden retriever."

"What does that make Dad?"

He laughed. "A mountain lion?"

A hawk flies overhead, letting out a sharp cry, and Greta watches her dad stumble again. It's unfamiliar territory, to feel this flicker of worry for him. Physically, he looks the same: the broad shoulders and lined face, the neat haircut and flinty eyes. But ever since her mom died, there's been something diminished about him. She supposes even mountain lions get old.

One of the other guides—this one clean-shaven and impossibly young—falls into step beside her. "You've gotta watch out for that stuff," he says, pointing out a tall green plant covered in spikes. "It's called devil's club."

"What does it do?" Greta asks, intrigued.

"If you brush up against one and those spiny suckers get stuck in your leg?" He shakes his head and whistles. "Not even tweezers'll do the trick."

"So what," she asks, "you're just half-hedgehog from then on?"

"You have to wait a few days till they fester, and then you can kind of start working them out." He grins. "If it sounds gross, that's because it is. Trust me, I know."

"I'm guessing that's a mistake you only make once," she says, but he doesn't answer; he's squinting at her, his head cocked to one side.

"Have you been here before?"

"To these woods in the middle of Alaska?" she says. "No."

"I meant on this tour—maybe last summer?"

She shakes her head, but she already knows where this is going. And she can see by the way Conrad half-turns to glance at her that he does too.

"Huh," says the guide. "Well, I'm Bear. It's just a nickname.

I'm really Preston, but that doesn't sound as impressive when you're living out in the bush all summer."

Greta nods as they start moving down a steep slope. "Nice to meet you, Bear."

For a second, he lingers, still eyeing her with a curious intensity, clearly hoping she'll introduce herself too, and that it might be enough to jog his memory. But she doesn't give him the satisfaction. Her father probably thinks she's reluctant because of the dull orange life jacket and the rubber boots and the paddle she's using like a walking stick as she half-slides down the hill. But it's not so much that she doesn't look like Greta James at the moment; it's more that she doesn't feel like her. Not right now. Not for a while.

At last they catch a glimpse of a brownish-green river at the bottom of the trail and crunch their way down to it over the pebbly beach. When they're clear of the trees, the glacier comes into view on the other side of the water, flat and white between gray mountains. In the stillness of the river, three orange canoes sit waiting for them.

As Tank explains this next part of the journey, Bear sidles up to her again.

"You're not from Texas, are you?" he asks.

"No," Greta says as, beside her, Conrad folds his arms over his chest, staring straight ahead. She can almost feel the irritation radiating off him.

Once, when her parents were visiting New York, they went out for dinner at an old-fashioned steak house in Brooklyn and the waitress went wide-eyed when she spotted Greta. It was still early days for that sort of thing; her first album hadn't even come out yet, so the only people who recognized her were hard-core fans who'd listened to her EP or seen her play with other bands over the years.

"Holy shit," the girl said, nearly dropping a water glass. She was in her early twenties, with a nose ring and at least a dozen tattoos. Not someone who seemed like she'd be easily flustered. "You're Greta James."

Helen let out a surprised laugh as she looked over at Greta, but Conrad—who had been eyeing the rib eye at the next table—began to examine his menu.

"I saw you play that indie showcase at the Knitting Factory last summer," the girl said. "You're a total badass on the guitar."

Greta smiled. "Thanks. You play?"

"A little," she said. "Mostly I sing."

"That's awesome."

It being New York—where people are either far too cool to fawn or else want to seem like they are—that was the extent of it. But Greta had glowed through the rest of dinner, privately elated by the interaction.

As they left the restaurant, her mother had hooked an arm through hers. "My star," she said, beaming.

"Mom," Greta groaned. But they were both grinning like crazy.

"Wasn't that something, Con?" Helen asked, and for a second, Conrad's face went soft. That was the thing about him: every so often, the pride would shine through.

"It's always nice to be recognized for your work," he admitted stiffly. But he couldn't help adding, with a note of disapproval, "Though applause shouldn't be the point."

"Well, in my line of work," Greta said, "it quite literally is."

This made Helen laugh that unexpectedly big laugh of hers. "She's got you there," she said to Conrad, untangling her arm from Greta's to walk over to him. "If you ever need a standing ovation, honey," she said, giving him a kiss, "you let us know."

Now, as Tank finishes up his demonstration on how to get into the canoe, Bear is still frowning at her from beneath the brim of his hat. "Are you an actress?"

"No."

He looks disappointed. "A model?"

Greta laughs. "Definitely not."

"Come on. I *know* I know you from somewhere."

She gives a noncommittal shake of her head as Tank claps his enormous hands. "Okay, you six come with me," he says, pointing to a family standing off to the side, "you six with McKee, and you six with Bear."

Bear grins at Greta, now part of his designated group. Conrad grunts as he moves toward the first of the large canoes. When they've all clambered in—the narrow vessel tipping from side to side—Bear shows them how to hold their paddles, and then Tank shoves them off, the bottom scraping over the rocks. They're the first to float out into the calm waters, spinning in a leisurely circle before Bear gives the command and they all start to row.

Greta is the smallest, so Bear placed her up at the bow. Behind her, Conrad sits on the next bench, followed by two couples: a pair of athletic gay men in their fifties and an older-looking husband and wife with a ridiculous amount of fancy outdoor gear, including a compass the size of a golf ball that the woman is wearing like a necklace.

The day is perfect, all blue sky and crisp air, and as they get farther from shore, the other voices fade; there's only the slap and dip of the paddles and the ripple of the water as they push through it, moving toward the giant glacier a few yards at a time. Above, a bird makes a slow loop, and Greta tips her head back, letting the calm wash over her, allowing the peace to—

"I've got it," Bear cries from the other end of the canoe, and she snaps back again. "I *knew* it. I knew you were someone."

Behind her, she can hear Conrad let out a sigh, and there's a rustling of coats as the others turn to look at each other, confused.

"You," Bear says, his voice ringing triumphantly across the quiet water, "are Greta James."

There's a beat of silence.

And then another.

And then the woman with the compass says, "Who?"

# Chapter Twenty

Theirs is the first canoe to reach the opposite shore, a barren stretch of windswept silt that leads right up to the base of the glacier. The minute they bump up against the sand, Conrad jumps out.

"Wait up," Greta says, but he's already charging across the beach, clumsy in the awkward life jacket and the stiff rain boots, his head down against the racing wind.

"It's okay," Bear says, hopping out to hold the canoe steady as the others step carefully over the side. "He probably wants to be first. It's a thing. Being alone with the glacier."

Greta suspects it has less to do with getting to the glacier than with getting away from her, but she doesn't say so. Bear is still looking at her with slightly starry eyes.

"So are you playing one of the ships?" he asks as he drags the canoe up onto the firm ground. "I wouldn't have thought—"

"No, I'm just . . . on a cruise." She points. "With my dad."

He straightens again, wiping his hands on his waterproof pants. "Huh."

"Yeah."

"You know, one of my roommates is obsessed with you." He takes out his phone and grins at her. "Would you mind if we . . . ?"

With a sigh, she glances over at the receding figure of her father, then nods and brings her face close to Bear's, flashing a quick, perfunctory smile. In her baseball cap, she looks less like someone famous than someone's kid sister, but he doesn't seem to mind.

"So," he says, slipping the phone back into one of his many pockets. "Are you, like, seeing anyone?"

"Yes," she says flatly, her eyes once again on her dad, who is getting smaller in the distance, dwarfed by the huge wall of bluish ice.

Bear looks disappointed. "That producer guy?"

Greta's surprised he even knows that, though just before they got together, Luke had dated a high-profile reality-TV star—famous more for her Instagram account than anything else—and between that and Greta's own dramatic ascent while they were dating, they'd become frequent targets of party photographers and the occasional paparazzo.

She's about to tell Bear that it's really none of his business, but she can feel the woman with the compass hovering nearby, phone in hand.

"Sorry, but do you think I could get one too? To be honest, I don't know who you are, but I figure my daughter might. She's into . . ." She waves a hand around vaguely. "Pop culture."

In spite of herself, Greta smiles. "I'm a musician."

"She's a rock star," says Bear.

The woman snaps a photo, then studies it for a moment with benign interest. "Cool," she says with a shrug, then walks off to join her husband, who is gazing out at the glacier through a pair of enormous binoculars.

The other two canoes are still faraway specks of orange on the water, so their group begins the hike in a small cluster, moving slowly across the hard-packed sand and scattered stones. The glacier is starting to feel like a mirage, like no matter how far they sail or row or walk, they'll never actually reach it. But after a few minutes, it looks less blocky and more intricate, like some sort of confection, delicate as a meringue.

Conrad is nearly there, his shadow tiny against the sheer bulk of it. Everyone else peels off, following Bear over to the opposite end of the glacier's broad face, where a small cave has formed in the ice. But Greta keeps walking straight ahead, her eyes on Conrad, who has stopped to take it in. His life jacket is still buckled tight, like he might have to hurry back to the canoe at any moment, and his hands are on his hips, and he looks somehow both irretrievably lost and entirely at home.

When she's close enough, she clears her throat. "Dad," she says, but the word is returned to her by the wind. She steps up beside him and tries again: "Hey."

This time he turns to look at her, his expression inscrutable.

"It's beautiful, huh?" she says, her eyes roving over the ice. From afar, it had looked clean and white, but now she can see that it's streaked with dirt and sand. Underneath that, though, the bluish tint is even more brilliant up close, like the whole thing is glowing from the inside out. And the size of it is staggering; the column in front of them—so unremarkable from a distance—is as tall as a two-story house, glinting in the abundant sunshine.

It takes Conrad a second to answer. "I can't decide," he says, his head tipped back to take it all in, "whether it's the most extraordinary thing I've ever seen, or the least." He turns to her. "It's obviously a natural wonder. But it's also just a bunch of ice, you know?"

Greta smiles at this. Down by the water, the second canoe is coming ashore. Excited voices tumble across the barren stretch of beach, carried by a gust of wind. Farther along the glacier, the rest of their group is posing for pictures, which Bear dutifully takes for them, squatting to get the best angles.

She nods in their direction. "Should we . . ."

But Conrad doesn't answer. Instead, he walks up and lays his bare hand flat against the ice. It looks like a piece of abstract art, its curves not governed by any sort of logic except for the water streaming down in rivulets, forming muddy pools along the base of it.

"Listen," she says, "I'm sorry about . . ."

"What?" he asks, turning to her, his eyes shadowy beneath the brim of his cap.

"I know it bothers you when people recognize me," she says with a shrug.

He squints back up at the ice. "Not everything is about you, you know."

"I know," she says. But then, after a pause, she can't help adding: "Though, in fairness, it feels like most things are. When it comes to you, anyway."

He turns to her again. "What's that supposed to mean?"

"Just that we obviously have our differences."

"And?"

"And you like to point them out."

There's a pause, and then a funny smile appears across his face. "I think I preferred your sullen teenage years."

Greta can't help laughing at this. "That's because I hadn't discovered therapy yet," she says. "I just put all my feelings into terrible, overwrought songs."

"Which you played incredibly loudly at all hours."

"Come on," she says with a grin. "You have to admit that 'Life Sucks Hard' was kind of a classic."

Conrad shakes his head. "For a comfortable suburban kid, you sure had a lot of angst."

"Well, the good news," she says, "is that I figured out how to make a living off it."

Right away, his face shifts. And right away, Greta feels herself bristling in response.

"Just because I don't sit behind a desk all day," she says in a hurry, forever on defense, "doesn't mean it's not hard work."

"Hard work?" he repeats in a voice heavy with scorn.

"Yes."

"You play the guitar."

Greta balls her hands into fists at her sides. "Yeah, Dad, I play the guitar. Every single day. For hours and hours. I also write my own songs. And produce them too. I'm in the recording studio, and I deal with the business end of things, the branding and the publicity, not to mention that I'm on the road two hundred days a year and—"

"Not anymore."

She narrows her eyes at him. Her nose is running from the cold, and she swipes at it with the back of her hand. "What do you mean?"

He shrugs. "You're not on the road anymore."

There's a knot in her stomach, and it winds itself tighter now. She didn't think he'd noticed. She didn't think he'd been paying attention.

"I know you canceled your shows for the past few months," he continues, raising his voice over the wind. "And that you postponed your tour."

Greta swallows hard. "So?"

"So," he says with infuriating patience, "if this dream job of yours is to play music, and you're not even doing that, then what *are* you doing?"

"That's not . . ." she begins, then realizes she isn't sure how to finish the sentence. "That was . . . temporary. I'm playing Governors Ball on Sunday." Before he can ask what that is, she adds, "It's a festival. In New York. A big one."

He studies her for a moment. "And what happens," he says eventually, "if this doesn't go well either?"

It's bad enough, thinking about that last show she played.

It's a million times worse hearing about it from her dad.

She assumed he was at least generally aware of what happened. It was hard not to be. But up until now, she had no idea if he'd actually seen the video.

Now she knows.

"The last one didn't *go well*," she says, choosing her words carefully, "because it was a week after Mom died. And because she wasn't there that night, which just about killed me. And because I wrote that song for her, and that was the moment I realized she would never hear it." Greta shakes her head, trying to tamp down her frustration. "I know you don't get it. How could you when you've never even been to one of my shows?"

He looks offended by this. "That's not true. I came out for the—"

"The album release? Yeah. But only because Mom insisted."

"We both know that's not exactly my scene," he says with a shrug.

"You think it was Mom's scene? She came to all those shows because she wanted to support me. Not because she was some huge closet indie music fan."

His face softens a little. "Yeah, but she loved it."

"That's because she loved *me*," Greta says, half-shouting at him over the wind. "How do you not get that?"

"I do," he says, surprisingly contrite. "That's why I went."

"Well, it was hard to tell. You spent the entire night in the corner of the bar, looking like you'd rather be anywhere else."

He gives her a level look. "Can you blame me?"

Greta opens her mouth, then closes it again. The wind is like static all around her. She's tempted to pretend not to understand what he means, but she knows that's not fair. That this conversation was inevitable. Even so, she doesn't feel ready for it.

She remembers the first time she played "Told You So" for her mom, the way her mouth had tightened as she listened to the music come thumping out of Greta's phone. The opening notes were harsh and propulsive; the opening lines too: *Here's to all the haters / the ones who didn't think I'd get here.* By the time they reached the chorus, Greta's hands were damp, and she couldn't bring herself to look up. It didn't matter, anyway. Helen, her gaze fixed on the phone, was frowning as she listened to the song, which was tinny and vibrating and full of anger, a middle finger in musical form.

When it was over, the silence felt loud. Greta was already brimming with arguments in her own favor; she'd been preparing her case ever since those first few lines came to her on a trip to London, when she sat in a café and watched a father patiently teaching his daughter how to draw a caterpillar on the back of a children's menu and thought: *That's the way it should be.*

It spun through her head, that thought, until it eventually became a song. One she had every right to play. One she'd earned many times over.

But when Helen finally looked at her with a face full of disappointment, all of Greta's defiance melted away, and her face went hot and prickly.

"I would never tell you what to feel," her mom said slowly, each word precise, "and I would certainly never tell you what to do when it comes to your music."

Greta dug her nails into the palm of her hand as she waited for the next part, the part she'd known would be coming ever since she'd jotted down those first few words.

"But what I will tell you," Helen said, "is that this will hurt him. And before you continue down this road, I just want to make sure you know that."

Greta nodded once without meeting her mom's eyes. "I know" was all she said, and they never talked about it again. Not when it was released as the first single off her debut album and squeaked onto the very bottom of the indie charts. Not when the video dropped and the song continued to gain momentum. Not when the album came out and her parents flew to New York for the launch party, and she saw the way her dad looked so out of place in that bar, with his jeans and plaid button-down, scanning the room like he already knew what everyone was thinking: that the song they were all there to hear was about him.

And he was right.

She'd expected to feel triumphant. *See?* she imagined herself saying to him that night. *I did it. You didn't think I could, but I did.*

*I told you so.*

But instead, she was surprised to feel sad.

Everyone there knew Helen as the mom with the sign.

They knew Conrad as the dad in the song.

The "Told You So" guy.

Standing there on her big night, she tried to summon all the feelings that had gone into the song, the memories she'd thrown into it like kindling. There was the time he marched her guitar out to the garbage can after a fight. The time he told her he wouldn't help with college if she planned to study music. The time he didn't show up to the sixth-grade talent show. The application for a business program he left on her pillow in high school. The pride he took in Asher becoming manager at the bank. The indifference when Greta told him about her own achievements.

He wasn't on board with any of this. She knew that. In a way, she even took a sort of pride in it, wearing his disapproval like a coat of armor. It was meant to steer her off course, but instead it only made her work harder all those years. It made her try more, care more, play more. It gave her something to push against. It just hadn't occurred to her until that night that without all that friction, she might not be where she was. She might not be *who* she was.

But it was already too late for them.

Her mom had insisted on a toast. "To dreams coming true," she said, beaming at Greta as she lifted her glass. "I always knew you could do it."

They both turned to Conrad, who held up his beer a little awkwardly. "Congrats," he managed, and for once, he sounded sincere. But later, when it was time for her to play, she noticed him standing stiffly in the back, and when she segued into the first notes of "Told You So" and a huge cheer went up in the room, he bent his head to Helen, then slipped out the door.

Now the sun moves behind the clouds, and her dad's face darkens along with the sky. Behind him, she can see the crags in the glacier, ragged and hollow. Farther down the beach, the rest of the group is still busy exploring the ice cave, their voices thin in the distance.

"You wrote that song about me," Conrad says, his eyes flinty, "and then expected me to come to the party and smile about it? How was I supposed to feel?"

"*Proud,*" she says. "You were supposed to feel proud. That was a huge night for me. It wasn't about you."

He laughs, a humorless laugh. "You made it about me when you decided to release that song."

Greta stiffens. "Art is about telling the truth. And expressing how you feel. That's all I was doing. It isn't personal."

He gives her a look like *Come on,* like they both know that isn't true. "You wrote a love song for your mom," he says. "And I get that. Believe me, I do. If I had the words, I'd write one too. But what you wrote for me . . . it was more like a battle cry. And I don't know what I'm supposed to do with that."

"Dad, you act like you're blameless in all this," she snaps at him. "Like that song came to me out of thin air. Maybe if you'd been more supportive—"

"I bought your first guitar!"

"I *know*," she roars back. "That's why it hurts so much. Because I loved it, and at one point, so did you. And then somewhere along the way, you decided my dreams weren't practical enough, and you stopped cheering me on. I was twelve years old, and I was *good*, but rather than be in my corner like any sort of normal parent, you discouraged me. And when that didn't work, you just took yourself out of the equation entirely. Do you have any idea how that felt?"

"No," he says, and for a second, she thinks that's it. He scrapes at his chin, his mouth a thin line, his eyes on the sky. But then he turns back to her with such a flat, pained look that she feels her stomach go tight. "But I do know how it feels to worry about money. And I wanted you to be realistic."

"To give up on my dreams, you mean."

"To find a more sensible pursuit."

"To settle."

He sighs. "To start thinking in a more stable direction. I'm not going to apologize for that."

"You know what the worst part is?" she says coolly. "That it never occurred to you I might be successful at this."

Conrad kicks at the gray silt, his toe leaving an indent. "What do you want me to say? Other people's kids—they get real jobs. Jobs with benefits and security. Jobs that make sense to me. I know how to give Asher advice on managing a team and how much to put in his 401(k). I'm happy for you that you've made it this far in a tough business. I am. But your life doesn't look the way I thought it would when I imagined what you could be."

"Yeah," Greta says. "It's *better*. Why are you the only one who can't see that?"

"Because no matter how hard I squint at it, this whole thing seems like it's built on guesswork and fairy dust. Like it could all fall apart at any moment. Maybe it's even falling apart right now.

And I can't lie and say it doesn't scare me that my daughter has a *job*"—here, he uses air quotes—"where there's no backup plan and so much uncertainty and absolutely no guarantees."

"Dad," Greta says, and to her surprise, her throat goes tight. This conversation feels like being stuck in the mud, all spinning wheels and no forward movement. They've had it so many times it's like they're in a play, each simply repeating their lines. But somehow, they can't bring themselves to stop. "There aren't supposed to be any guarantees. It's *supposed* to be a one-in-a-million kind of thing. It's like I won the fucking lottery and you'd rather I give the ticket back and sit in some drab office crunching numbers just because the work is steady." She shakes her head. "It's impossible to talk to you about this. We're on completely different planets."

"We are," he says with a grunt. "On my planet, there was no fancy summer camp. Or guitar lessons. You know how many jobs I had by the time I was your age? I delivered newspapers and mowed lawns and stocked groceries. After the navy, I bartended and worked construction and—"

"Dad," she says. "I know all this."

"When I finally got to the Yellow Pages, I might've only been making copies and running errands, but I was the first one in my family to work in an office. The first one to wear a tie every day. Maybe it wasn't glamorous, but I always knew where my next paycheck was coming from, and that's a big deal. I fought my way to solid ground, and I thought I taught you the same."

"You did," she says, startled. "That's why I work so hard at what I do. Every day. I want for this to work out. Badly. I want to keep playing music, and keep making better and better records, and putting on better and better shows."

"Yeah, but what if it all falls apart? You have absolutely no Plan B."

"Dad," she says with some amount of amusement. "Of course I do. I grew up under your roof, didn't I? There's also a Plan C and D and E."

He allows himself a flicker of a smile—a brief moment of pride—before his mouth goes straight again.

"Do you know how often I'm asked to write for other musicians?" Greta continues. "Or how many people have wanted me to produce for them? I have a standing invitation to teach a class at NYU, for godsakes. I know this business can be fickle. And that nothing is certain. And I also realize I'm not exactly having my finest hour right now. But the odds of getting to where I am—they're astronomical. And I did it. I made it."

"For now," he says morosely.

Greta stares at him, trying not to feel so deflated. "Why is it so hard for you to believe in me?" she asks. "Didn't you ever have a dream?"

"Yes," he says simply. "Your mom was my dream."

His answer is so unexpected, and so heartbreakingly obvious, that it knocks her back a step. She inhales sharply, trying to regain herself. "Well, this is *my* dream. And at the end of the day, it doesn't matter what you think. Because I'm fine. I'm *fine*. I'm going to be fine."

She says it three times. Like a magic spell. Like she's trying to conjure something.

Like she's trying to conjure *someone*.

But all she's got is her dad, staring at her with stony eyes, the straps of his life jacket flapping madly in the wind. It's never worked before, looking to him for reassurance. She hates herself for needing it, for caring what he thinks even though she's told herself a thousand times that she doesn't. But here they are yet again.

"Haven't you ever taken a chance on anything?" she says, her voice cracking. "What ever happened to the kid who loved magic?"

"Life," he says, looking at her incredulously. "*Life* happened. I grew up. Had a family. Got a job, one where I could put food on the table." He shrugs. "I always had my priorities straight. Which is obviously something that's hard for you to understand."

Greta blinks at him. "What's that supposed to mean?"

He walks a few paces along the face of the glacier, stepping over the stream that's formed from the runoff. Then he whirls around and comes back, his jaw set and his eyes hard. "You chose your music," he says, and for a second, Greta is confused. But then he practically growls the next part, and her stomach drops. "When it really counted, you put that first."

There's nothing she can say to this. Because he's right.

She hadn't thought about it like that, of course. In the moment, she wasn't really thinking about anything. She'd just arrived in Berlin, and the festival was a few days away. She and Luke had plans to go to some museums and wander the city and drink a whole lot of beer. The call from her dad felt vague and faraway: her mom was having headaches and he was worried. It was rare for him to phone her; that alone should've been warning enough. But there was also a hitch in his voice, something subtle and hard to define.

"She hasn't mentioned anything to me," Greta had said. She was in the lobby of the Berlinische Galerie, and it was noisy with voices and footsteps. "Has she gone to the doctor?"

"Not yet, but we have an appointment on Friday," he said. "Asher is coming. Maybe you should be there too."

Luke had gotten the tickets and was standing near the entrance, waving them in her direction. When she glanced over, he mouthed, *What?* She shook her head and turned around again.

"Dad," she said, putting a finger to her other ear as a group of German schoolchildren shuffled past. "I'm in Berlin. I'm playing a festival this weekend."

"Oh," he said. "Right. I forgot."

"How worried are you? I mean, if you think I should can-cel . . ." She was regretting the words even as they came out of her mouth. On Saturday afternoon, she'd be headlining in front of forty thousand people. It wasn't that she *couldn't* cancel. It would be costly, and it would take a lot of explaining, but she could do it if she had to. If it was important.

She just didn't want to.

"I'm sure it's nothing," Conrad said briskly. "She'd probably kill me if she knew I was even calling you."

"Listen," Greta said, "I'm supposed to fly back to New York on Monday, but I can switch my ticket to come straight to Colum-bus instead."

"It's okay," he said, but his voice was tight. "We'll be okay."

"Well, if anything changes," she says, "I can be there. I *will* be there. I promise."

"I know."

Greta felt a tug of uncertainty. "You'll let me know how the appointment goes?"

"Of course," he said. "Good luck with the festival."

"Thanks," she started to say, then realized he'd already hung up.

Now he's looking at her with a slightly bewildered expression, like he's not exactly sure how they've waded into this. They haven't actually talked about it before, not outright, and suddenly here it is, dropped onto the sand between them like something heavy and lifeless.

"Dad," she begins, her mind racing, but she doesn't actually know what to say. There are no apologies big enough. She's thought about that conversation constantly over the last few months; it's a small blinking light in her chest that never seems to dim. But she's only now realizing how much her dad has been an afterthought. There's the guilt that her mom needed her and she wasn't there, the heaviest thing of all, and then just behind that, a razor-sharp grief that she didn't get a chance to say goodbye. But for the first time, Greta can see that she's been feeling sorry for her mom, and sorry for herself, and at the end of all that, there simply hasn't been anything left over for her dad.

Conrad's shoulders are hunched, and his face looks wind-burned. "It doesn't matter now," he says, though of course it does. It matters more than anything. That moment, that phone call, that missed opportunity: all of it is as elemental to their lives as this glacier is to the beach, huge and imposing and receding so slowly, so gradually, that you might be forgiven for assuming it would be here forever.

"Dad," Greta says again, and this time he looks disappointed when she can't seem to locate a follow-up sentence. But she feels entirely empty.

In the distance, Bear is walking their way. He's beaming at them, his smile so at odds with the moment it's almost humorous. Almost.

Conrad turns to follow her gaze, then lets out a heavy sigh.

"It all went so fast," he says, watching the younger man cross the beach. Greta isn't exactly sure what he's talking about, but when he turns back to her, his eyes—the same color as hers—look very tired. "I'm not going to be around forever either."

"Dad," she says for a third time, feeling hopelessly ill-equipped for whatever this conversation is. "You have to stop—"

"I told her I'd make sure you were okay. I promised."

Bear is getting closer now, and Greta can see that he's holding a small chunk of ice in one hand. She turns back to Conrad, feeling oddly panicky.

"I *am* okay," she says in a way that makes her sound precisely the opposite. "We just have different definitions of that."

His mouth tightens at the corners, but he doesn't say anything.

When Bear is close enough, he calls out to them: "Couldn't let you miss all the fun." He waves the piece of ice in the air. "You have to taste it. There's nothing like glacier ice."

Greta shakes her head, still too full of emotion to manage a smile. Conrad, too, looks at him, stone-faced. "No thanks," he says, but it's not enough to dissuade Bear, who lopes the final few yards with all the eagerness of a puppy.

"Trust me on this," he says, pushing the ice into Conrad's hands.

For a second, nobody moves. They all three stand there in the middle of all that wilderness, their cheeks pink and their boots sunk deep into the sand, staring at the piece of blue-gray ice like it's some sort of oracle.

And then, to Greta's surprise, Conrad gives it a single lick.

"See?" Bear says with a grin. "Now you'll always remember this as the day you tried glacier ice."

There's a flash of something on Conrad's face. "I doubt it."

But Bear is insistent. "Sure you will. What could possibly top that?"

"My anniversary."

For a few seconds, this doesn't quite land; it skirts the edges of Greta's crowded brain, the word moving through her head like music: *anniversary, anniversary, anniversary*.

And then, all at once, her heart falls.

It was today. Of course it was today.

This whole trip was meant to be a celebration. But today was the actual day. Forty years since they walked down the aisle in a small wooden church in Ohio; forty years since they said their vows and, laughing, smashed cake into each other's faces.

Forty years, and they were supposed to be spending this day together.

Forty years, and Greta completely forgot.

She turns to her dad, mouth open, feeling suddenly undone. But before she can say anything, Bear gives him such a hard thump on the back that Conrad pitches forward a step.

"Happy anniversary, man," Bear says. "How many years?"

Conrad's eyes meet Greta's, and then he says, in a voice like gravel, "Forty."

What he doesn't say, what she can practically feel him not saying is: *At least it would've been.*

"Wow," Bear says, shaking his head in wonder. In his hand, the piece of ice has started to melt, one slow drip at a time. "Forty years. What's your secret?"

Again, Conrad looks at Greta.

"We always kept our promises," he says.

## Chapter Twenty-One

When Bear heads over to round up the others, Greta starts to follow. But Conrad hangs back. She turns to face him, not sure what to say. All the heat between them has dissolved; what's left is something heavier, something slower to burn.

Her face is numb from the wind, her hands so cold they feel hot. An image of her uncomfortable bed in her windowless room on the ship flashes in her mind, but the thought of getting from here to there—hike to canoe to bus to boat—feels insurmountable, like she might as well be on the moon right now.

Conrad pats at his pocket again, then reaches inside and pulls out a small plastic bag, cradling it carefully in his palm. To her alarm, he looks like he might cry.

Still, it takes Greta a second to realize what he's holding.

When she does, she walks back over to him, staring down at the contents of the bag, which don't look all that different from the grayish sand they're standing on.

Her mouth falls open.

"It's not all of them," he says quietly. "The rest are still at home. But it seemed only right to bring some here."

Greta's heart is racing beneath all her layers. She glances toward the rest of the group, then at the plastic bag, at this piece of her mom that he's carried here from Ohio, that he's held in his pocket all day. It knocks the wind out of her, seeing it there like that.

"I thought you might want to help," he says, and she nods, though she's not entirely sure. Her brain is moving slowly; so are her feet, which feel unaccountably heavy as she starts to move back toward the glacier, head bent against the wind.

Conrad surveys the area. "What do you think?"

There's the ice in front of them, towering and slick, and below that a series of puddles between patches of sand. Greta is shivering now, though she can't tell if it's from the cold or something else. He's right: this is what she would've wanted. But it's still hard to imagine leaving any part of her here in this windswept place.

It's hard to imagine leaving any of her at all.

"Maybe over there," Greta says, pointing to a small shelf in the ice, just about eye level, because it looks sturdy and even and somewhat protected from the elements.

Conrad nods solemnly. "Do you want to go first?"

She accepts the bag from him, feeling the small and precise weight of it, then picks her way over to the ice, her wellies sinking into the puddles. She's not sure whether she should pour straight from the bag or put some into her hand first. In the end, she's afraid the wind will blow it away, so she reaches inside and scoops a little into her palm, then tips it gently onto the ice. Some of it drifts off anyway, scattering into the air like snow, there and then gone. But she feels surprisingly lighter as she watches it go, and when she turns to her dad, she can see that he's crying too.

When it's his turn, he stands there for a long time, his head bowed as if in prayer. Behind him, Greta quietly says a prayer of her own: "I love you, I love you, I love you."

This, too, is carried off by the wind.

Afterward, Conrad tucks the empty bag into his pocket and wipes a sleeve roughly across his face. Down by the canoes, Bear is shouting for them, his voice faint. But they take their time anyway. About halfway there, Greta is seized by a sudden impulse.

She loops an arm through her dad's, and he stiffens for a moment, then relaxes. So they walk the rest of the way like that.

They've barely left the banks of the river, the glacier already starting to recede, when Greta feels a drag on the canoe. She turns to see Bear with his oar braced in the water, his eyes on a line of spruce trees. "Shh," he says, though none of them are speaking. He half-stands, the canoe tilting beneath him, and the rest of them lift their dripping paddles, trying to follow his gaze. One of the men passes over a pair of binoculars, and Bear lets out a soft laugh as he looks through them.

"Holy shit," he says. "I heard there was a Steller's sea eagle spotted in Juneau last month. He must've made his way up here."

"A what?" says the woman with the compass.

Bear hands the binoculars to her. "A Steller's sea eagle. They're incredibly rare. Especially around here. This one is a vagrant."

"A vagrant?" the husband asks. "What does that mean?"

The binoculars reach Conrad, and Greta watches as he lifts them to his eyes, scanning the trees. She can tell when he's spotted the bird by the way his whole body goes still.

"Just that it's way off course," Bear explains. "They're usually only found in Asia."

"Wow," says one of the other men. "So what's it doing all the way over here?"

Conrad hands Greta the binoculars, which are heavier than they look. When she peers through them, the world skids madly before righting itself. She searches the feathery tops of the trees until she sees a pop of orange: the great curved beak of the bird, which looks enormous in a way that has nothing to do with magnification. It's huge and black with white-tipped wings, and it sits placidly in the branches, its beady eyes alert, its head moving mechanically back and forth.

"Well, that's just it," Bear is saying. "We don't know. But legend has it that these birds are messengers from the land of the dead, returning to visit their loved ones."

Greta lowers the binoculars and turns to Conrad, her heart beating fast. He's looking at her in disbelief, his face suddenly pale. For a moment, the canoe spins slowly in the water, everything so quiet it almost feels loud. And then Bear begins to laugh.

"No, I'm just messing with you," he says with a grin. "It probably got lost. Or blown off course in a storm."

All the tension floods back out of Greta. She wants to laugh along with the others, but she can't. When she looks back at her dad, he gives her a slightly embarrassed smile, and it makes her feel less alone, imagining that he believed it too, even though they both know better, even though they both understand that it's far easier to get lost than to reach across such impossible distances.

Later, they're returned to the cruise ship, and Greta follows Conrad back up the long ramp in silence. It's the same silence they've been carrying between them for hours now, from the canoe to the hike to the picnic area—where they ate their strawberries wordlessly, both thinking of Helen—then back to the bus, which got stuck in the mud halfway down the mountain, so that they all had to climb out and collect sticks to shove under the wheels, watching them spin uselessly until something finally caught, and the bus gave a little buck, fishtailing a few feet down the road before coming to a stop so they could all pile on again.

It's a complicated silence. But not an unpleasant one.

Back on the ship, they pause at the elevators to look at each other. Greta can think of nothing to say, not after all that. Neither can Conrad, apparently. When the elevator arrives, he steps on, reaching out to hold the door for Greta. But she gestures toward the hallway.

"I think I need a walk," she says.

He nods. "I'll see you tomorrow then."

"What about dinner?"

"I'm sure you've had enough of me today."

Greta laughs. "Does that mean you've had enough of me?"

"It means we survived the wilderness safari," he says with a hint of amusement. "Which was not necessarily a given."

And with that, he lets his hand slip and the doors close between them.

Greta stands there for a long time in her muddy sneakers, sunburned and bone-tired and restless. Her reflection in the silver doors of the elevator—blurred and distorted as if in a fun house mirror—looks alarmingly close to how she feels right now.

She still hasn't moved when there's another ding and the doors slide open to reveal Todd Bloom in a blue rain jacket, his curly gray hair tousled from the wind.

"Oh," he says with mild surprise. "Hi. I didn't know you guys were back."

Greta steps aside so he can get off the elevator. "Just."

"Was it good?"

"It was," she says, thinking that she wouldn't be able to explain it any better if she tried. "How was fishing?"

"I skipped it," he tells her with a guilty smile. "There's an eagle preserve in Chilkat that I wanted to—"

"Oh," Greta says, remembering. "We saw one too."

"A bald eagle?"

"No, this kind of sea eagle that's really rare. Seller's, maybe?"

Todd's eyes go wide. "You saw a Steller's sea eagle?"

"Yeah. It was mostly black, but it had white around the wings and—"

"You saw a *Steller's sea eagle*?" he repeats as a large extended family comes pouring out of the elevator, midway through a raucous argument over who was supposed to have booked today's floatplane tour. They stream around Greta and Todd, but even once they're gone, his face is still frozen, like his brain has short-circuited from this information.

"I guess they're usually from Asia?" Greta offers in an attempt to jog him out of it.

"*You saw a Steller's sea eagle?*" he says for a third time. "Do you know what the odds of that are? There can't be more than two or three ever spotted around here. Ever! They're hard to find even in their natural habitat. And to stumble across one on a completely different continent when you're not even looking for it?" He shakes his head. "That's lucky. That's, like, buy-a-lottery-ticket lucky. I can't even begin to tell you how jealous I am."

"Well, if it makes you feel any better, he was pretty far away . . ."

"No, I'm glad you saw it," he says sincerely. "It's something really, really special. Not just the bird itself, but it's like . . . if you see a gyrfalcon in the Arctic Circle, it's still an amazing thing, right? But when you spot one in Ohio, well, that's something different altogether. It's that it's wandered so long and far, that it's made it to such an unlikely place. The fact that it doesn't belong is what makes it stand out. It's what makes it even more extraordinary."

An image of Greta's mother flashes in her head, dancing in the crowd at one of her shows, looking entirely out of place and radiating happiness. She swallows hard.

"It should've been you," she says quietly, but Todd smiles at her.

"No," he says. "I have a feeling it was meant for you."

# Chapter Twenty-Two

Greta isn't sure where she's headed after that, but she finds herself crossing through the indoor pool, which is crowded and stuffy, the windows fogged and the air heavy with chlorine. There are still hours left to explore the town before they're due to leave port again, yet half the passengers are idly leafing through magazines on lounge chairs or bobbing around in the hot tub, oblivious to the towering mountains at their backs. They could be anywhere right now, at a cheap hotel in Vegas or a community pool in the summertime, even in their own backyards, and Greta has a sudden and uncharacteristic impulse to scream at them for missing it all, this trip that others would give anything to be on.

Feeling claustrophobic, she weaves through the chairs and out the door on the opposite side, back into the fresh air, where she stands gripping the rail of the ship, looking out over the bay and listening to the incessant crying of the seagulls.

"Hey," someone says behind her, and when she turns to see Ben, her heart lifts. He's wearing fishing gear—orange waders and rubber boots—and a Boston Red Sox cap that's bleached from the sun. Beneath the brim, he's watching her with a slightly puzzled expression.

"Hey," she says, turning to lean against the rail. "Catch anything?"

He nods. She waits for him to say something more, to make a

joke or step forward and kiss her. But he keeps frowning at her like something is wrong.

"What?" she says finally, her pleasure at seeing him—and at the memory of last night—melting into something far less patient. Because this day has already felt like a thousand years, and she doesn't need whatever this is too.

"I just . . ." He trails off uncertainly, then pulls his phone out of the pocket of his waterproof jacket. "You're not . . . I mean . . . you would've told me if . . ."

"Ben," she says with a sigh. "Just spit it out."

There's a flash of annoyance on his face, or possibly something more than that. Finally, he says, "You're engaged?"

She stares at him. "What?"

This time, he doesn't pose it as a question: "You're engaged."

"I'm—what?" she says again, her mind moving slowly. "No, I'm not."

"It says so right here." He holds out his phone. On the screen, there's a picture of Greta and Luke kissing on a street corner. She recognizes it immediately, the night coming back to her in a hurry. It was two years ago, not long after they'd started dating. Greta had played a surprise set at a smallish venue in Brooklyn, previewing a few tracks from her album several weeks before it was due to come out. She and Luke had spent the day arguing about the bridge on one of them, and though she'd agreed to try it his way, she'd changed her mind once she was onstage. This happened often during her live performances; anyone who played with her knew she had a tendency to call audibles once she was out there. Sometimes the changes were successful, sometimes not. But they always kept her shows interesting. That night had been a good one, and afterward, elated by the reception—the mad applause from the crowd—she'd charged back into the greenroom only to find it empty. Out on the street, Luke was waiting for her, pacing around in the frosty air, his hands deep in his coat pockets. Greta was expecting a fight, but instead he pulled her close and kissed her.

"You were brilliant," he said simply.

The picture had appeared online the next day. The photographers were mostly there for the band going on after her, far more famous at the time than Greta, so it hadn't gotten much pickup. But later, once the album came out and interest in her romance with the handsome Aussie producer started to be of greater interest, the photo resurfaced.

And now here it is again: under a headline that inexplicably announces her engagement to Luke Watts.

She takes the phone from Ben and stares at it.

"That's not . . ." she says, then starts again. "I'm not . . ."

"Then why would they say that?"

"I don't know," she says, pushing the phone back into his hand. She starts to walk along the rail of the ship, not exactly sure where she's going. "Because they're trying to get you to click."

He follows her. "Well, there must be some truth to it. Or else why would they—"

"Ben," she says, spinning around. "I'm obviously not engaged."

His face is hard. "Maybe that's not as obvious as you think."

"What's that supposed to mean?"

He shrugs. "We only just met. How would I know if you're really—"

"You're one to talk," she says, sparking with sudden anger. She pushes open the door to the inside of the ship, her ears ringing as she leaves the rushing wind behind. "You're the one who's married."

"That's different."

"Yeah," Greta says, "it's worse."

"We're separated," Ben hisses as they pass a family on their way to the buffet. Greta ignores him, continuing down the red-carpeted hallway toward the elevators. "And that's not really the point here. I don't think it's crazy to see a headline like this and wonder if my—"

"Your what?" she asks without turning around. At the elevators, she hits the button too hard. Ben appears at her side, blocking the doors.

"Are you seriously so immature that we can't even talk about this?"

"I guess so," she says, and when the bell dings and the door opens behind him, she raises her eyebrows. "Are you seriously so immature that you're not going to let me on?"

With a look of profound disappointment, he steps to the side, and Greta hurries into the elevator. She presses the button for the seventh floor, her heart pounding faster than it should, and for reasons she can't quite explain. Ben's face, as he stands there, is caught somewhere between baffled and disappointed.

"For the record, I'm not engaged to anyone," she says, and then, right before the doors close, she adds: "It's just me."

All the way up, those last few words thrum through her head. She's not even sure why she said them, but she feels them all the same, deep in her bones, in some true and unexamined place.

It's just her.

In her room, she takes out her phone, which she'd turned off earlier to save the battery. As it powers up, it begins to buzz madly with notifications. The texts pile up one after another, from Howie and Cleo, from her agent and publicist, even from Atsuko and Nate. There's one from Asher that says, It's not true, right? and another from Yara that says, This better be fake news.

There's nothing at all from Luke.

She switches off the phone again, her heart thumping, and peels off her hiking pants and sweatshirt, throwing on the same black dress she'd worn the first day. Then she grabs her jean jacket, stuffs her feet into a pair of Vans, and walks with purpose back down the hallway, as if she knows exactly where she's going, as if she ever does.

To get off the ship, she has to show her plastic passenger ID card to one of the officers, who scans it on a computer, then gives her a sharp nod. "Make sure you're back by six P.M.," she says, and Greta starts to walk out into the sunlight. But after a few steps, she turns back.

"What happens if I'm not?"

The officer looks surprised. "Well, the ship leaves without you."

"And then what?"

"You either find your way to the next stop, or you go home," she says, then adds with a grin, "Or I guess maybe you live here now."

It's nearly four, and the water is glinting in the late-afternoon sunlight as Greta walks along the harbor. At the end of the pier, two kids in wellies are selling bait from a metal bucket. A fishing boat glides into the bay, tiny against the backdrop of the cruise ship. Everything feels muted by the impossible scope of the landscape around them, and she imagines what it would be like to actually live in a place like this, to wake every morning in a little red house huddled beneath the enormous sky and the towering mountains.

Greta finds it almost painful sometimes to think about all the different lives she could be leading, to know that every choice she's made has meant the loss of so many other possibilities. Every day, more doors close. Without even trying, simply by moving forward, you end up doubling down on the life you've chosen. And the only way to survive is to commit to it fully, to tell yourself it's the right one. But what if that's not true?

Closer to town, a little girl has set up a lemonade stand with a plate of Oreos and a jar for tips. At her feet, a husky puppy is chewing on an antler like something right out of an ad campaign for the state of Alaska.

Greta stops at the table and points to the blue plastic pitcher. "How much?"

"You're from the ship, right?" the girl asks, squinting up at her from beneath thick brown bangs. She must be nine or ten, with pale skin and dark eyes, and she's wearing a yellow T-shirt with a ladybug on it.

"Do I look like I'm from the ship?"

The girl considers this. "No, but you're not from here."

"How do you know?"

"Because I know everyone who lives here. Literally."

Greta smiles. "So you're gonna charge me the tourist rate, huh?"

"Those are the rules," the girl says very seriously.

"Fair enough." Greta hands over a twenty-dollar bill. "Guess I'll have to move here to get the discount."

"You would never," the girl says matter-of-factly. She stands up to pour the lemonade, heaving the pitcher over a trembling paper cup. "Nobody ever does. At least nobody like you."

"What does that mean?"

"Someone cool," the girl says a little shyly. "From someplace cool. Probably."

"I'm from Ohio, actually," Greta says, and the girl looks disappointed. "But I live in New York City."

"Knew it." She hands over the cup and Greta takes a sip, trying not to wince at how tart it is. But the girl is watching her closely. She shrugs. "I know it's not that good. But it's something to do."

"It's great," Greta says, waving away the change. "Keep it. Consider it a down payment for next time."

A smile twitches on the girl's face, but then she shakes her head and busies herself stacking the cups. "You're not coming back here."

"Maybe I'll see you in New York, then," Greta says, and the girl looks up in surprise, her face full of delight.

Greta waits until she's walked a few blocks to toss the mostly full cup into a garbage bin. Then she stops to look around. The main street is lined with dusty bars and gift shops. There's a statue of a wooden bear outside one of them, and a neon sign that says WILD ALASKAN SALMON in the window of another. A large black dog watches her from the bed of a muddy blue pickup truck, and across the street is the Hammer Museum, which Greta assumes contains artifacts from some great frontiersman named Hammer, until she notices the literal ten-foot sculpture of a hammer and nail out front.

Up ahead, she spots a wood-beamed brewery and heads toward it. Inside, the whole place smells of grain and hops, and it's crowded with tourists from the ship. Greta waits in line to order the signature lager, then carries her pint to the garden out back, which isn't nearly as busy.

For a long time, she just sits there, letting the events of the day recede. The beer is crisp and refreshing, and the sun is warm on her face. She listens to the rise and fall of conversations around her, and watches a bee circle an empty glass. Then, after a while, she takes out her phone and does something she swore she'd never do again.

She calls Luke.

# Chapter Twenty-Three

"It wasn't me," he says the moment he picks up the phone, which is when Greta catches the eye of a harried waiter and points to her glass. The guy nods and starts to head back into the brewery, but she makes a frantic motion and he turns back again.

*Two*, she mouths, holding up two fingers.

"Greta?" Luke says on the other end of the phone, and she hates herself for missing the way he says her name, the *e* drawn out so that it sounds more like *Greeta*. It's so specific, so unique to him, and the familiarity makes her stomach twist. "You there?"

"Yeah. Listen—"

But, of course, listening has never been his strong suit. "I swear I didn't do it," he says. "I didn't even know till I got off the plane in Sydney a little while ago and had a million texts. It's everywhere. My brother said it's even trending on Twitter."

"Fantastic," Greta says flatly.

"Look, I know you're probably not thrilled, but it's obviously not true, so who cares, right?"

She grits her teeth. "I do."

"Well, I don't."

"That sounds familiar."

"So does *that*," he says, but he seems more amused than anything else. "You have to admit it would've been a clever way to get you to ring me." A few seconds pass as he tries to wait out her silence, but he can't manage it. "How are you, anyway?"

"I'm fine, Luke," she says with a sigh. "That's not really the—"

"I saw you're doing Gov Ball. That's huge. Wish I could be there to see it."

Greta adjusts her grip on the phone. "Yeah."

"Are you ready?"

She doesn't want to talk about this with him.

At least, she doesn't want to *want* to talk about this with him.

But the truth is, nobody will ever understand her as well as Luke, at least musically speaking. Those years they were together, he could be an asshole about so many things—not making enough of an effort with Yara and playing devil's advocate when they talked about politics and always needing to have the last word in a fight—but when it came to her music, they were almost always in sync.

They'd met in L.A., where Greta was opening for a bigger band at the Wiltern. Her EP had been out for a few months by then, and she was in the middle of recording the album. Cleo had paired her with a producer back in New York, a sixty-something white guy with hairy ears who had produced three platinum rock albums in the last decade. But on every track, his feedback was the same: "A little less."

Greta didn't quite know it then, but what she needed was someone who would ask her for more.

Luke was at the show that night with a couple of musician friends. When they came backstage to meet her afterward, he was the only one not wearing a porkpie hat. Later, once the other two had left and Luke somehow remained, perched on the arm of the ratty sofa in the greenroom, she asked if they'd forgotten their monocles.

He laughed, a surprisingly big sound. "They're singers. What do you expect?"

"I'm a singer," she said, arching an eyebrow, still unsure whether or not she was flirting with him. He was wearing all black that night—T-shirt, jeans, and boots—and had one of those haircuts you only ever really see on actors, the kind that seem to defy gravity.

"You sing," he said matter-of-factly. "But you're not a singer. At least not primarily."

She gave him an even look. "I can't decide if I should be offended by that."

"You shouldn't," he said. "You have an interesting voice. It works. But at the end of the day, you're mainly a guitarist. And a damn good one."

If he'd told her she was smart or cool or pretty, if he'd said he liked her eyes or her hair or her outfit, she might've been pleased. But no other compliment could've worked as well as that one did. Nothing could ever mean half as much.

*A damn good one.*

She carried those words around with her for months.

Afterward, they went for burgers at a nearby diner, then drinks at a dive bar around the corner, then back to her hotel, ostensibly for the bottle of champagne the concierge had left for Greta. But a few hours later, they were still in bed—the bottle still unopened—when Luke asked if he could hear the third song from her set again. "That'll be the single, right?" he asked as he traced her collarbone. "'Told You So'? I think I figured out the problem with it."

She frowned at him. "Who said there's a problem?"

"You're pulling your punches," he said, undeterred. "It's not meant to be a ballad. It's not even meant to be a power ballad. It's an anthem. You wrote a big song, an angry song, and now you're too afraid to play it that way. Which is a shame because it's a great fucking track. Or at least it could be if you'd stop worrying what people might think and just play the hell out of it."

If anyone else had said this to her, she might've kicked them out of bed. But there was something mesmerizing about his certainty. Already, she understood that he was right. That maybe she'd even known this. She'd just needed to hear someone else say it. And so, with only a sheet wrapped loosely around her, she climbed out of bed and stooped to unlatch her guitar case.

"You look like a badass Statue of Liberty," Luke said with a lazy grin as he propped himself up on one tattooed arm to watch.

"The Statue of Liberty *is* a badass," Greta said, and then—although the room was mostly dark—she closed her eyes and began to play. At first, she had trouble finding the right tempo. She stopped and started twice, but on the third try, the music and lyrics began to match up again. There was something cathartic about playing such a familiar song at such an unfamiliar pace, something in the quickness that gave it a whole new intensity, an electricity that matched the feeling behind it.

Midway through, she opened her eyes and her heart picked up speed, a drumbeat all its own. She didn't know if it was the song or the way Luke was watching her, with a look that fell somewhere between arrogance and awe, a look that said of course he'd been right, of course he'd known it would be better this way. But he hadn't imagined it could be quite like this.

Now the waiter returns with two beers, and Greta takes a long sip from one of them. He'd asked if she was ready for Gov Ball, and she isn't sure how to answer that. To anyone else, she'd lie and say yes. To Luke she says, "I honestly don't know."

To his credit, he doesn't promise she'll be fine, as so many others would. They haven't spoken in months, but still he knows her.

"It's not like you haven't done this before," he says. "It's not like you don't know how."

"Yeah, but it's been a minute."

"I noticed that," he says, his voice softer now. "You okay?"

Greta tips her head back to the blue Alaskan sky. For a second, she feels like laughing. Is she okay? Right then, it seems an impossible question.

Luke clears his throat. "Have you at least been playing on your own?"

"A little."

"Well, you should be. I mean it. You need to go out there this weekend and light that place up."

She tries to think of a response to this, but her heart is too loud in her ears. She realizes then that this isn't a pep talk. He's not just being nice.

He's trying to save her.

He's trying to tell her she needs saving.

"I've seen you do it loads of times," he says. "The way you go out there and play like you don't give a fuck about anything. Like you're all alone up there."

Greta is silent for a moment. "But I should, shouldn't I?"

"What?"

"Give a fuck. About all of it. This show. My career." She waits for him to say something, but he doesn't. "What if I can't do it?"

"Jesus, Greta," he says, and he seems genuinely distressed. "You don't sound like yourself."

"I don't feel like myself."

"The Greta I know is too stubborn to listen to what anyone else thinks."

"Well," she says, swirling the amber-colored beer around in her glass. "I'm listening now."

"You don't need me to tell you anything. You already know what you should do."

"Play it faster?" she teases, and he laughs.

"Not this one," he says, and then more somberly: "It was for your mom, wasn't it?"

She nods, though he can't see her. "I shouldn't have tried it."

"You took a swing."

"It was reckless."

"It was emotional," he says. "There's nothing wrong with that."

She takes a sip of her beer, then sets it back down on the table. "They want to approve the set list. They want me to open with 'Prologue.' "

"And you don't," he says. It's not a question.

"I hate leaving things unfinished," she tells him, and they both know she's not talking about "Prologue" anymore. She rests her forehead in her hand. "There's a part of me that wants to try again, but it feels impossible to go back to it."

"I know it was just a skeleton," Luke says. "But from what I heard, it has good bones. You'd just have to be willing to take it the rest of the way."

"They made me promise to leave it out."

"Fuck 'em," he says so quickly it makes her laugh. "I'm serious. That video didn't make the rounds just because everyone was taking the piss. You made people feel something, even if it wasn't what you intended. You were magnetic up there. You always are."

Greta feels a knot form in her throat. "And if it happens again?"

"It won't," he says. "But if it does, well . . . that's just part of it."

"Part of what?"

"Making art. You know that better than anyone. And the worst thing you could do right now is pull your punches. Fuck the suits. Take another pass at it. Double down. Get it right. Then get up there and play it true."

"Next you're going to tell me to sing my heart out," she jokes, but he doesn't laugh.

"Pretty much," he says. "Listen, if you're not ready on Sunday, you're not ready. But just make sure it's your decision. Not theirs. And whatever you decide, you've got to pick up the goddamn guitar again, okay? As soon as possible. Just play."

"Okay," she says, and right then, she realizes she misses him. Really misses him. She remembers when they landed back in New York, still foggy from the funeral and the muddled days that followed it. At the airport, Luke had automatically started to get into the same cab as her, but Greta shook her head. "I think I need to be alone right now," she said, and he nodded, leaning in to give her a kiss before closing the door.

She couldn't sleep that night, and around four A.M., she finally gave up and went for a walk, tracing a path down through Nolita and then Chinatown, the streets empty and the storefronts covered by grates. Eventually, she wound her way to the river, where she stood looking out at the Brooklyn Bridge, the lights from the cars twinkling as they streamed into the city.

She stopped only once to gaze up at the towering stone arches as she crossed. Ahead of her, the sun was rising in slices between the buildings, yellow and then orange and then pink, and by the time she made it to Luke's apartment in Dumbo, it was fully light out. His voice over the intercom was groggy, and he was waiting in the hallway—barefoot and bleary-eyed—when she got to the top of the stairs.

As soon as she saw him, she knew for sure. They both did.

"Don't do anything hasty," he said, but it didn't feel that way to her. It felt like something that had been coming for a long time. She and Luke were like a wave that had crested too soon. There was the early madness of falling in love, and when that burned off, they still had the music, which seemed like enough. But Greta had been in the world for six days without her mom by then, and already she knew she needed something more.

"Thanks, Luke," she says into the phone now. It's not just for the call, but for everything.

"See," he says, and she can hear the smile in his voice, "I'm not the worst person to be fake-engaged to."

"Not the worst," she agrees.

"Good luck this weekend," he says. "Burn it all down, okay?"

"I'll try," she says, and then she ends the call.

It's getting late now, so she takes one last sip of beer, pays her bill, and walks back up the main street of the tiny town. Her mind is a jumble, her thoughts too scattered to parse. All she knows is that for the first time in a while, she's itchy to play, and that's no small thing.

When she makes it back to the ship, the same officer is standing at the door.

"Glad you decided to keep going," she says, like she knows something Greta doesn't, like she's managed to peer directly into her brain.

"Keep going?" Greta asks as she passes over her key card.

"With the cruise," the woman says, as if this should be obvious. "You know. Instead of moving here."

Greta half-turns to take one more look at the little town and the great mountain behind it, then, once the card is scanned, she slips it into her pocket and hurries onto the elevator. She's about to press 7, then thinks of her tiny room with its thin walls and hits 2 instead.

When she gets out, she looks left and then right down the corridor, trying to remember where it is, the jazz club they'd passed that first full day at sea. She wanders by the piano bar and the casino before she finds it tucked back beside the nightclub. There's no door, no rope, just an easel advertising tonight's shows, one at eight and one at ten. For now, the tables are bare and the lights are dim.

Up on the stage, there's a keyboard and a drum set, surrounded by various speakers and microphones and wires. Above those, just as there'd been last time, six electric guitars hang in a row. Before she can think better of it, Greta walks up the aisle, steps onto the stage, and peers up at the first one, a red-and-white Yamaha. She looks around before lifting it gently from the hook near the lighting bar. There are several amps behind her, but she doesn't plug it in. Instead, she runs her fingers over the strings, her heart giving a little skip.

When that first chord fades out, she stares out over the room.

There's no audience. Just dozens of empty seats.

She looks down at the guitar again.

Then she takes a deep breath.

And begins to play.

She doesn't bother with the words; those will have to come later. For now, it's just the music, and it's different this time, fuller somehow. She closes her eyes as she plays, and when she reaches the end, when the last notes fade out, it's like emerging from a dream. She comes out of it slowly, and as she does, she notices Preeti standing uncertainly by the door. The room falls silent again as she lays a hand on the still-vibrating strings of the guitar.

Greta has been playing in front of people since she was twelve. She's headlined festivals with tens of thousands of fans, recorded in some of the most famous venues in the world, jammed with some of her childhood heroes, and enjoyed more encores and ovations than she can count.

But right now, nothing—*nothing*—can match the look of awe on this one girl's face.

"Wow," Preeti says softly, and Greta smiles, because the guitar could use some tuning, and the bridge didn't really work without someone on keys, and she still needs to come up with the words to match whatever it was she just played. But even so, it was good. She could feel it.

Preeti takes a few steps into the room. "That song is . . ." She shakes her head, not finding the words. "Do you think you'll ever try it again? In public, I mean."

"I don't know," Greta admits, taking the guitar off. "It didn't go so well the last time."

"Yeah, but it might be my new favorite," Preeti says so earnestly that Greta has to swallow the lump in her throat before speaking.

"Thank you," she manages.

"Those chord changes in the middle—how did you do them?"

"Here," Greta says, holding out the guitar. "I'll show you."

Preeti looks momentarily dumbstruck. Then she hurries up the steps to the stage, loops the strap over her head, and places her fingers carefully on the strings. She's wearing a Blondie T-shirt and jeans that are torn at the knees and her dark hair is pulled back into a messy bun and it nearly takes Greta's breath away, how much it's like seeing her former self, right down to the way her tongue is sticking out in concentration.

She looks up at Greta, suddenly shy. "It's the part between the second verse and the bridge," she says. "Your hands were flying."

"Use your middle finger," Greta says, which makes Preeti laugh. But she adjusts her hands on the fret. "There. Try it now. Start with E."

The first note comes out with confidence; the second, more tentatively.

Which is sometimes how it goes.

"It's not supposed to be easy," Greta reminds her, and Preeti looks up.

"What's it supposed to be then?"

"I think fun?" Greta says with such a lack of conviction that they both start to laugh. "Yes. Fun. It's definitely supposed to be fun." She glances down at the guitar in Preeti's hands again. "Here," she says, hooking her own fingers around an imaginary set of strings. "Try it this way."

Preeti's eyes dart between Greta's hands and the guitar she's holding. Then she starts again. This time, when she plays it, the notes ring out across the empty room with such satisfaction that neither of them can keep from grinning.

"Good," Greta says, hopping down from the stage. "Now keep practicing."

She's still buzzing all over as she starts to walk back up the aisle, her heart beating fast, like it hasn't given up the song just yet.

Preeti glances up. "Where are you going?"

"I've got somewhere I need to be," she says, but before she hurries out, she turns around one more time, looking at the girl on the stage—all elbows and grim determination—and she smiles. "Burn it all down, okay?"

## Chapter Twenty-Four

"So I figured something out," Greta says the moment Ben opens the door, and if he's got any follow-up questions, he doesn't ask them. He just stares at her for a second, the air charged between them, and then he takes a step forward, and so does she, and suddenly they're kissing—softly at first, then more urgently— as they stumble into the room and onto the bed, letting the door fall shut behind them.

A minute later, he pulls away. "Wait, what did you figure out?"

She smiles. "How to play again."

"You'd stopped?"

"It's a long story."

"I'd like to hear it."

She ignores this, tracing a circle around one of the buttons on his shirt. "Hey," she says. "You know I'm not really engaged, right?"

He nods. "And you know I'm not really married."

"Well, yeah . . . but I'm more not-engaged than you are not-married."

"That's fair," he says; then, after a pause: "But I don't feel married."

Greta laughs. "I'm sure nobody does when they're sleeping with someone else."

"It's not that," he says, tucking her hair behind her ear in a way that makes her stomach dip. They both still smell like the outdoors, like sunscreen and salt water and earth.

"I know," she says, and kisses his shoulder. He pulls her close then, and she rests her head on his chest, feeling the rise and fall of his breathing. Her eyes drift over to the table in the corner, where his typewriter sits, entirely incongruous beside his phone and computer and other more modern devices. "I still can't believe you use a typewriter."

"I know it seems pretentious," he says sheepishly, "but it's the only way I ever get anything written. No distractions. Just words on a page. You should try it sometime."

"I'm writing rock music, not trying to crack the Watergate scandal," she says with a grin. "I use voice memos to catch any melodies. And then notebooks for the lyrics."

"I'm a notebook guy, too," he says. "Nothing beats pen and paper. Though I guess it depends on the pen."

She nods. "Rollerball all the way."

"You're not serious," he says, shifting position so he can look at her. "You don't use a fountain pen? There's nothing better."

"Yeah, there is. A fine-tip Pilot V5."

He laughs. "What, do you have a sponsorship deal or something?"

"No, but I should really tell Howie to—"

Before she can finish, he kisses her, and when he pulls back again, his face is lit with such simple happiness that Greta's heart does a little judder.

"Can I take you out tonight?" he asks.

"We're on a boat."

"It's a ship," he says. "And I realize that. I just meant on a date."

"A date?" she asks skeptically.

"What?" he says. "Too formal? Too nerdy?"

She smiles. "No. A date would be nice."

When she gets back to her room to shower and change, Greta glances through the pileup of messages on her phone. Pretty much anyone who's ever been on the payroll has been trying to reach her. She calls Howie, and he picks up right away.

"Jesus," he says. "Where have you been?"

"On a boat," she reminds him.

"I know that. I meant— Never mind." He sighs, and she can picture him pinching the bridge of his nose as he does when he's stressed. Which is often. Howie manages only a small number of musicians, but most of them are significantly more famous than Greta, and he always seems to be on call. "Just tell me this. Did you do it?"

"Do what?" she asks coolly. "Get engaged to Luke?"

"No, did you—"

"Plant it? God, Howie. Of course not. What would be the point?"

"To get some publicity ahead of this weekend," he says flatly. That's the thing about Howie. He's not like some agents and managers. He isn't slick, and he doesn't try to charm you. He's a straight shooter all the way. Which is why she likes him. Usually.

"This is *not* the kind of publicity I want," she says. "And for the record, we're not even together anymore. I haven't seen him in months. And I'd never leak something like this. Even if it were true."

"Fair enough. Had to ask," Howie says matter-of-factly. "Next question: Now that it's out there, do you want me to kill it or wait till after this weekend?"

A knot forms in Greta's chest, because she knows exactly what he's saying.

That it could be helpful.

That maybe she even needs it.

It hasn't even been an hour, but already the joy of playing

again—the feel of the strings beneath her fingers and the reassuring weight of the guitar around her neck—is starting to fade.

She's silent for a long time. On the other end of the line, Howie clears his throat. "Okay," he says. "Roger that."

"I didn't say anything."

"You don't have to."

Greta sighs. "Let me think about it a little more. I'll call you later."

"Right-o," he says, and then he hangs up the phone.

There's a dress code in the dining room tonight, so Greta pulls out the nicest thing she brought, a short black dress and a pair of heels. On her way down, she spots Davis and Mary sitting on a small sofa near a panel of windows, faces pressed together as they beam into a phone. As she gets closer, Greta hears the sound of Jason's voice. She's about to make a U-turn when Davis looks up.

"Greta," he says so loudly that she jumps. "We're talking to Jase. Come say hi!"

For a second, she considers saying no. But there's no graceful way to escape this situation, and so—grimly, awkwardly—she walks around the back of the couch and stoops to see Jason's face on the screen.

"Well, don't you look nice," he says with that dazzling smile of his, his eyes dancing with amusement. "How's life at sea?"

Davis hands Greta the phone, then hauls himself off the couch. Mary stands too. "You two catch up," she says. "We've got to get ready for dinner."

"What about your phone?" Greta says, holding it out to him, but Davis waves this off.

"We'll get it later," he says, and then—almost as an afterthought—he adds, "See you, son," before walking off down the hall.

When they're gone, Greta lifts the screen again, and suddenly it's just her and Jason, who is laughing. "Typical," he says. "Always trying to pawn me off."

"Hey," Greta says. "Congrats on the engagement."

"Congrats on *yours*," he says, and on the screen, she can see very clearly how quickly her face turns pink.

"Yeah, that's not actually—"

"What?"

"Real. We broke up. Months ago."

He looks surprised. "Oh. I guess you can't always believe what you read online."

"Shocking, I know."

"Well, mine is one hundred percent verified," he says gently. "You're hearing it straight from the source."

"I'm really happy for you."

He nods. "I'm sorry I didn't tell you sooner. I wasn't sure how."

She peers at him through the screen, thinking how odd this is. They've never even really talked on the phone before. "You don't owe me anything," she says, but not unkindly, and he ducks his head and runs a hand over his close-cropped hair. When he looks up again, his expression is hard to read.

"I do, actually. That night in Columbus, I wasn't just messing around. I need you to know that," he says, suddenly serious. "Olivia and I were on a break. I'm not saying it wasn't still a shitty thing to do, but we'd been going through a rough patch, and I wasn't sure we'd make it, and I'd been thinking about you. A lot. And then your mom died, and I came back to see you, and I guess maybe I was trying to figure out if we could ever . . . you know."

"What?" she asks, trying to keep her face neutral.

"If we could ever be something," he says. "Something real."

Greta resists the urge to put the phone down. It's too hard to look him in the eye right now. She thinks back to that day, the way he stood there in her childhood bedroom, running a hand over her old guitar. "And then you found out I was with Luke."

"No. I mean . . . yeah. But it wasn't just that," he says, clearly eager to be understood. "It was more that I remembered how things are with you and me."

"How's that?"

"I don't know." He shrugs. "I guess you've always sort of kept me at a distance."

"Jason," she says, impatient now. "My mom had just died."

He holds up a hand. "I know. But that's how it's always been. Ever since we were kids. You keep things light."

"So do *you*."

"Maybe when we were younger," he says. "But things change."

Greta feels her face get hot, thinking about all the years he snuck out of her bed while it was still dark, all the times he was careful not to leave anything behind. She remembers walking up the Bowery on a freezing cold night after too many drinks, the two of them shouting at each other because she'd found out that he hadn't invited her to a Christmas party he'd thrown, and then—in the course of the argument—he found out that she hadn't invited him to her birthday dinner either, and they went back and forth like that, before both stalking off in opposite directions, each stubbornly waiting several days for the other to make peace, until Jason finally showed up at her apartment with a bottle of wine and a sheepish grin, his coat dusted with snow, and they fell into her bed and spent the rest of the weekend there, only to part again on Monday morning with the casual, business-like air of two people with no attachments or responsibilities to each other.

She'd always assumed there was a mutual understanding between them, but maybe she'd been wrong. Maybe it was just her.

Things change. So do people, apparently.

He's still watching her from the other end of the video, his eyebrows slightly raised, and she realizes the panic she's been feeling—it's not about losing Jason, who is no more hers than she was ever his. What she's lost, really, is her closest ally: someone just as fiercely independent, just as passionate about his work, someone who—not that long ago—would've shuddered at the thought of wedding registries filled with fancy china and fondue sets.

It's a smaller loss. But it's still a loss.

"I'm sorry," he says, his face a bit pixelated now. Outside, the wind is whistling past the window, and a group of people in evening wear walk by in a cloud of perfume.

"It's okay," she tells him, though she's not exactly sure what he's apologizing for. "We're okay."

"I'm glad," he says with a smile. "Let me know when you're back in the city. Maybe we can all get brunch sometime."

"I'd love that," Greta says, trying to imagine making conversation with her ex-something-or-other's new fiancée over avocado toast at some trendy Tribeca hotspot.

Jason laughs. "No, you wouldn't."

"No, I wouldn't," she agrees. "But we'll do it anyway."

He starts to say something else, but the picture is frozen now, capturing him there in profile, his handsome face tipped to one side.

"Jason?" she says, moving the phone around. But nothing changes. She waits a second, then another, then says, "Jason, I think I've lost you," and to her surprise, her eyes prick with tears. But once she's said it, once it's out there, the next part is somehow easier. "Goodbye," she says, and then she ends the call.

## Chapter Twenty-Five

When she gets to the dining room, Ben is waiting at the entrance in a sports coat. He's trimmed his beard, and his hair is neatly combed, and suddenly—improbably—this feels like an actual date.

He looks oddly amused as she walks over to him.

"What?" she asks, glancing down at her outfit. She'd thrown a bomber jacket on over her dress, but looking around at the other passengers, most of them wearing more formal attire—floor-length gowns and expensive-looking suits—she wonders if she should take it off.

Ben shakes his head. "I was literally just thinking about what might've happened if I'd met you in New York." He gestures at her outfit. "And then I realized you probably wouldn't have given me the time of day."

Greta smiles. "You never know."

"Maybe not," he says, leaning to kiss her on the cheek. He lingers a moment, his mouth close to her ear, and adds, "I'm gonna try not to overthink it."

They're seated at a table near the window. It's supposed to be for four, but Ben convinced the maître d' to let them have it to themselves, and they sit looking out over the water and the gray scroll of shore.

Once they've ordered, Greta lets out a yawn, which makes Ben laugh. "You're worse than my students."

"Sorry," she says, rubbing her eyes. "It's been a really long day."

"How did it go with your dad?"

"I don't even know how to answer that," she tells him. "It was . . . a lot. A lot of fighting. A lot of emotion. Maybe even a lot of progress. But it was exhausting. I don't think we're built to spend that much time together. At least not without my mom."

He nods. "She was your translator."

"She was," Greta says. "Now it's like we're yelling at each other in two completely different languages." She twists her napkin in her hands. "I've spent so much of my life sparring with him. That's just always been the dynamic between us, even when I was younger and we got along better. He and my brother—they watch baseball for fun. He and I—we argue. But it feels different now."

"How so?"

She shrugs. "He's old. And sad. I am too. Honestly, I just didn't feel like fighting with him today. I didn't have the heart for it. Don't get me wrong—I still think most of this is his fault. He's the parent. But I'm obviously not blameless either. And this morning it was like . . . I don't know. For the first time maybe ever, I guess I wished things were easier between us."

"You should tell him that."

"I can't," she says, shaking her head. "There's way too much water under that particular bridge. And we're both much too stubborn."

"People change."

Greta looks over at him. Not even an hour ago, Jason had said pretty much the same thing, and she wonders if she's the only one who hasn't changed, if she's the only one who can't.

Her phone buzzes on the table and she flips it over to see Howie's name. She ignores it, taking a sip of her wine. "Tell me about your fishing trip," she says to Ben. "Did you catch anything?"

"Yeah, I got a sockeye," he says proudly. "I was the only one. It was big too."

"Wow," she says as her phone begins to jitter again. This time, when she looks, she sees it's from Charles, Howie's husband, a trick he uses whenever a client is ignoring him. But she still doesn't answer. It doesn't matter anyway; a moment later, he texts her a link to an article in *People*. The headline reads: GRETA JAMES ENGAGED TO MUSIC PRODUCER. Beneath it, Howie has written: It's getting a lot of pickup. Everyone wants a quote from you. I'm on now with Cleo and Anna and Miguel. They said we need something by tomorrow at the latest.

Anna and Miguel are both publicists, one for the label, one hired independently. The fact that they're all on the phone together means this is serious.

*A quote,* she thinks. What would she even say? *Luke and I are thrilled to start the next chapter of our lives together?*

It was one thing not to correct it. It would be entirely another to lie about it.

When she glances up again, Ben is watching her. She sets the phone down.

"My manager," she says, by way of explanation. "The story is apparently everywhere."

"And he's getting it fixed?"

"Sort of," she says, and Ben raises his eyebrows. "It's just an issue of timing."

"What does that mean?"

She picks up her fork, then sets it down again, avoiding his gaze. Her stomach is churning. "I think the idea is to wait a few days."

"What for?"

"It's a strategic thing."

"What, like for publicity?"

"No," she says, then shrugs. "I don't know. Maybe."

Another text comes through from Howie. We need to either give them something or kill the story. What do you want to do?

Ben stares at her. "Please tell me you're not serious."

She glances back up at him, suddenly annoyed. "Please tell me you're not going to be a jerk about this because you're currently sleeping with me."

"That's not why—" He stops and shakes his head. "It's because you're better than this. Pretending to be engaged to some guy just to—what? Get some press? Some extra likes? That's not you."

"You hardly know me. It's only been a few days."

"Well, it doesn't feel that way. At least not to me." He picks up his wine glass and takes a swig. "Anyway, time is just a construct."

In spite of herself, Greta laughs. But Ben is still serious.

"Look, I'm sure it's more complicated than it seems," he says, leaning toward her again. "And it's not like you owe me an explanation. But I can't help thinking you don't want to deny it because you're still in love with the guy."

"I'm not," Greta says flatly.

"Then what?"

"You *just* said I don't owe you an explanation."

He opens his mouth, then closes it again, looking caught out. "Well, I guess I lied. Can you at least tell me more about Luke? Why'd you end things with him?"

She sighs. "Why do you want to know?"

"I just do."

"This isn't a relationship. We don't have to do the thing where we talk about our exes. Especially when yours isn't quite so ex."

"Okay, fine. What do you want to know about her?" he asks, looking like someone about to submit to a drug test. He downs the rest of his wine, then pours himself some more. "I'll tell you anything."

Greta gives him an exasperated look. "I said we *don't* have to do that."

"Come on," he says, and then he actually claps his hands. "Give me your best shot."

"Fine. What was her least favorite thing about being married to you?"

He looks surprised, then he laughs. "Okay, I changed my mind. This is a terrible idea."

"I told you," she says, smiling at him. His eyes are shiny in the light, and he looks younger in his shirtsleeves, undeniably attractive, but also so unassuming it's easy to miss it.

Greta thinks about what he'd said earlier, about what would happen if they'd met in New York. She'd gone straight to picturing him at one of her shows, a fish out of water, but now a new image starts to assemble itself in her mind: Ben making a pot of tea at her stove, the two of them reading in bed together, walking through Tompkins Square Park with ice cream on one of those perfect New York days.

The fact that she's never done—or even wanted—any of this before doesn't strike her as odd. It wouldn't have made sense with any of the other guys she's dated. Jason, because he was always working. And Luke, because he thought he was too cool. Her college boyfriend, Wesley, existed almost entirely in his dorm room, smoking pot or playing videogames. And the few minor relationships she'd had in her twenties—Ryan the digital ad guy, and Pablo the coder, and Ian the hedge fund manager—hadn't lasted long enough to reach that phase where even the most mundane things feel special in the right company.

But with Ben, she can somehow imagine it. And though she knows it's less a personal fantasy than an amalgamation of every romantic comedy she's ever seen, every love story she's ever been told, that doesn't mean it doesn't come from someplace hopeful or wistful or true. Maybe even someplace genuine.

Underneath the table, she bumps her knee lightly against his, a conciliatory gesture. "It's not about Luke," she says. "This whole thing. It's about me."

"What do you mean?"

"I'm in kind of a weird moment. It's hard to explain. Or maybe it's not. Maybe it's just embarrassing." She sighs. "I hate this part."

"What?" Ben asks. "Being embarrassed? If it makes you feel any better, right before you got here, I realized I had toilet paper stuck to my shoe."

Greta shakes her head. "No, opening up to new people. Don't you ever wish you could skip forward, like on a record, and know everything without having to go through the motions?"

"God, no," he says. "I love this part. It's like conducting research before you sit down to actually write. You find all these interesting facts and random ideas, but you still don't know exactly what they'll turn out to be yet. It's all possibility."

Without thinking about it, Greta kisses him, one hand on his knee, the other on the table, the starry lights all around them. When she leans back again, she takes a deep breath and says, "My mom died suddenly, and then I broke up with Luke, also suddenly, and then I tried to perform a song I'd only just written and fell apart onstage—like, *really* fell apart—and the video went viral, and the critics trashed the song, and my new album got pushed, and I completely stopped performing, which is the part I've always loved most, and it was only supposed to be for a little while, but now it's been three months, and I haven't been onstage once, and I've got to play Gov Ball this weekend, and the label is worried I'll go rogue again, so they want me to stick to the script, showcase the new album, play some of the hits, and basically make a clean break from what happened last time, since they're counting on the livestream to get things back on track, but I'm starting to wonder if that's not the right move here, if maybe Mary is right and the only way out is through, and I owe it to myself to try again, but at this point, I'm worried that no matter what I play, I'll fall apart for a second time because I'm still kind of a mess, and if it goes badly again, I'm honestly not sure my career can survive it, and then everything else will come crashing down too because it's pretty much my entire identity, and honestly, I really hate the idea of my dad being right about it all, not to mention everyone else who doubted me along the way, especially Mitchell Kelly, who heckled me when I played 'Lithium' at the eighth-grade talent show, even though he's probably working some depressing desk job now and would never listen to music as cool as mine, and before you say anything, I realize this is all psychological, but it feels very, very real at the moment, especially the fear, which is something that was never an issue for me before, and yeah, maybe I'm lucky to have gotten this far on hard work and sheer nerve and blind fucking faith, but it doesn't mean I don't want more, because I do, I want *so much* more, and I keep thinking about this profile that *Rolling Stone* did of me a little while back, with the headline GRETA JAMES IS FLYING HIGH, and this picture of me floating up in the clouds, and how lately, it's felt like just the opposite, like I'm sinking fast, and if I don't do something, I might never be able to pull out of it, which I have to— I *have* to—because the only thing I know for sure is that I'm not ready to come down yet. Not by a long shot."

She pulls in a shaky breath, and Ben stares at her for what feels like a long time.

"What," he says finally, "is Gov Ball?"

## Chapter Twenty-Six

By the time they order dessert, Greta has made Ben watch at least a dozen different performances from some of her favorite artists, an unofficial highlight reel she didn't even know she was in possession of: Green Day at Woodstock and Prince at Coachella, Radiohead at Bonnaroo and the Stones at Glastonbury. Something has loosened inside her again as she skips from video to video, showing Ben the ones she loves most, the volume turned low, the two of them huddled so close over her phone that she can feel the warmth of his breath.

As the last notes of "Wild Horses" carry out into the night, Mick Jagger raises his hands in the air, and the crowd cheers, and Ben leans back in his chair with a dreamy smile. "That was really nice."

Greta laughs. "Really nice?"

"It was," he says with a shrug.

When they finish watching Arcade Fire play Lollapalooza, the algorithm that shuttles viewers from one video to the next suggests Greta James at Outside Lands, and Ben sits forward so fast he nearly knocks over the bottle of wine.

"Play it," he says, clearly a little drunk now.

Before she can object, he's already reached forward to jab the button, and there she is, wearing black leather pants and a white tank top, her lipstick already smeared from the mic, beads of sweat on her forehead as she plays the opening chords of "Done and Done," the first song she ever released, the first song that got her noticed. Seeing herself on that stage, all angles and edge, her hands flying over the strings so fast it looks like a magic trick, her eyes glinting with defiance as the audience roars back at her, you wouldn't know she'd started writing it after she and Jason had ended things for the thousandth time, alone in her apartment in the middle of summer with a broken air conditioner, the heat pushing up against the windows so that everything felt damp and heavy and hopeless. The song had started as an elegy but had gradually become something more forceful than that, something more empowering, and that day she debuted it—somehow both forever ago and no time at all—it swept out over the crowd with a pulsing energy that felt almost magnetic.

Even now, on a screen the size of a deck of cards, she can feel the power of it. Not just the song but the performance, and she brings the phone closer and studies the video like it's someone else entirely up there, trying to locate the confidence behind her face the way you'd use a metal detector on a beach.

She rarely watches her own performances, and there's something strange about seeing this one now. She feels both immensely proud and also wildly distant, as if it doesn't belong to her anymore. As if someone else made that track. Someone else sauntered across that stage and absolutely crushed it. Someone else took a formal bow at the end, and then—as the applause continued to grow—waved at the crowd as she walked offstage.

Someone else. Surely it had to be someone else.

"Wow," Ben says when it's over, and Greta sets the phone down. The waiter appears behind them with their desserts: a slice of cheesecake for Ben and a strawberry tart for Greta. She tucks in right away, but Ben is still watching her. "That was . . . it was . . ."

"Really nice?" she suggests, and he laughs.

"And then some."

She reaches over for a forkful of his cheesecake. "Isn't it weird?" she asks once she's done chewing. "Achieving your dreams?"

"How so?"

"It's like, if I'd shown that to my twelve-year-old self," Greta says, gesturing at the phone, "she would've lost her mind. To be playing up there in front of all those people?" She shakes her head. "It would've been a total dream come true. Just that one song alone. Did you feel the same way when you published your book?"

"I guess so," he says thoughtfully. "But after watching that, it feels . . . quieter."

Greta laughs. "But if twelve-year-old Ben could see you now, what would he think?"

"He'd be pretty psyched I'm in Alaska," he says with a grin. "And he'd think the book was cool. But that kid was also kind of a nerd."

"The odds are so crazy, right?" she says, taking another bite. "To actually make a go of it. To be one of the best. It doesn't matter if you're a guitarist or a writer or a soccer player or whatever. It's all so unlikely."

"Until it's not," Ben says, and she smiles at him.

"I remember a few years after college, this hotshot manager came to a gig I had at a bar on the Lower East Side. My best friend, Yara, was playing keyboard with me then, and I told her that all I wanted was for this guy to sign me. I didn't care if anything else happened after that. I was waiting tables at the time, and I thought I just wanted some validation—some sign that this was all going somewhere. That would've been enough, you know?" She looks out the window at the perpetual dusk. "Yara— she laughed at me. She said, 'If you sign with him, you'll want to make a demo. And if you make a demo, you'll want a label to pick it up. And if a label picks it up, you'll want to hit the charts. Nobody ever wants just the one thing.'" She turns to Ben, who is watching her intently. "And she was right."

"So what do you want now?"

She smiles. "What a question."

On the phone's screen, the algorithm is suggesting the next video: *Greta James Loses It at BAM*. She watches Ben's eyes fall on the words, then flick away again.

"You've seen it," she says, "haven't you?"

He's quiet for a moment; then he nods. "I looked you up that first night."

She reaches over to switch off the phone, and Ben leans forward.

"For what it's worth," he says, "I don't think it's as bad as you think. It was real and it was human and you should never apologize for that."

"Thanks," she says in a voice full of emotion as she reaches over to take his hand. They're still sitting there like that, eyes locked, when Greta hears her name being called and looks over to see Eleanor Bloom.

She's waving as she approaches them, her huge earrings swinging like chandeliers. "There you are," she says as Greta disentangles her hand from Ben's and stands to give her a hug. But a few feet short of the table, Eleanor stops dramatically, her eyes going wide. "You look just like your mother in that dress."

Greta glances down, disoriented. "She never wore anything like this."

"You don't remember her when she was your age," Eleanor says as the rest of the group makes their way over: Todd and Davis and Mary, followed by Conrad, who is wearing his one good shirt, with its wrinkled collar under a sports coat.

Ben smooths his tie as he stands up. "Hi, I'm—"

"Jack London," Eleanor says, beaming. She winks at him, and Greta realizes she's a little drunk. They all are. "We know."

"Oh, well—" he begins, but Davis cuts him off.

"This looks mighty romantic," he says, surveying the half-filled wine glasses and the two place settings arranged side by side. "Anything you care to tell—"

Mary thumps him in the stomach, and Davis coughs. Greta takes the opportunity to hand back his phone, which he tucks into his jacket pocket with a grin.

"I'm glad you're having fun," Mary says to Greta. "Did you try the duck?"

"I did," Ben says cheerfully. "It was just ducky."

Greta lets out a sudden laugh at this and promptly realizes she's drunk too. She glances over at Conrad, who has been standing behind the others, his eyes bouncing from the floor to the window to the table in an effort to avoid her, and she can't help feeling a little disappointed after their breakthrough this afternoon. But at last he looks at her and—with a strained casualness—asks, "Anything new with you?" and it clicks.

If she'd thought the rumor might reach him, she would've headed it off. But he doesn't exactly pay attention to the types of news outlets that would have a story about the engagement between an indie musician and a well-known music producer. She has no idea how he saw it. He didn't even buy a data package for this trip.

A waiter sweeps by with a tray of empty plates. Around them, the room is buzzing with laughter and conversation. But here in this little scrum, everyone is quiet.

Conrad stares at Greta. And Greta stares back at him.

"If you're talking about—" she begins, but he cuts her off.

"Your engagement?"

Ben looks from one to the other, and then, slowed by the bottles of wine they'd just finished, takes it upon himself to helpfully interject. "Oh, she's not *actually* engaged," he says, "if that's what you're wondering."

Eleanor's eyebrows shoot up on her forehead. "What?" she says, her voice rising above the din. "You two are *engaged*?"

Ben—who had been looking pretty pleased with himself—now scuttles backward a step, glancing at Greta, who says, as calmly as she can, "I'm not engaged to anyone."

Conrad frowns, but he doesn't seem angry. To her surprise, Greta realizes he looks hurt. "That's not what I heard," he says. "Your aunt Wendy saw the news on Twitter."

His sister—the most excitable member of their family—was always reading up on Greta's life, tracking it like a reality show. "Tell her she shouldn't believe stuff like that," Greta says, then adds, "You shouldn't either."

"I don't have much choice. It's not like you bother to keep us informed."

If he notices the *us*, he doesn't show it. But it takes the edge off Greta's impatience. "Well, now you know," she says, "so you don't have to worry about—"

"You marrying that Australian jackass?"

"Dad," Greta says, exasperated. "Come on. You can either be upset about the possibility of me getting married or upset about the fact that I'm not. Pick a lane."

He grunts. "All I'm saying is that it would be nice to hear the news before Aunt Wendy. And Twitter."

"I told you, there isn't any news."

"Well, clearly there was."

"But it wasn't true."

"Still."

They scowl at each other for a second, both frustrated.

After a moment, Mary clears her throat. "We were on our way down to the piano bar," she says, seizing the opening to escape. "Maybe we'll see you guys there?"

"Maybe," Ben says a little too brightly.

Conrad gives Greta one last look, unreadable as always, then turns and starts walking toward the exit. Eleanor hurries after him, giving his arm a comforting pat. Greta watches him go, her mouth screwed up to one side.

"Don't worry about him," Davis tells her. "It's a tough day."

"I know," Greta says. "But he doesn't have to take it out on me."

"And you don't have to take it out on him either," Mary says, her voice firm in a way that reminds Greta of her mom. "He loves you. You know that."

"Yeah," Greta mutters. "It's just that he doesn't always like me very much."

Mary hesitates for a moment, then walks over and kisses the side of her head. "The love part," she says, so quietly that only Greta can hear, "is more important."

## Chapter Twenty-Seven

Afterward, Ben suggests they go to the casino.

"You don't strike me as a gambler," Greta says, looking at him doubtfully.

"I'm not," he says with a grin. "But I'm feeling lucky tonight."

They start with blackjack, and each manages to lose fifty bucks by the time their drinks even arrive. Greta knocks hers back and suggests they quit while they're behind. But then her phone rings.

"Be right back," she tells Ben, weaving through tables and slot machines, trying to find an exit amid all the mirrors and flashing lights.

"Where are you?" Asher asks when she picks up. "It sounds like Vegas."

"It feels like Vegas. What's up?"

"Oh, nothing much," he says. "Just calling to see if I should be picking out a tux for your upcoming nuptials. Thanks for writing me back, by the way."

Greta ducks into the hallway. "Sorry, it's been a long day."

"Sure," he says, his voice full of mirth. "Wedding planning can be stressful."

"Asher."

"What?"

"You know it's not true."

"Well, it's nice to hear it straight from the source," he says, relenting. "I bet Dad was excited about the possibility."

She can't tell whether he's kidding or not, and she doesn't bother to ask. "Have you talked to him?"

"Not today."

A ship's officer walks past, and Greta returns his crisp nod before shifting to face the wall. "Did you know?" she says to her brother. "About the ashes?"

"He brought them?" he asks, surprised.

"Not all of them."

"Good, because the girls want to spread some in our garden."

Greta frowns. "Isn't that a little morbid?"

"They're ashes. Of course it's morbid. All of this is. Where did you spread the rest of them?"

"On a glacier."

He whistles. "Wow. She would've loved that."

"I know," Greta agrees, her throat suddenly thick.

"How was it?"

"Hard," she says. "Really hard."

"I bet." Asher's voice is so soft it makes her want to cry. "I wish I'd been there. But it's better that you were."

"What does that mean?"

"You know what it means," he says, and she does. They both do. They've just never said it out loud before. Helen didn't play favorites the way Conrad did; her affection for Asher was never in doubt, her love for both of her children a seemingly infinite resource. But everyone knew the bond she had with Greta was special.

"Thanks, Ash," she says quietly.

"For what?"

"I don't even know."

"World's best brother?"

She smiles. "Something like that."

When Greta returns to the casino, Ben is at the roulette table. As she walks up, he pushes a small pile of chips onto number 12.

"Your birthday?" she asks, and he shakes his head. "One of your daughters' birthdays?"

The dealer spins the wheel, and they both watch the ball bounce around madly. It lands on 00. Everyone at the table groans.

"Jack London's," Ben says sheepishly as they cash in their remaining chips and get up from the table. Around them, the slot machines are dinging and beeping, and a cheer goes up as someone makes their point at craps.

"What is it with you and that guy?" Greta asks, amused.

Ben shrugs. "He's an incredible writer."

"I mean, I realize *Call of the Wild* is a big deal and all, but it can't be *that* good."

He stops and turns to her. "Wait. You haven't read it?"

She shakes her head, and his mouth falls open. It's like she's told him she killed someone.

"Seriously?"

"Seriously."

"But you raised your hand," he says, wide-eyed. "At my lecture."

"Oh," she says. "Yeah. Sorry. I lied."

He looks utterly scandalized. "Why would you lie about something like that?"

"I think I once saw the movie and figured that was enough. Besides, I know the basics: the gold rush, and Alaska, and the wolf, and—"

"The wolf?" he asks, indignant. "You think Buck was a wolf?"

"Wasn't he?"

Ben looks like his head is about to explode. "He was a *sled dog.* That's, like, the whole point of the book," he sputters. "How can you not— It's one of the foremost— I mean, every kid should have to—" He stops and shakes his head. "It's a classic!"

Greta holds up her hands. "Okay, okay. I'll give it a read."

"Great," he says, suddenly businesslike. "I have an extra copy in my room, in case of emergency. Should we go get it now?"

"I appreciate your enthusiasm, but I don't think this qualifies as an emergency."

"Fine," he says, still looking determined. "You can read it in the morning and then I'll buy you a drink tomorrow night and you can give me a full report."

She holds up her empty glass, rattling the ice. "The drinks are free, remember?"

"I remember," he says, his eyes shining as he takes it from her. "But I'll buy you one anyway."

They get refills at the bar, then leave the noise of the casino behind, making their way unsteadily down the starboard passageway. At the piano bar, they pause to peek inside. There's an old white guy with gray hair joyfully plunking out a Billy Joel song, and Eleanor Bloom is perched on top of the piano with a microphone, her eyes closed as she belts out the words. She's almost completely out of tune, but she's singing with enough gusto that it doesn't seem to matter. Todd lifts a glass in her direction, a little red-faced, and Davis roars with laughter. Mary and Conrad are behind them at the bar, swaying in time with the music.

"Let's get out of here," Greta says, because it's all a bit too much right now, and so they scoot past the entrance, their drinks sloshing in their clear plastic cups.

Farther down the corridor, the sound of a saxophone drifts from the jazz bar, rich and full and thrilling, and without thinking about it, Greta finds herself leading them inside.

"Is this where you played before?" Ben whispers as they find a spot in the back.

Greta nods, her eyes drifting to the guitars above the stage. Underneath them, the jazz trio—which consists of keys, sax, and drums—moves seamlessly from one tune to the next, the crowd clapping their hands and tapping their feet. The music is lively and unpredictable, and Greta closes her eyes and lets it course through her, wishing for a second that she were up there too. But for now, it's enough to listen.

After a few minutes, she takes a step back, then another, then turns and heads out into the hallway, the music still pulsing through her. Ben follows her down the dimly lit corridor with a dreamy smile.

"I don't know why I never go see live music," he says. "It's so exhilarating. Is that what it's like when you play? Because I'd love to see you sometime."

He sounds so earnest, so unassuming, that Greta's not really thinking when she says, "All you have to do is buy a ticket."

"I think I will," he says, and she stops walking and spins to face him. He's not smiling anymore. In fact, he looks surprisingly serious. "I've always wanted to go to Gov Ball."

She stares at him. "Seriously?"

"No," he says with a sheepish grin. "I didn't even know what it was until tonight. But I *would* like to be there. If it's not too—"

"No," she says quickly. "It's not too . . ." But her heart is beating fast, and she addresses this next part to the floor: "Actually, I don't know."

"You don't know what?"

"It's just—there's a lot at stake."

"And I make you nervous?"

This is clearly meant to be a joke. It's meant to sound preposterous. But Greta nods. "Sort of," she says, though when she tries to imagine what it would be like to see his face in the crowd, she feels more reassured than anything. It's the rest of it that makes her nervous.

Ben looks amused now, maybe even a little pleased. "Another time then, maybe."

"Another time," she agrees.

He takes her hand, and they continue down the hall, winding

along the edge of the ship. Outside, it's fully dark now, and all she can see in the windows is their reflection, Ben in his sports coat and Greta in her dress. She pauses for a second to look at the blurry image, but then Ben steps forward and cups his hands against the glass.

"Wow," he says, and Greta does the same, peering out at the wash of stars, glinting above the darkened water. He turns to her, just slightly, and puts a hand on her hip, and she takes a handful of his shirt and pulls him closer. When they kiss, it's long and slow and hungry, the two of them leaning there against the cool of the window, pressed up against the world, and it isn't until someone lets out a whistle that they break apart again.

"Steamy," says the old lady with a mischievous grin, and when Greta glances back at the glass, sure enough it is.

Eventually, they end up at the ship's only real nightclub, a black box of a bar that's pulsing with pink and purple lights and playing mostly disco music. There are a few intrepid couples on the dance floor, none of them younger than sixty, including one duo that's somehow managing to execute proper ballroom moves to "I Will Survive." When the next song comes on, they're joined by two men she recognizes from the other night's ill-fated musical; they gaze deeply into each other's eyes as they sway, arms around each other.

Ben's shoulder is pressed against Greta's on the velvet banquette, and his breath smells like cherries from the cocktail he ordered. She's busy studying his profile, the way his head bobs to the beat of the music, when he turns to her.

"What?" he asks with a little frown. "Why are you looking at me like that?"

"I was just thinking that my mom would've loved you."

"I've always been extremely popular with moms," he jokes, but she can tell he's happy.

"She read your book, you know."

His face brightens. "She did?"

"Mary told me at your lecture. They were in a book club together."

"Did she like it?"

Greta smiles. "Apparently, she did."

"Isn't it funny, the way you make a thing and put it out into the world and then it drifts so much farther than you ever could've imagined?" he says. "Like a lost balloon."

"Or a message in a bottle," Greta says. "Since the whole point is to let it go."

Ben leans away, just slightly, but enough so that there's now a space between their shoulders. "I've never been very good at that part," he admits, his face troubled beneath the speckled light of the disco ball.

"It gets easier," Greta says. "You'll see when you finish your next book, and you start—"

"We're supposed to have a talk when I get back."

"Who?" she asks, though she already knows.

He downs the rest of his drink. "I don't know what to do. Sometimes I think it doesn't matter whether or not I still love her. That there are more important reasons to stay. Not just the kids, but there's so much history there. And it's hard to close the book on that, you know? But other times . . ." He looks over at her, his eyes pleading. "I don't know. It's like I want to take this last week and bottle it up so I can remember how it feels in case I ever start to lose my nerve."

When he looks at her, Greta isn't sure what to say. What she's thinking is: *Of course he'll go back. He has a wife and kids and a mortgage.* She can picture his life at home: the yard full of plastic toys and the basement with pipes that burst in the winter. The PTA meetings at the elementary school and the group of friends they make plans with every month, promising themselves they'll try that new place in the city but ultimately settling for their usual spot in the suburbs because one of the kids has a sore throat and it's been a busy week and it's easier that way. He probably has a lawnmower. And a grill. And a special voice he uses when reading bedtime stories. He has a whole world.

It's not easy to turn such a big ship.

A new song comes on, slower this time, and around them, several couples wobble to their feet. After a moment, Ben stands too. "I think we should dance," he says, holding out a hand, and then he leads her solemnly out onto the floor and pulls her close.

Greta can't remember the last time she danced like this. It was probably with Jason at Asher's wedding, the two of them leaving enough space to maintain the illusion that this was just a neighborly friendship, even as he slipped the key to his hotel room into her hand. But this is different. She wants to think it's corny, her cheek pressed against his chest, his hands knotted against the small of her back, but she can't muster any kind of cynicism right now.

"Can I tell you something?" Ben says, leaning back to look at her, his eyes searching hers. "It's not just because of his writing."

"What?" she asks, confused.

"The reason I'm so inspired by Jack London. It's because he lived this great big life."

The song ends, and the DJ puts on something faster, and the dance floor begins to empty again. Greta stops moving, and Ben does too, their arms still around each other. They just stand there under the swirling lights.

"He wasn't only a writer," Ben says with an odd sort of urgency. "He was a sailor, an explorer, a boxer, an oyster pirate, an activist. He went up to the Klondike when he was only twenty-one to seek his fortune, which sounds so wild and romantic, but in the end it was writing that really did it for him. He was this gutsy, intrepid adventurer, you know? But he was also just a guy with a pen."

Greta watches the lights flicker across his face. He lowers his arms and takes a step back. Above them, a disco ball twirls, bathing the room in silver.

"I mean, look around," he says, and she does: at the last few swaying couples, the people at the bar, the man falling asleep in the corner. "How many people really live? Like, really and truly do something big with their lives?" His eyes find Greta's again, and there's an intensity to them she hasn't seen before. "I have a good life. But until recently, it's been a small one too. And mostly I'm okay with that. But every once in a while, I look around and it sort of cracks me over the head. How contained it all is. How safe. And it makes me realize how few risks I've taken." He reaches for her hands, both of them. When he speaks again, his voice is determined. "I want to take more risks. I want to make it count."

She doesn't know if he's talking about this night. Or this moment. Or something altogether bigger. But either way, she understands.

Either way, she wants to make it count too.

# THURSDAY

## Chapter Twenty-Eight

Sometime in the night, Greta must've agreed to go on some sort of excursion with Ben this morning. She has absolutely no memory of this, but nevertheless she wakes to find him standing over the bed in a green hooded sweatshirt that says SAVE THE WHALES, looking entirely too enthusiastic for seven A.M.

"Hey." He nudges her shoulder. "We've got fifteen minutes."

She yawns. "What's happening now?"

"Whale watching," he says, beaming, but then his smile slips. "You didn't forget, did you?"

"Can you forget something you don't remember knowing in the first place?"

He sits on the edge of the bed and leans over her, smelling of mint toothpaste. "Trust me, we're going to have a whale of a time," he says. Then—even as she rolls her eyes at him—he kisses her on the nose.

Looking out the window, she can see that the ship has docked flush up against a huge wooden pier, beyond which there's nothing but forest, everything green and thick and wooded. A seagull flies low past the veranda, and they can hear laughter from the people next door.

"Where are we again?" Greta asks, rolling onto her stomach. Her head is pounding, her mouth full of cotton. "And how much did we drink last night?"

"Icy Strait Point," Ben says as he stands and walks over to the dresser. "And a lot."

When he turns around again, he's holding a small worn paperback. He hands it over carefully, almost reverently, and she sees that it's an old copy of *The Call of the Wild,* the spine cracked, the pages foxed and yellow.

"I thought you said you had a spare."

He shrugs. "I have plenty of others."

"Yeah, but this one . . ." She looks up at him. "It must be worth something."

"Only to me," he says with a smile. "It was my first ever copy."

She stares down at the cover, a faded illustration of two dogs locked in battle. *A classic story of the frozen North,* it says.

"Ben, I can't take this."

"It's just a loan," he insists. "But that copy—it's magic. It changed my whole life."

"It's too important," she says, trying to hand it back to him.

But he only smiles. "I trust you with important things."

A few minutes later, she has it tucked under her arm as she sneaks out into the hallway in a pair of Ben's sweatpants and an oversized Dave Matthews Band hoodie. She pauses to check her phone. Six new messages from Howie. Her heart sinks a little further with each one.

If you want to go along with this, I need a quote ASAP.
I'm happy to write it for you.
Something vague, maybe?
Or we can shut the whole thing down.
Let me know what you want to do.
Like, now.

She turns the phone off again and hurries down the hall. To her relief, the only people she passes—a group with matching family reunion shirts—are too busy arguing to notice her. It isn't until she reaches the elevators that her luck runs out. Of all people, her dad is there, waiting with a newspaper tucked under his arm. Greta briefly considers darting away, but it's too late. He glances over, raising his eyebrows at her disheveled appearance: wild hair, bare feet, heels dangling from one hand.

"I'm going whale watching," she announces, because her brain is still too fuzzy to come up with anything better.

"In that?" he asks with an entirely straight face.

She steps up beside him, and they both turn to the elevator doors, hands clasped behind their backs in the exact same way. Above them, something soft and classical plays from the speaker, and Greta lifts her eyes to the ceiling, trying to come up with something else to say.

"I'm sorry I forgot your anniversary," she tells him eventually, and he looks over at her in surprise. "It's weird. Sometimes all I can do is think about her. And sometimes it hurts too much."

His voice, when he speaks, is like sandpaper. "Me too."

The elevator dings, the doors sliding open in front of them. It's empty, but neither of them moves to get on. After a moment, the doors shut again.

Somehow, they're still standing there. Together.

"She kept a picture of Glacier Bay taped to the fridge," he says without looking at her. "Every morning, when she went to get the milk for our tea, she'd smile and say, 'That looks just like heaven.'" He turns his watery green eyes to Greta. "I have no idea how to do this without her."

Before she can say anything, the doors open again, and this time, a family in swim gear is waiting on the other side, two moms with three kids, the toddler in the midst of a tantrum, red-faced and furious. All five of them shift to the side in a cloud of tears and sunscreen, leaving room for two more. But Conrad is still watching Greta, and Greta is still watching Conrad.

She's about to let this one go too—not yet ready for the conversation to be over—when he looks between her and the elevator, his face flickering with indecision. Finally he gives his head a shake, and then, just like that, he turns and walks off down the hall without saying a word.

"Totally understandable," says one of the moms with a grin. The other one catches the door before it closes, so Greta steps on.

When she arrives at the meeting spot outside on the pier, Ben is already there. He's wearing jeans and sneakers and a puffy vest over his hoodie, and his eyes are shielded by the brim of a navy Columbia cap. There's a moment before he sees her where she stands there watching him, and it's a little dizzying, honestly, to feel her rib cage expand like that, to feel every inch of her heart inside it.

"What?" he asks, as she walks over and fits herself under his arm.

"Nothing," she says.

The whale watching boat is bigger than the one she took yesterday, and she and Ben file aboard behind people with serious binoculars and even more serious cameras. Most of them huddle inside; the morning is chilly, and it'll be a while before they're far enough out to see any whales. But Greta and Ben head straight for the top deck anyway, their eyes already stinging from the wind.

They stand near the rail as the boat peels away from the dock, watching the cruise ship recede, their gloved hands wrapped around the metal railing. As they get farther out from the shore, they can see the whole of Icy Strait Point, a small collection of red wooden buildings on stilts and a rocky beach, all tucked beneath the cascading evergreens.

The tinny voice of a guide greets them through the speakers positioned around the boat. He walks them through the safety instructions, interrupting himself to point out a family of otters floating on their backs. Greta squints but can't make out the shapes. Ben nudges her with his elbow and hands over a pair of binoculars.

"You're so prepared," she says, peering out at the sunbathing otters.

"I was a Boy Scout."

"Of course you were." She hands them back. "Have you ever seen one before?"

"A whale? Not up close." He looks a little wistful. "I really hope we do. They seem impossible, don't they? Something that big. That ancient. There's something almost holy about them."

Greta turns to face him. "How are you having trouble writing about Melville? You clearly love this stuff."

"Well, it wasn't all whales with him."

"Want to know what I think?"

"Do I have a choice?"

"I think you're afraid to move on," she says. "You had a good thing going with Jack. He's what you've always known. So it's daunting now, the idea of figuring out someone new."

"Are we still talking about dead authors or is this a metaphor?"

She laughs. "You're the writer."

"I think I prefer subtext," he says with a grin as a few people in brightly colored jackets begin to emerge from down below, clanging up the metal staircase.

They sail deeper into the wilderness, the tiny speck of Icy Strait Point getting more and more distant in their wake. Everything in Alaska feels like the middle of nowhere, but they're especially isolated now. The guide comes over the loudspeaker to point out a bald eagle overhead, and Greta can see the flash of brown and the white head. Ben hands over the binoculars again, and it takes her a minute to find the enormous bird as it slices through the sky.

"Okay, folks," the guide says over the loudspeaker as the engine sputters off and the ship bobs like a cork in the sudden quiet.

"We got word there was a pod here this morning, so we're gonna hang out for a while and see if they feel like saying hello."

Greta leans against the cold railing, her eyes raking the water. Ben wraps his arms around her, and she's grateful for the warmth, and for the weight of his chin on her shoulder.

"Sometimes it just takes time," the guide says over the speaker, and so they wait, everyone on the boat unnaturally quiet, everything around it too. It feels like they're all holding their breath, like someone has hit pause on the world.

And then, just like that, there's a break in the water.

From a distance, it could almost be anything. Just a dark smudge amid all that blue. A dorsal fin, moving in a slow, graceful arc as a humpback whale breaks the surface before disappearing again.

Greta surprises even herself by letting out a cry of delight. Around her, others exclaim too. Cameras shutter and click and beep. And everyone from the other side of the boat rushes over, eyes on the water, hoping for another glimpse.

"Did you see it?" Ben whispers excitedly, moving to stand beside her at the rail. Greta nods but can't bring herself to talk. She's too busy keeping watch.

The entire boat is silent again.

They wait. And wait.

Finally, there's another slight disruption in all that blue, and then a faint spray from the blowhole. But nothing else.

Greta's eyes start to water. She's afraid to blink.

When the humpback surfaces again, there's nothing subtle about it. The whale comes bursting out of the water, tall and straight as a torpedo, its body sleek and powerful, and Greta watches in astonishment as it does the world's most dramatic belly flop, sending up an explosion of white. Everyone is gasping and cheering like it was a show put on just for them, a feat of athleticism or an especially impressive magic trick.

*A classic story of the frozen North,* Greta thinks, looking out at the place where it disappeared.

They spot the whale only one more time before they move on. A flash of tail so perfect that it almost seems cartoonish. It's rare to see something in real life that actually matches up with all the many imitations you've seen, Greta thinks. It's rare to get that chance, to watch a whale's tail disappear into the peaceful water in a place like this, the sky like a deep blue bowl set down above them, the mountains and trees as soft and blurred as watercolors around the edges of it.

She and Ben look at each other, but neither says anything, and she knows that he's moved by it too, that whatever happened out here was almost too big for words.

She takes his gloved hand and gives it a squeeze.

On the way back, they pause once more for another pair of whales, who mostly just float, their enormous backs cresting every now and then. But it's nothing compared to that first one.

As the boat picks up speed, Greta watches the churning wake. They're once again alone on the upper deck, and though her fingers are frozen and her nose is running, she doesn't yet feel ready to go inside, to break the spell. She leans into Ben, and under her breath, so quietly she's not even sure he can hear, not even sure she wants him to, she begins to sing.

*"Baby beluga in the deep blue sea . . ."*

It's not the jaunty version, the one children sing. It's slower and softer than that, something entirely new, something she's halfway making up as she goes, and it's almost haunting, the way it mixes with the wind.

*"Swim so wild and you swim so free . . ."*

Greta closes her eyes.

*"Heaven above and the sea below . . ."*

Ben's head is cocked as he listens.

*"And a little white whale on the go."*

When she's finished, she opens her eyes again, and Ben leans forward, resting his elbows on the rail. Beneath them, the boat sways.

"I sing that to my girls sometimes," he says.

She nods. "My mom used to sing it to me."

"It's beautiful," he tells her, "the way you did it."

They're still far from shore. Everything out here feels untouched and pristine, clean and uncomplicated. She turns to face him, her heart quickening.

"My dad asked me to come back," she says. "Just before my mom died."

He looks at her but doesn't say anything.

"She'd been having these headaches, and he was worried. I was in Germany for a show I'd been looking forward to." She closes her eyes. "We've always had this way of hurting each other, of pretending we don't care what the other thinks. I figured he was trying to make me feel guilty because I was so far away."

Ben looks stricken. "You couldn't have known what would happen."

"Maybe not. But I could've been there."

"It wouldn't have changed anything."

"No," she says, her heart like a weight in her chest. "But at least I would've gotten to say goodbye."

His eyes are full of sympathy. "I'm sure she knew how you felt."

Greta thinks of the last text exchange she'd had with her mom, which was—of course—completely ordinary. At work, Helen had run into the music teacher, who had gushed about Greta.

I offered you up for the winter recital, Helen had written, and Greta could so clearly picture the face she'd be making, that gleeful, slightly devilish look she got whenever she teased her daughter. It'll just be you and a couple dozen first graders. I figured you'd be fine with it.

Sounds delightful, Greta had responded. Wish I could.

Helen's reply was quick: I bet!

Greta had typed the next part without really thinking. It was late in Berlin, and Luke was already asleep beside her and she had to be up early the next day for sound check. Thanks for thinking of me, she wrote, and then she switched off her phone. It wasn't until she turned it on again the next morning that the response came through.

I'm always thinking of you.

Hours later, while Greta was onstage in front of thousands of fans, something ruptured deep inside her mother's brain, sending her into a coma.

And that was it.

The end of the only conversation that had ever really mattered to her.

On the boat, they're both quiet for a long time, Greta and Ben, their eyes fixed on the blue-gray water.

"I've never told anyone that," she says eventually, and he puts an arm around her shoulders.

"Thanks for telling me."

She nods. "I trust you with important things."

## Chapter Twenty-Nine

They're not quite to shore when Greta's phone starts buzzing again. She slips it out of her jacket pocket and scrolls through her messages. It's been only a couple hours, but there are a lot of them, still mostly about Luke: a flurry of interview requests and messages from friends. But it all feels so far away right now, out on the water, silly and insignificant.

She glances over at Ben, who is looking at his own phone with an unreadable expression. "I missed five calls from Emily."

"Who?"

"My wife," he says, then grimaces. "My ex-wife. I'm just gonna . . ."

"Of course," Greta says as he brings the phone to his ear, his jaw set and his face suddenly businesslike. But after a second, he shakes his head.

"My service cut out again."

"Want to use mine?"

"No, that's okay," he says, looking off toward the spit of beach, with its huddle of red buildings, which they're fast approaching, the boat tipping up and down over the chop. "I'll try again in a few minutes."

"Hey," she says, turning to him as the pier comes into sight and the boat begins to slow. "I changed my mind."

"About what?"

"Gov Ball."

He frowns at her. "You're not doing it?"

"No," she says, taking a deep breath. "I am. I'm definitely doing it."

"Good," he says with a small smile. "That's really good."

"And I'd like you to come."

He looks surprised. "Yeah?"

"Yeah."

"I thought I made you nervous."

She laughs. "You do."

"But?"

"You also make me calm," she says, and he pulls her close. Even before she says this next part, there's a piece of her that can't believe she's saying it at all. "You make me . . ."

"What?" he asks with a grin, like he already knows what she's going to say.

"Happy."

When he kisses her, his lips taste of salt. "Are you going to play that song?"

"What, 'Baby Beluga'?"

He laughs. "The one from the video."

" 'Astronomy,' " she says, and even just the word sends a ripple of anxiety through her. "I doubt it. They want me to focus on the new album. It's a safer bet."

Ben raises his eyebrows.

"What?"

"You don't strike me as someone who goes in for safe bets," he says, and Greta wishes she could be as sure as he sounds.

On the dock, people are waiting in line for the next tour. Below them, there are children playing on the beach, tossing rocks into the water and squealing when the surf comes up too high, their laughter carried by the wind.

The boat bumps up against the wooden pier with a thud, and Greta and Ben make their way down from the top deck, nodding at the crew as they pass through the interior and back out into the sunshine. A little boy looks up at them urgently as they weave through the assembled crowd.

"Did you see any?" he asks, shuffling around in his excitement.

"A few," Greta says. "You'll have to say hi to them for us."

He frowns at her. "Whales don't talk."

"No, but they wave," she tells him with a grin.

At the end of the dock, there's a sprawling red building filled with gift shops and restaurants. Ben tries his phone again as they walk inside, their eyes adjusting to the light beneath the lofty wood-beamed ceiling. Near the entrance, a small cannery museum is set up, and Greta wanders over to look at the huge cast-iron structures, which were apparently once used to cut and clean the fish before stuffing them into cans.

She turns around, ready to make a joke to Ben—something about close quarters and sardines; she hasn't quite gotten there yet—but she sees that he's still standing near the door, the phone pressed to his ear. From this distance, it's hard to read his face. The barnlike building is filled with noise and chatter, and between them, people crisscross the wooden floors, carrying bags from the gift shops or eating crab cakes out of paper boats. Still, she can tell by the hunch of his shoulders that something is wrong.

As she watches, he lowers the phone and looks around. When his eyes find hers, there's something wild about them. He hurries over to where she's still standing beside the canning machine.

She doesn't ask if everything is okay. She already knows it's not.

"Hannah broke her arm," he says, his voice cracking. "It's really bad."

Greta swallows. "What happened?"

"She fell at the playground. They're at the hospital now." He glances around, his gaze unfocused as he takes in the odd collection of fish-related contraptions. "I don't know what to do. She must be so scared." He blinks a few times, his eyes glassy. "I can't believe I'm not there right now. I can't believe I'm not home."

Greta isn't sure what to say. Everything that occurs to her feels woefully inadequate: *I'm sorry* and *That's awful* and *I hope she'll be okay.*

She says it anyway: "I'm so sorry."

But Ben is distracted now, looking at something on his phone, rubbing the back of his neck with his other hand. It's a gesture she hasn't seen before, maybe something he does when he's upset or worried or both, and as she watches him, Greta is suddenly aware of how little they actually know each other. At the end of the day, they're just two strangers who've spent less than a week together in a place that's about as far from their real lives as it's possible to get.

Her heart is thudding for reasons she can't quite explain.

"I should go," Ben says, snapping his head up.

Greta nods. "Right. Sure. I'll go back with you."

For a split second, he looks bewildered by her response. But then he shakes his head. "No," he says. "I meant . . . home. I should go home. I should be there with her."

She stares at him, feeling like she's misread something important, like she'd accidentally gone straight to sympathy on some invisible continuum, when perhaps the situation warranted something more serious. "She's going to be okay, right?" she asks, and a flicker of impatience passes over Ben's face.

"I don't know," he says tersely. "That's the whole point of going there."

"Yeah, but a broken arm isn't"—she fumbles for the right word—"*serious* serious. Right?"

"They heard the bone snap," he says. "That's . . . serious. She might need surgery. Anesthesia . . . that's definitely serious."

Greta looks around, still trying to recalibrate. "How would you even— I mean, we're in the middle of nowhere and—"

"I don't know yet," he says. "I have to go figure it out."

"We'll be in Vancouver in less than forty-eight hours," Greta says. "By the time you find another way back—"

"I can't just sit here in the middle of Alaska and drink beers with you while my daughter is in the hospital."

She reels back. "That's not what I'm saying. I meant—"

"You wouldn't understand," he says as he starts for the door.

Outside, the sky is still a hard, clean blue. Greta follows him up the wooden boardwalk that leads back to their ship, which is docked on the other side of a small peninsula, hidden behind an outcropping of spruce trees.

"Wait a second," she says, half-trotting to keep up as he walks straight through someone's family photo, charging ahead, each footstep loud on the wooden planks.

"I can't wait a second," he says, spinning around. "You don't get it because you're not—"

He stops himself, but they both know what he was about to say.

*You're not a parent.*

It's only a fact. And not even an unpleasant one to Greta. At least most days. Still, something about the way he says it stings, and she has to work to compose her face to disguise this.

"I'm sorry," Ben says. "But this is the part where you drop everything to be there."

Greta stares at him, stricken. It takes a few beats for him to realize what he's said. When he does, his face goes slack.

"I didn't mean . . ." he begins, but he doesn't seem sure where to go from there. "I wasn't talking about what happened with . . ." He stops again and shakes his head, flustered now. "I'm sorry," he says finally. "But I really have to go."

"It's fine," Greta says, because what else is there to say at this point?

"I wish . . ." He falters, then tries again: "I wish it didn't have to end this way."

The word *end* lands with a thud between them, and Ben looks as if he's trying to decide whether or not he should take it back.

"I really hope your daughter's okay," Greta says, and to her surprise, he reaches for her hand. There's something automatic about it, the way they fit, and she thinks how strange it is that they woke up together this morning, and how empty it will feel without him tomorrow.

"Thank you," he says, and then—just like that—he turns and walks off toward the ship.

Later, sitting on the cold sand, Greta does a search on her phone: there's a flight from the nearby town of Hoonah straight to Juneau, and from there, a red-eye to New York. All afternoon, as the sun slides across the sky, and the tourists move in and out like the tide all around her, she tries to picture where he might be at that moment, imagines him sitting in a taxi, then waiting at an airport, then flying across the barren landscape, doing everything he can to get home.

# FRIDAY

## Chapter Thirty

The last day at sea is cold and gray. The wind has fallen flat, making everything eerily still, and a low-hanging fog sits atop the water so that it almost feels like they're sailing straight into a cloud. Looking out the rain-specked window from a reclining chair in the Crow's Nest lounge, Greta thinks of ghost ships, of pirate ships, of all the ships that have come before, sailing these waters when they were still uncharted. She wonders if Jack London might've been on one of them, or if he made it up here some other way. She wishes she'd asked Ben.

Tomorrow, they'll be back in Vancouver before dawn. But today, there's only this: water and mountains and sky. Gray on gray on gray.

She has no idea how long she's been there when her dad walks up, glass in hand, and sits down in the chair beside her. He's wearing a fleece vest with the logo of the cruise ship on it, and his cheeks are a little ruddy.

"Let me guess," he says. "You're here for the Macarena."

"What?" Greta asks wearily, and he nods over his shoulder, where a group of people have started to gather for a lesson on the small dance floor in front of the bar.

"It's your big chance to learn all the moves."

She glances over at him. "Please tell me that's not why *you're* here."

"No, I was looking for you."

"Why?"

"Do I need a reason? It's our last day. I thought we should spend some time together."

Greta gives him a skeptical look.

"Fine," he says. "It was Asher's idea."

It's almost enough to make her laugh. But not quite. "I'm probably not the best company right now," she tells him.

He gives her a once-over, taking in the leggings and sweatshirt and lack of makeup, the messy knot of her hair and the way her knees are drawn up to her chest. "Rough night?"

"Something like that," she says, returning her gaze to the window.

"How was whale watching?"

There's a hitch in her chest as yesterday comes back to her: the sound of the wind and the taste of the salt, the sheer size of the whales as they broke the surface of the water, and the splash as they came down again. And, of course, Ben: his arms around her, his beard rough against her cheek, the sound of his delighted laughter as that giant tail disappeared into the water.

"It was amazing," she says truthfully.

"You saw some?"

"A few," she says. "How about you?"

"We went bear watching. Only spotted one, but it was worth it. He was huge."

"Almost as big as Davis," says a voice behind them, and Greta feels two hands on her shoulders. Mary leans over and gives her a feather-light kiss on the top of her head. "Hi, sweetie."

For some reason, this makes her feel like crying. "Hi."

"Where's your fella?" Mary asks, walking around the chairs to face them, silhouetted against the window.

"Good question," Conrad says. "Shouldn't you be at his lecture?"

Greta had forgotten that Ben was due to give another talk today. She wonders if the cruise director replaced him with someone, or whether the auditorium is empty right now. Thinking about him onstage in that tweed jacket sends a zip of nervous electricity through her, and she glances down at her phone almost involuntarily.

All night, she'd wanted to text him, but she hadn't. Because what was there to say, really?

Even so, she'd been disappointed to wake up this morning and find no message from him. Not even a simple update. She debated reaching out to ask how Hannah was doing, only she wasn't sure about the etiquette in a situation like this. Would it be intrusive to check in? Was it rude not to? She even considered calling the local hospital in the hope of getting an answer without having to be in touch with Ben at all, then decided that was veering alarmingly close to stalker territory. Probably they couldn't tell her anyway. So she'd done nothing. And now it's been twenty-four hours since he left, and not a word.

She turns the phone over in her lap.

"He had to leave," she tells them. "Family emergency."

"What do you mean, leave?" Conrad asks. "We're at sea."

"He went from port yesterday."

"But how—"

"I don't know, but I'm sure he figured it out."

"Well, that's too bad," Mary says. Something about the look on Greta's face must be enough to warn her from asking anything more, because she's quick to move on. "Hey, I bet this will cheer you up. Davis and I decided to do a medley for the variety show tonight."

Greta raises her eyebrows. "A medley of what?"

"I don't know," she says with a laugh. "He's in the piano bar trying to figure it out as we speak. You'll be there, won't you?"

"Wouldn't miss it."

"And listen, don't shoot the messenger, but I promised Eleanor I'd check one more time to see if you want to—"

"No," Greta says flatly, aware that she sounds like a petulant teenager. But she doesn't know how many more times she can say it. "Please tell her in the nicest way possible that I *still* have no interest in performing at a cheesy cruise ship variety show." She pauses. "No offense."

"None taken," Mary says. "But you should know the reason she's been pushing so hard is that your mom promised we could all come see one of your shows this summer."

Greta's caught off guard by this. "She did?"

"She was always telling us how great they were. How they made her feel like she was twenty-one again." Mary smiles wistfully. "We were going to plan a girls' trip to come see you play on tour. And now that she's gone . . ."

She doesn't finish the sentence. She doesn't have to.

"I suspect," she says after a moment, wiping her eyes with the sleeve of her shirt, "that Eleanor is thinking this might be the closest we get."

Greta reaches for Mary's hand and gives it a squeeze. "It won't be," she says. "I promise. Tell me when you want to come, and I'll take care of it."

"We'd love that," Mary says, looking down at her fondly. "Your mom would be so proud of you, you know that?"

Greta nods, but what she's thinking about is her sixth-grade talent show, when she got such cold feet that her mother had to come backstage. "Ah," she said when she saw Greta perched on an overturned recycling bin, miserably hugging her guitar. "I see the problem now."

"What?" Greta asked, lifting her head.

"You're not playing." She stooped down so that their eyes were

level. "You just need to play. Once you start, you'll be fine. I promise."

"How do you know?"

"Because," she said, giving Greta a kiss on the forehead, "that's
your superpower."

And she was right.

But now, for the first time in a long time, Greta is scared to play
again. And nobody is here to tell her it will be okay.

When Mary is gone, Greta and Conrad sit listening to the in-
structor call out directions for the Macarena—*Palms up, one then
the other!*—as the dancers dissolve into laughter, feet thumping
on the wooden floor. Out the window ahead of them, the fog is
starting to burn off, making everything sepia-toned in the afternoon light.

The threadbare copy of *The Call of the Wild* is sitting on the
table between them, and Conrad looks over at it with interest. He
picks it up and opens to the title page, where Ben's name is written in the neat blocky handwriting of a child. He glances over,
eyebrows raised, the significance of it becoming clearer. "Did he
leave this for you?"

"It's more of a loan."

"Which means you'll be seeing him again?"

Greta gives him a sideways glance. "I don't know, Dad."

"Well, for whatever it's worth—and I know it's not usually
worth a whole lot—I thought he seemed like a good guy." He
pauses, and Greta can almost see him biting back the phrase *for a
change*. To his credit, he doesn't say it. Instead, he taps the book
gently, then sets it back on the table. "With good taste."

"He is," she tells her father. "But he has a wife and kids."

Conrad's mouth falls open. "He does?"

"Well, he's separated. But that's still a lot of baggage."

"Everyone has baggage," he says. "Even you. Just because

yours is a different shape and size doesn't mean it's not heavy too."

Greta narrows her eyes at him. "When did you get so philosophical?"

"I think it's all this water," he says, turning back to the window. "It's getting to me."

"It's not just about . . . baggage," Greta says after a moment. "Our lives are so different. He's worried because his daughter might need surgery. I'm worried because—"

"You have to play the guitar this weekend."

Greta stiffens automatically, searching for the usual air of dismissal inside the words. But it doesn't seem to be there. So she nods.

Conrad considers this for a moment. "But that's what makes you happy."

"I mean, it will if it goes well," she says cautiously, still unsure where he's headed with this. She gives him a funny look. "Are you drunk right now or something?"

He laughs and shakes the ice in his glass. "It's after noon and I'm on the last day of a cruise I was supposed to be taking with my late wife to celebrate our anniversary. Of course I'm drunk. But I'm still allowed to have a chat with my daughter, aren't I?"

"I guess," she says flatly. "It's just . . . kind of weird."

"Asher told me you've been having a hard time," he admits. "That's why he thought this trip would be a good idea."

Greta frowns. "For who?"

"For you," he says as if this should be obvious. "He thought it might help if you came along."

"Right," she says. "Help *you*."

Conrad looks confused. "No, help *you*. Why would it be to help me?"

"Because you were supposed to be here with Mom," Greta says, feeling like she's fallen into some sort of alternate reality. "It would've been too sad for you to come by yourself."

"I wouldn't have been alone," he says slowly, as if explaining something to a very small child. "I would've had the Fosters and the Blooms."

Greta throws up her hands. "That's what I said!"

"To who?"

"It's what I said to Asher when he asked me to come on this trip to keep you company."

"He told *you* to come here to help *me*?" Conrad asks, and Greta nods, relieved that they're finally on the same page. "And he told *me* that it would help *you*?"

"Pretty much."

Conrad sits with this a moment. "Wow."

"Yeah. He basically Parent Trapped us. On a boat."

"It's a ship."

"Oh my god. Who *cares*?" Greta says, tipping her head back with a groan. "Why is everyone so concerned about this? Are you worried I'm going to hurt the ship's feelings?" She searches for her phone. "What time is it anyway?"

Conrad checks his watch. "Twelve-thirty."

"Great," she says, looking around for a waiter. "Because I could really use a drink too."

When she turns around again, he's laughing at her.

"What?"

"Nothing," he says with a grin. "I just . . . I don't mind that he tricked us."

Later, Greta will give Asher all sorts of grief for this. She'll call him a puppet master. She'll tell him he owes her. But right at this moment, and much to her surprise, she has to admit that she doesn't mind either.

## Chapter Thirty-One

Before the variety show, they go for a drink at the Starboard Saloon, and Greta spots a stray pack of cards on one of the tables.

"Let's see what you got, Houdini," she says, sliding them over to Conrad as they sit down. He shakes the cards from the box, looking handsome and relaxed in his shirt and tie.

"It's been a while," he says as he begins to shuffle, but then he fans out the deck with businesslike precision, nodding at the cards in his hands. "Pick one."

She does. "Now what?"

"Now you give it back," he says. "But don't tell me what it is."

He's got this funny little half-smile on his face as he starts to shuffle again, like maybe he's enjoying himself. But then he loses it mid-bridge and the cards go flying everywhere. Greta slides off the chair to start picking them up, while Conrad sits there, surveying the mess.

"I think I'm too old for this."

"You're not," she says, lifting her head.

He studies his hands. "Well, I *feel* ancient."

Greta stops what she's doing. "This doesn't only have to be an ending, you know. It could be a new beginning too."

He shakes his head, his expression sober. "I don't want a new beginning."

"I'm afraid you don't have a choice," she says softly as she sweeps the cards from the floor. When she looks over again, his expression is vacant. He sets down the queen of hearts and stares at it for a while.

"We were in the middle of a puzzle," he says, and Greta sits back on her heels to listen. "It's been on the dining room table ever since. We hadn't done very much. It's a hard one. A thousand pieces. But now—now it's like I can't stand working on it without her, but I also can't bear to put it away."

Greta slides back into her chair. "Dad," she says, and her voice breaks on the word; all at once, it feels like more than that is breaking too. She thinks of the ice cleaving off the glacier, pictures something inside her falling away. "I should've come home."

"What?"

"When you called."

Something snaps into place behind his eyes. "You didn't know. No one did."

"I wish I would've been there." She rests her elbows on her knees, her forehead in her hands. "I'd give anything to go back and redo it. I'd give anything to rewind so I could get on the first plane out of there and make it home in time."

She's crying now, and Conrad—so unaccustomed to this, so out of practice—half-stands as if to comfort her. But then he sits down again, lowering his eyes. A waiter comes around with a bowl of peanuts, which he sets in the center of the card-strewn table, then leaves again in a hurry.

"I stayed," Greta says quietly, "so I could play the fucking guitar. Like that even matters."

Conrad shrugs. "It's what you do."

"What?" she says, bracing herself, waiting for him to say that what she does is choose her career over her family. What she does is choose her music over everything else.

But he doesn't. Instead he says, "You play the fucking guitar," and it's so unexpected, so uncharacteristic, that they both laugh in spite of themselves. "How many people get to do that for real?"

"Thanks," she says, which feels at once too small and too big. She wipes her eyes and lets out a long breath, then straightens the messy pile of cards and pushes the deck toward her dad.

"Here," she says. "Try again."

Later, they find Eleanor and Todd waiting outside the auditorium. He's wearing a tux and she's wearing a sparkly ball gown with a tiara-like hairpiece. It's the kind of ensemble that makes you want to roll your eyes, but you can't, because on Eleanor, it actually looks beautiful.

"Listen," Eleanor says from inside a cloud of perfume. "I had a word with Bobby."

Greta frowns. "Who's Bobby?"

Eleanor laughs, then realizes Greta is serious. "The cruise director," she says, clearly unable to fathom not being on a first-name basis with such an important figure by the final night. "He promised to save a slot for you. Just in case."

It's clear she's bracing herself for another no. So she looks surprised when, instead, Greta folds her into a hug.

"Is that a yes?" Eleanor asks, confused.

"It's still a no," Greta says. "But thank you for asking."

In the theater, they settle into seats near the front and listen to Bobby explain how things will go. Around her, everyone but Conrad is nervous; Davis plays an invisible piano with his fingers, Mary hums under her breath, and Eleanor and Todd keep tapping their feet.

"This was a terrible idea," Mary whispers to Greta as the first act—an eight-year-old kid nervously clutching a set of juggling balls—steps onto the stage.

The poor kid drops the balls a total of twelve times in three minutes, two of which could be chalked up to the swaying of the ship, the rest of which he just fumbled. But when he's done, the audience claps enthusiastically anyway, and beside her, Greta can feel Mary relax.

After that, there's a family of Irish step dancers, a sixty-something guy who lip-syncs to "We Didn't Start the Fire," and a magician, whom Conrad watches with a slightly judgmental frown.

"Amateur stuff," he mutters, but he looks riveted anyway.

Next up are a couple of Christian singers with ukuleles, followed by the old lady Greta has run into everywhere. She reads an original poem about feminism and the resistance that's so powerful and so full of curse words even Greta is blushing by the end. Greta applauds madly and swears she sees the woman wink at her as she leaves the stage.

"So much talent on one ship," Bobby says after pretty much every act. When it's their turn, Mary and Davis scoot out of their row and walk up to the stage, where they launch into a medley of songs from the sixties—everything from Marvin Gaye to the Beach Boys—that gets the whole place clapping along. It's been years since Greta has heard Davis play the piano, and Mary's voice is clear and strong. The whole time, they never take their eyes off each other.

Afterward, a comedian does a too-long bit about fishing, and an old man gives a dramatic reading from *Ulysses*. Then it's time for Eleanor and Todd, who glide around the stage to huge applause, so graceful it almost seems like they're floating, and Greta realizes she's actually enjoying herself at this stupid variety show on this stupid cruise ship.

Later, she's so busy whispering with Mary about the eighty-three-year-old identical twins who did a scene from *Much Ado About Nothing* that when Bobby introduces the next act, she almost misses the announcement. But then she sees Preeti climbing the steps, an acoustic guitar already strapped over her shoulder, and she goes very still.

There's no reason for her to be nervous. Preeti certainly doesn't look it. She walks straight to the center of the stage, where she stands behind the microphone, adjusting the guitar. The excitement radiating off her is almost palpable, and when she looks up, it's to beam out at the audience, all confidence and enthusiasm.

She takes the pick from between her teeth and leans close to the mic. "I'm going to play a song by one of my musical heroes," she says, her eyes raking the crowd. "It's called 'Birdsong.'"

Whether or not she expected this line to be met with applause, Greta doesn't know. But there's only silence, and a bubble of laughter in Greta's throat. Because it's her song, and nobody here knows it. Of course they don't. Even her own group has no clue. Conrad scratches his ear. Mary digs in her purse for a mint. Todd yawns once, then again.

Preeti plays the opening chords, and Greta doesn't know whether she's more flattered or anxious. Probably a bit of both. The song is old by now, the fourth track on her EP, her very first recording, and one that she rarely even plays herself anymore. It's more like a study of a song than a song itself; she was fiercely proud of it at the time, but she knows now that it's too self-consciously flashy, full of complicated riffs and tricky sequences. It's not a crowd pleaser, but it's a hell of a lot of fun to perform, and she feels a twinge of pride as she watches Preeti—her eyebrows knit and her tongue sticking out—tackle the first progression, and realizes she's having fun with it too.

"She's pretty good," Mary whispers, and all Greta can do is nod, unable to tear her eyes away. It's odd to see someone else take such simple pleasure in something you conjured out of thin air, and Greta's heart is lodged in her throat as she watches Preeti make her way across the too-thin tightrope of the song, her fingers moving fast on the strings, her head bent over the instrument.

It's not until the second verse that it starts to get away from her.

At first, it's just a wrong note.

She pauses. Readjusts. Plays a few chords, then pauses again, gears grinding.

It's strange to watch it happen in real time, to know exactly what it is the girl's heart is doing in her chest up there, to feel the sudden hollow where her nerve had only just been. It's one mistake, then another, and then—just like that—the hesitation has moved in like a fog, and it's hard to see past it. You start to overthink it, every piece of it, from the drilled-down elements of the song all the way to the energy in the room, which is falling flat all around you like the wind after a storm. And your fingers, which had just been flying, have now gone numb.

Preeti looks up. It's only for a moment, not long enough to focus on anything, but Greta knows exactly what she's looking for.

She's looking for help.

She's looking for *her*.

"Poor thing," says a woman behind her, and someone else murmurs in agreement. The whole audience has begun to fidget. There's nothing more uncomfortable than watching someone fail right in front of you. Greta understands this better than anyone.

She doesn't know what she plans to do when she stands up. She only knows she has to do something. Onstage, Preeti is completely frozen, and a stillness hangs over the auditorium, awkward and interminable.

Greta slides out of the row, ignoring the baffled looks from Conrad and Mary and the others, and the muffled grunt from the woman whose toe she steps on a bit farther down. As she hurries up the aisle, she pauses only to grab a ukulele straight off the lap of the man from the Christian duo. "Hey," he says, startled, but she doesn't stop. Instead, she bounds up the steps and makes her way across the stage to Preeti, who is standing wide-eyed and entirely motionless.

Greta's footsteps sound much too loud.

But not nearly as loud as her heart.

"You okay?" she asks when she gets there, putting a hand over the microphone, and Preeti manages a nod.

"Okay," Greta says, with more certainty than she feels. She glances out at the audience, a sea of people, each of them with a phone in their lap, hundreds of tiny cameras ready to capture this moment.

She swallows hard.

*Just play the fucking guitar,* she thinks.

The ukulele feels tiny in her hands, more toy than instrument, and there are fewer strings, but her fingers still find the right places. She glances over at Preeti, who looks close to tears. The room is still completely silent. Greta manages a grin.

"Let's do it," she says, and then she begins to play. The song sounds all wrong on the ukulele, too high-pitched and jangly, and there aren't enough strings to match the notes, though it doesn't matter because then Preeti joins in, picking up right where she left off, a little wobbly, a little stilted, and not nearly worthy of the applause that immediately starts up, but it's enough to get them through it, which is sometimes all that matters.

When they're done, the crowd gets to their feet, and Greta lets out a breath. Beside her, Preeti is laughing, her face slack from relief.

"Holy shit," she says, which pretty much sums it up.

Greta grabs her hand and they take a bow together, and then she steps back and motions to Preeti and the cheering intensifies as someone yells, "Encore!" and for some reason, it makes her feel like crying. But she doesn't. Instead, to her surprise, she finds herself saying, "One more?" and Preeti bobs her head and places her hands on the guitar again—carefully, carefully—and plays the opening notes to "Done and Done," and Greta laughs and joins in, and the audience stays on their feet, clapping along, and—impossibly, unexpectedly—it's pure joy, all of it.

Afterward, Preeti gives her a hug and says, "I owe you big-time," which is exactly what Greta had been thinking about her.

"I've been there too," she says. "You'll be better now that you've been through it."

"You think?"

Greta nods. "It's not supposed to be easy."

"Right," Preeti says. "It's supposed to be fun."

She grins and gives the girl one more hug, then returns the ukulele to the Christian singer—who is too impressed to be annoyed—and sidles back along the row to her seat, where she's greeted with a second standing ovation from Mary and Eleanor and Todd and Davis and even her dad. *Especially* her dad, who is smiling and shaking his head as she slides in next to him to watch the last few acts with a slightly sheepish grin.

Afterward, they all head to the piano bar to celebrate. Mary and Eleanor laugh over drinks, and Todd nods off in the corner, and Davis looks over the shoulder of the piano player with raised eyebrows.

"He's got nothing on you," Greta says when she joins him, and he roars with laughter and heads off to the bar to get the next round of drinks. The first of many.

At some point, Greta reaches for her phone to send Howie a text: Kill the story, okay? He writes back immediately: You got it.

And for the first time in a while, she thinks maybe she does.

When she looks up again, her dad is standing beside her. "What you did up there," he says, "was pretty amazing."

"I was only trying to help her out. She's a nice kid."

"I don't just mean that," he says, and the way he says it—so full of sincerity—makes Greta's throat go tight. "It was beautiful, what you played."

"I'm sorry yours wasn't." It isn't something she was planning to say, not at all. But there it is anyway. Conrad blinks a few times, looking as surprised as she is. She clears her throat and starts again: "I can't apologize for writing it. It was how I felt. But I *am* sorry I hurt you. And that it took me until now to say that."

He stares at her for what feels like a long time, so long she's convinced he might walk away. Instead, he says, "You were just being honest. You were being . . ."

"What?" she asks when he trails off.

"Look, we both know I tend to play things safe. Your mom wasn't like that. When she came back to my bar that night, nobody in her life thought it was a good idea. Things would've been a lot easier for her if she'd stuck with the other guy. But it turned out he wasn't her dream." He smiles. "I was."

Greta nods. "And she was yours."

"Right, but for me it was easy," he says. "Wanting to be with her? It was the easiest thing I've ever done. For her, it was more of a risk. She had to take a leap, a big one, but she wasn't afraid of that." He closes his eyes for a moment. "What I'm trying to say is that sometimes I forget how brave she could be. How fearless." When he opens them again, he looks right at Greta. "Just like you."

She stares at him, lost for words. "Thanks, Dad," she manages, blinking a few times, though she doesn't feel particularly fearless right now. In fact, it's the opposite. She's been too afraid to revisit "Astronomy" because it would mean revisiting not just the hope she'd been holding on to when she wrote the song but the grief that's now a necessary part of it too. Finishing it would mean saying goodbye. And she hasn't felt ready for that. So instead she's been hiding. But it's time to take her own kind of risk.

"You know how you could really thank me?" her dad is saying. "You could write me a new song. Maybe call it 'Oceanography.'"

Greta laughs, unsure what to make of this. "Why?"

"Because your mother's was called 'Astronomy,'" he explains, looking pleased with himself, "and oceanography is sort of the opposite of that. It's as far as you can get from the stars. But it's still interesting in its own way."

She doesn't know if he came up with this on the fly or whether he's been thinking about it for a while now. She's not sure it matters.

"To opposites," she says, clinking her glass against his, and even as he tips his head back to drink, she can see that he's smiling too.

Later, as she makes her way back to her tiny box of a room for the last time, Greta realizes she hasn't thought about Ben in hours. And maybe that's okay. They had a week, and now that week is over. Sometimes that's all you get. Maybe it was enough.

But when she unlocks the door, the first thing she sees is the book, right where she'd left it, in the middle of the bed. She sits down and picks it up, turning it over in her hands. Her brain is still hazy from the cocktails, her body still buzzing from the show. But when she opens it to the first page, she finds herself yielding to the words anyway, and by the time she closes it again, hours later, she can hear the attendants starting to collect the luggage in the hall, as beyond the walls of her room, the ship glides into the Port of Vancouver.

# SATURDAY

## Chapter Thirty-Two

Greta is on the observation deck, elbows on the railing, watching the city grow closer, when a text comes in from Ben.

She's okay, it says. No surgery.

That's all it says. But she's relieved to know.

I'm so glad, she writes back, and then she waits, watching the screen for a few seconds, hoping more of the little bubbles will appear. But they don't.

The air is chilly, and though it's only the beginning of June, it smells of fall, like leaves and wood smoke and damp. Greta stays there for another minute, soaking it all in, then slips the phone back into her pocket, picks up her guitar case, and heads inside.

Everyone else is at the buffet, having one last meal before they're set to disembark. Greta's flight is the earliest, which means she'll be getting off soon, with the first group. So she grabs an apple before walking over to say goodbye.

Conrad stands up when he sees her. "You off?"

She nods and hands over a bag from the gift shop. He reaches inside uncertainly, then pulls out a puzzle.

"A new beginning," she tells him as he studies the box, a thousand pieces of blue-and-white glacier.

"Wow," Davis says, peering over his shoulder. "That looks like a complete and total nightmare."

"It does," Conrad agrees; then he looks up at Greta, his eyes damp. "Thank you."

Greta smiles. "Thank *you* for a great week," she says, and to her surprise, he begins to laugh. She does too, then tries again: "An unexpected week?"

"That works," he says, giving her a hug, but the truth is so much more complicated than that. This was a strange week. A sad week. A hard week.

It was a week that could've easily sunk them.

But somehow, it didn't. Somehow, they're still here. Still trying.

She says goodbye to the others too, high-fiving Davis and promising Mary she'll come visit over Christmas. She laughs when Todd suggests that she join them for their next trip, and promises a beaming Eleanor that there'll be a couple of backstage passes waiting at her show in Cincinnati this fall.

They all wish her luck for tomorrow, and when Mary folds her into one last hug and whispers, "Your mom would be so proud of you," Greta has to blink back tears, even though she's said it a dozen times this week.

When her group number is called, she slings her guitar over her shoulder, says goodbye one more time, and then winds her way through the maze of the ship. There's baggage everywhere, and people too, a flurry of preparations. Strange to think that this will start all over again this afternoon, that an entirely new set of passengers will step on board. At the ramp, she turns in her key and then walks off the ship, glancing back only once at the breathtaking size of it, her unlikely home for the past seven days.

Afterward, there's a wait in the line for customs, then another one to get her suitcase, and then she hops onto one of the many buses going to the airport. As soon as she sits down, she gets a text from Asher. It's a blurry picture of Greta and Conrad at the piano bar last night that Mary must have sent him. Underneath it, he's written: I have so many questions. But the first is . . . am I still the favorite??

She laughs, then types: Don't worry. I'm pretty sure your spot is still safe.

Phew, he writes back. I was starting to think I need to have another kid.

As the bus pulls out, she presses her forehead to the window, watching the city of Vancouver whip by, a blur of gray, and she thinks how odd it is to start the day at sea and end it in New York City, to go from calm waters and endless sky to brownstones and bodegas. And tomorrow, a music festival.

On the plane, she pulls out her notebook to work on her set list, which she still hasn't sent to Howie for approval. At the top, she writes "Prologue" and stares at it for a long time. Then she flips back a few pages to a different song she wrote on a different plane traveling through a different sort of night. She closes her eyes, and what swims to the surface is an image of the glacier the other day, all those ashes floating off, black pinpricks against a stark white sky, like the opposite of stars.

Her heart gives a great lurch, and she lets herself feel it.

But only for a moment.

Then she begins to write.

She finishes just in time to nudge open her window shade and see the tip of Manhattan appear, the clusters of silvery buildings bounded by two rivers, one of her favorite views in the world. Even the first time she ever came here, nervous and hopeful, it had somehow felt like home. It's the kind of place you can fall in love with even before clapping eyes on it. Now she feels her heart swell at the familiar sight, and as the plane veers away from the city and toward the airport, she takes a few long breaths.

It's dark by the time she gets home. She drops her keys on the side table and surveys the little apartment. Her latest attempt at keeping a plant alive has failed, but otherwise, everything looks the same. She hasn't been there for three minutes when Howie calls.

"The story is officially dead, your car will be there at eight A.M. tomorrow, and the label wants to confirm that you won't be playing 'Astronomy,' " he says without even a hello.

Greta glances down at the notebook sticking out of her bag. Then she says, "Thank you, okay, and fine."

There's a brief pause on the other end of the line. "Fine?"

"Fine."

"To which part?"

"The car."

"Oh."

"Howie, I'm kidding. Tell them it's okay. I won't play it."

"You sure?"

"No," she says, and then she hangs up the phone.

# SUNDAY

## Chapter Thirty-Three

In the morning, Greta wakes early, even though the time change is working against her. She goes for a walk along the East River, returns to drink two cups of coffee—one after the other while standing in front of the machine—then takes a long shower. By the time eight o'clock rolls around, she's jittery and full of adrenaline, but she feels ready too.

As the car snakes up the FDR along the edge of Manhattan, she thinks about Ben, wondering what he's doing with his Sunday morning. She pictures him sitting in his apartment uptown, reading the newspaper with a cup of tea. Or out for a stroll in Morningside Park. Maybe he's at home in New Jersey. Or still at the hospital with Hannah, red-eyed and stubble-jawed. She hopes not.

Even after everything that's happened, there's a part of her that still wonders if he'll be there today. There are so many reasons she wants it to go well—bigger and far more important ones than impressing the nerdy professor she met on a cruise ship. But if she's being honest with herself, that's one of them.

When she gets to Randall's Island, the grounds are still empty. The grass has given way to mud, dotted by the previous day's footprints, and there's an expectant hush to the main stage. Howie meets the car near the entrance; Cleo is there too, resplendent in neon yellow, her braids swinging as she gives Greta a hug. Atsuko and Nate are waiting in the greenroom, where there are more hugs, some jokes about the tundra, and a few questions about her and Luke. But even with all the distractions, Greta can feel the nervous energy coming off them as they're ushered to the stage for sound check.

She's still dressed in street clothes—skinny black jeans and an old Metallica T-shirt—and facing nothing but an empty field, but as soon as she starts to play, some of the anxiety melts away. She always feels better with a guitar in hand, though she dives a bit too quickly into the opening of "Prologue," then pauses to make some adjustments to her earpiece and to the pedals.

"That's a hit for sure," says Cleo as they head back to the greenroom, and her bosses—a couple of white guys in suits and sneakers whose names Greta can never remember—both smile at this.

When she gets her makeup done, Howie paces anxiously behind her chair in his crisp button-down, looking entirely out of place amid the neon tank tops and band T-shirts. But she knows that's how he likes it. Howie is very good at what he does, which is managing overconfident rock stars with big egos. He hasn't had as much practice picking up the pieces when things fall apart. But he's been there for her anyway, his faith in her unwavering, even when it would've been understandable—maybe even sensible— for him to waver.

When the makeup artist steps away to get a different kind of eyeliner, he bends so that their faces are close together. "Don't look now," he says, "but I just found out who planted the story about you and Luke."

In the mirror, Greta can see the two execs huddled near the food spread. One of them smiles and lifts a bagel when their eyes meet.

"I told you not to look," Howie says, exasperated, but Greta doesn't care. Because the full meaning of it is settling over her:

that they thought she needed more publicity, a different story, a distraction in case things went south again.

That they thought her music wasn't enough on its own.

That *she* wasn't enough on her own.

"Listen," Howie is saying, "we'll deal with it all later. You can trust me on that. But for now, I just wanted to say . . ." He whispers this last part right into her ear: "Give 'em hell out there."

Then he winks at her through the mirror before walking off with a grin.

After that, the makeup artist returns, and Greta raises her eyes to the ceiling while she finishes applying mascara, and then a tour assistant does a final inspection of her outfit, a red dress and black boots, before she's joined by Atsuko and Nate. Outside, the festival is a shock to the system, a riot of color and noise. They're escorted through the grounds by a scrum of organizers in headsets and security guards with dark sunglasses, and all the while, Greta's heart is hammering so hard it feels like it's trying to escape.

When it's time, she hangs back in the wings while Atsuko and Nate walk out to take their places onstage behind their instruments. She can see them sitting there in the dark, waiting for her to join them, just like the rest of the crowd. Greta shifts from one foot to the other, the beat of this first song—this new song, this song that so much depends on—already thumping inside her.

Briefly, she thinks about that last disastrous performance, the feel of it never far away, and her face goes hot and prickly. It's still something visceral, the memory of all that emptiness rushing in where there had only just been music. The way the space had been filled by murmurs and then horror. The numbness of her hands and the chalkiness of her mouth. The lifting of thousands of cameras in the audience, capturing a moment that has been chasing her like a wild animal ever since that night.

But then someone hands her the guitar, and she lifts the strap over her head and feels the reassuring weight of it, and she realizes that's no longer her last performance. Not anymore. Her last performance was just a couple nights ago with Preeti, when she played a ukulele in front of hundreds of people on a cruise ship in Alaska. And they brought the house down.

On the stage, the lights begin to flash, changing from red to green to blue, and Greta can feel the anticipation like it's something buzzing and alive. When she walks out, the audience goes absolutely wild, with a cheer so loud it sends a shiver through her. But she doesn't show it. She makes her way to the center of the stage, lifts a hand, and then stands there, square to the crowd, her shoulders straight and her chin high as the music begins behind her, the first notes of a song she's never played in public before, a song nobody here has ever heard.

First there's the keyboard, then the drums, the tempo building as a roar goes up all around them, the energy moving from the crowd to the stage and back again like a closed circuit, like they're all out here inventing electricity, like the point is to light up this whole damn stage.

And even right then, even as she prepares to come in on the beat, even as her fingers hover over the strings—waiting, waiting—she's scanning the crowd, searching for a familiar face, wondering if he might be there.

Just before she begins, she sees him.

He's standing toward the front, a still point amid all the movement, the people hopping and dancing and swaying all around him.

And he's holding a sign.

It says GRETA'S DAD.

Behind her, the rhythm shifts, her cue to begin. But she doesn't. Instead, she lifts a hand, and the others stop playing. She can feel the collective intake of breath from the crowd as they wonder if history is about to repeat itself. But she doesn't pay any attention to that. She's too busy mouthing something to her band.

A moment later, the music swells again, slower now, more haunting, and the place erupts with wild cheers at the opening notes of "Astronomy," which had once been a song about hope, and then later sorrow, but underneath it all was always—always—about love.

This time, Greta doesn't hesitate. Not even for a second.

She just smiles and starts to play the fucking guitar.

# AFTER

# Chapter Thirty-Four

She reads the book one more time before she mails it back. It doesn't seem fair to keep something so personal, something dog-eared and marked up and well loved. Still, it's not easy to part with it. Dropping it into a mailing envelope, addressing it to Ben at Columbia, walking it over to the post office: all of it feels like saying goodbye.

She keeps his sweatshirt. That, she decides, he can live without.

Besides, she's taken to sleeping in it as the weather has started to turn cool again.

For the last few months, Greta has mostly been on the road, and it feels good to be back to normal: a blur of airports and hotels and venues, but also the clear reminder each night—as she stands before a crowd, guitar in hand—how rare and wonderful it is to get to do something you love.

She didn't read any of the reviews when the new album came out, but her dad continues to summarize them during their Sunday evening phone calls, a habit they've fallen into ever since he came to her show.

"You got a rave in the *Times*," he'll say. "They called it inventive and complicated and they especially loved—"

"Dad."

"Okay, okay. Well, it's in the scrapbook now if you ever change your mind."

The idea of him keeping up her mom's collection of articles and reviews would've been unfathomable only a few months ago. But now Asher tells her that he insists on showing it to anyone who comes over for dinner.

Conrad asks her only once if she ever hears from Ben, and she tells him the truth: it wasn't meant to last.

"Maybe the point isn't always to make things last," he says. "Maybe it's just to make them count."

The way she sees it, they did.

Then one day, she finds a package in the stack of mail left outside her apartment door. In the corner is a Columbia University address. She rips it open and finds a small blue clothbound book, with little huskies and snow-covered trees etched into its cover. Tucked inside, there's a note written on a piece of university stationery. *Thanks for sending mine back. Did you read it?*

Greta puzzles over that question mark for a while. It's open-ended; an invitation. She leaves the note on her desk, pausing to read it every so often when she walks by, though she's memorized each word. It isn't until a couple weeks later, when she stops by Powell's Books the morning before a gig in Portland and sees a different edition—this one snowy and simple, a blank landscape with only the shadow of a dog in the corner—that she realizes she's going to respond.

She considers what to say for a few minutes before writing, on a piece of hotel notepaper: *In fact, I read it twice.* And then she mails it off with the book.

He sends her another copy a week later, this one a close-up of a blue-eyed husky staring the reader down. His note says: *And?*

She finds her next one at the Strand, which she wanders into one day after having brunch with Jason and Olivia, which—in spite of the avocado toast—turned out to be more fun than expected. This one has a howling wolf on the jacket, snowflakes coming down all around him, and she dashes off a note on the back of a bookstore postcard: *And you were right*.

After that, he sends her a leather-bound edition with a message scrawled neatly inside the cover: *Welcome to the Jack London fan club*. She decides she needs to up her game and returns to a rare bookstore on the Upper East Side she once visited with Luke, who was trying to track down a signed Dylan album. It turns out they don't have any copies of *The Call of the Wild,* but there's a first edition of another book by Jack London called *The Cruise of the Snark,* which feels somehow appropriate. Inside, there's an inscription the author wrote to a friend: "Just a few places of a voyage that proved so happy."

She pays way too much for it and mails it off to him.

And then: there's nothing. Not for a long time.

All through the fall, Greta is still hopeful each time she gets back into town and picks up her mail. But by December, it's clear that whatever game this was, Ben is no longer playing. Maybe he's got other things to worry about, more important things. Maybe he's gone back to his family. Or maybe he's simply moved on.

For Christmas, she goes home to Ohio. It's their first one without her mom, but Helen is still everywhere: from the boxes of decorations they drag down from the attic to the carols that play on a loop. When it's time to hang the ornaments, Greta and Asher laugh at the ones she saved: popsicle-stick picture frames with thick globs of glue and chains of dried noodles with chipping paint. Each one feels like a gift she's giving them all over again.

On Christmas morning—much to Asher's chagrin—Greta gives her nieces a drum set.

Her dad manages to one-up her.

He gets them all guitars.

It's late at night when she arrives back in New York, the streets rain-slicked and mostly empty. She presses her face to the window of the cab as they come across the bridge, watching the mosaic of taillights, the dancing reds and yellows.

In the hallway outside her apartment, there's a sloping pile of packages, holiday gifts from friends and family, agents and managers, and, of course, the still-apologetic label execs. As she pushes open the door, a few of them fall inside along with her, and she sees a small brown box with Ben's address on it. She doesn't even bother to take off her coat before opening it. Inside, there's a book. But it's not *The Call of the Wild*. It's not even by Jack London.

It's navy blue with tiny white whales all over it.

She traces a finger over the title: *Moby-Dick*.

Even as she unfolds the note that's attached, Greta is thinking that she doesn't need to, not really; she already knows what this means.

Still, her heart wobbles at the sight of Ben's now-familiar handwriting.

*Time to turn the page,* it says, and she tucks it back inside the book with a smile.

A few days later, it begins to snow, so thick and fast it almost looks like a time-lapse, like the world outside has been sped up. Inside, everything is hushed and still. There's only Greta at the window, a mug in hand. She's been writing all day, and her fingers are streaked with ink.

Outside, the wind sends the snow whistling up the street in ribbons of white. Tomorrow, everything will be gray and slushy. But tonight, it's perfect, and she stays there like that for a long time, mesmerized by the way the flakes hover like static. Her window faces north, and she pictures Central Park, fifty blocks away: the trees cloaked in white, the drifts piling up, the lampposts with their dreamlike glow. And somewhere in the middle of it all— perhaps—another silent figure, slow-moving and bundled and equally full of wonder.

Her boots are under a bench in the entryway. She walks over and stares at them, weighing something, before slipping her feet inside. Then she grabs her coat and scarf, and a pair of mittens too.

By the time she gets outside, it's snowing even harder, and everything feels surreal and a little dizzying. For a moment, she just stands there, peering up at the twinkling streetlights and the velvety sky, her boots sunk deep in the snow.

And then she begins to walk.

# Acknowledgments

A great big thank-you to my brilliant and formidable agent, Jennifer Joel. This is our tenth novel together, and with each one, I feel even luckier to be working with you.

To my friend and editor, Kara Cesare, for embracing this book from the start and continuing to be its greatest cheerleader.

To everyone at Ballantine, it's been such a joy to work with you again. I'm especially grateful to Gina Centrello for the early enthusiasm, to Jennifer Hershey for always being so encouraging, to Kara Welsh for the vote of confidence, and to Kim Hovey for making it all happen. I also owe a great deal of thanks to Jesse Shuman, Allyson Pearl, Susan Corcoran, Quinne Rogers, Jen Garza, Karen Fink, Taylor Noel, Loren Noveck, Paolo Pepe, and Elena Giavaldi.

To Cassie Browne and Kat Burdon and everyone else at Quercus for being such wonderful partners in the UK, and for taking such great care of this story. And to Stephanie Thwaites, Jake Smith-Bosanquet, Roxane Edouard, Isobel Gahan, Savanna Wicks, and Tanja Goossens at Curtis Brown for finding homes for this book all over the world.

To Binky Urban, Josie Freedman, John DeLaney, and Tia Ikemoto at ICM for everything they've done for me over the years.

To Kelly Mitchell, my favorite sounding board.

To Marisa Dabice and Elena Awbrey for their musical expertise.

To Morgan Matson for the title, and Gretchen Rubin for the epigraph.

To Jenny Han, Adele Griffin, Sarah Mlynowski, Julie Buxbaum, Siobhan Vivian, and Morgan Matson for their early reads and invaluable advice. And to Anna Carey, Jenni Henaux, Lauren Graham, Rebecca Serle, Courtney Sheinmel, Elizabeth Eulberg, Robin Wasserman, Ryan Doherty, Mark Tavani, Andy Barzvi, Kari Stuart, Jocelyn Heyward, Allison Lynk, Hillary Phelps, and Summer Walker for the company and conversations while writing this.

To my readers, the ones who followed me here and the ones who are new. None of this would be possible without you.

And, of course, to my family—Dad, Mom, Kelly, Errol, Andrew, and Jack—for all the love and support.

Finally, this book wouldn't exist without the late Susan Kamil, who spent years lovingly badgering me into writing it. I remain so grateful for her unwavering belief and encouragement. I only wish she'd had a chance to read it; she would've made it infinitely better. This is for her.

## ABOUT THE AUTHOR

JENNIFER E. SMITH is the author of nine books for young adults, including *The Statistical Probability of Love at First Sight* and *Hello, Goodbye, and Everything in Between*, both of which have been adapted for film. She earned a master's degree in creative writing from the University of St. Andrews in Scotland, and her work has been translated into thirty-three languages. She lives in Los Angeles.

jenniferesmith.com
Facebook.com/jensmithwrites
Twitter: @JenESmith
Instagram: @jenniferesmith

## ABOUT THE TYPE

This book was set in Sabon, a typeface designed by the well-known German typographer Jan Tschichold (1902–74). Sabon's design is based upon the original letterforms of sixteenth-century French type designer Claude Garamond and was created specifically to be used for three sources: foundry type for hand composition, Linotype, and Monotype. Tschichold named his typeface for the famous Frankfurt typefounder Jacques Sabon (c. 1520–80).